HARPER'S JUSTICE BOOK I

THE RUSTLER HUNTER

R.J. SLOANE

desert life
media

The Rustler Hunter: Harper's Justice Book 1
By R.J. Sloane

Unless otherwise indicated, all Scripture quotations are from the Christian Standard Bible®, Copyright © 2017 by Holman Bible Publishers. Used by permission. Christian Standard Bible® and CSB® are federally registered trademarks of Holman Bible Publishers.

Publisher:
Desert Life Media, LLC
Gilbert, AZ 85295

www.rjsloanewesterns.com

Printed in the United States of America

ISBN: 978-1-960217-55-4

When justice is executed,
it is a joy to the righteous
but a terror to evildoers.
—Proverbs 21:15 CSB

1 - The Rustler Hunter

Trinidad, Colorado
January 10, 1898

J.J.

BEST I COULD tell, the thieving rustler was about twenty minutes ahead of me. The second I leaped onto the back of Magnus, my flaxen chestnut mustang exploded into motion before my spurs even touched his sides. When I pressed him harder, he surged to a full gallop, his powerful strides eating up the frozen ground between us and the steel beast thundering ahead.

"Yaw!"

My voice carried sharp and urgent beneath my navy blue bandanna as we closed the distance. Magnus and I had been partners for over a year, and he read my intentions better than most men. The moment I pointed him toward that train, he knew we were chasing down something dangerous. His ears pinned back with determination, nostrils flaring in the bitter air.

We had a train to catch. More importantly, we had to

bring down "Knife-Edge" Pete Kowalski.

Three days ago, Pete had slipped through my fingers when I'd raided his rustling operation outside Trinidad. Forty-seven head of stolen cattle, five dead cowboys, and a burned-out ranch house, but Pete had vanished like smoke. Word came this morning that he'd bought a ticket on the westbound Atchison, Topeka, and Santa Fe. The snake thought he could run to the Arizona Territory and disappear into the desert.

He thought wrong.

The locomotive's whistle shrieked through the early morning silence as we approached the caboose. Icy wind cut through my duster, making my eyes water behind the dark spectacles. The cold bit deep, but Magnus never faltered, his breath steaming like dragon's fire as he matched the train's speed stride for stride.

"Yaw!"

Magnus closed the final gap with a burst of speed that would've left lesser horses gasping. I measured my timing with the precision that had kept me alive through eight years of hunting the worst men in the territories by calculating speed, distance, and trajectory. Too soon, and I'd be paste on the railroad ties. Too late, and Pete would slip away to terrorize more honest ranchers.

My heart hammered against my ribs as I launched myself from the saddle. For one terrifying heartbeat, I sailed through nothing but frigid air and prayer. Then, my brown leather gloves caught the caboose railing, my body slamming hard against the cold metal with enough force to rattle my teeth.

Magnus veered away from the tracks, his hoofbeats fading as I hauled myself over the railing onto the vestibule. Through the sting of tears and wind, I watched him slow to an easy lope. That mustang had never failed me yet. Lord willing, he'd be waiting when this was over.

I yanked the bandanna from my face, sucking in a deep breath of the train's coal-tinged air. The familiar weight of my dark spectacles pressed against my nose, protection against the mountain sun that had been triggering those cursed headaches for months now. A weakness I couldn't afford, especially not today.

Slipping the glasses into my vest pocket, I squinted against the sudden brightness and eased open the door.

The passenger car buzzed with morning conversation. Traveling salesmen compared territories, a young mother soothed her crying baby, an elderly preacher read his Bible. Normal folks living normal lives, unaware that one of the West's most wanted men sat somewhere ahead of them.

I moseyed down the aisle like any other passenger, the soft *ching-ching* of my spurs barely audible over the train's rhythm. Years of practice had taught me to blend in, to be forgettable until the moment I wasn't. My eyes swept the car methodically, cataloging every face, every posture, but Pete wasn't among them.

The train lurched sideways as we hit a curve, and I grabbed the nearest seat back to steady myself. My spurs jangled softly as I approached the door to the next car, every nerve singing with anticipation.

I pushed through the door, and there he was. Third row from the front, tan duster draped over broad shoulders, red bandanna knotted at his throat. Pete kept his hat pulled low, but I'd memorized every scar on that face, every tell that marked him as trouble. The way he sat too straight, too alert, one hand resting near his gun while his eyes tracked the other passengers like a predator counting sheep.

This was the moment that separated legends from corpses. When planning met chaos and only skill decided who walked away.

I pushed through the door between cars, crouching low, and the mountain air hit my face like a slap. That's when everything went sideways.

Glass exploded above my head in a shower of glittering fragments as buckshot chewed through the window where I'd been standing a heartbeat before. Pete had spotted me, or maybe just gotten spooked by a passenger who moved too purposefully.

Didn't matter. The dance had started.

I rolled left and came up with my walnut-handled Remington already in my fist, thumb working the hammer as I searched for a target. Through the settling glass dust, I caught a glimpse of Pete's snarling face as he pumped another round into his shotgun.

The second blast shredded the door frame inches from my shoulder, splinters of wood joining the glass storm. Passengers in the forward car screamed, diving under seats as Pete roared something about not going back to prison.

Trapped between cars with nowhere to run and a madman with a scattergun ahead of me. Shoot. It was like being stuck between a rattler, a bear, and a coyote. Couldn't go forward. Couldn't go backward. Obviously, either side meant leaping off a train at full speed.

Most men would have panicked, made the fatal mistake of rushing forward or falling back. But eight years of hunting killers had taught me patience was the deadliest weapon I carried.

I spotted the maintenance ladder welded to the car's exterior and made my choice. Up and over. The kind of desperate maneuver that would either end this fight or end me.

The metal rungs burned cold through my gloves as I hauled myself up the side of the swaying car. Wind tore at my duster, threatening to rip me loose and feed me to the wheels below. The train bucked and rolled over uneven tracks, each jolt trying to shake me free like a bronc dumping an unwelcome rider.

Belly-crawling across the roof, I gripped the shallow ridges of the curved metal surface, my fingers already going numb from the cold. Below me, Pete's voice carried through the thin roof as he shouted threats at the terrified passengers.

"Anyone tries to be a hero, and I'll blow their head clean off!"

The familiar pressure started building behind my eyes as mountain sunlight reflected off the snow-covered peaks around us. Those cursed headaches that had been plaguing me for months, getting worse every time I worked a job above the tree line. I squeezed my eyes shut for a moment, fighting through the pain.

Not now. Not when innocent folks needed me to be sharp.

I reached the gap between cars and peered down through the vestibule. Empty, thank the Lord. Pete was still inside, probably using the passengers as shields while he figured out his next move. Smart, but not smart enough.

Easing down the ladder, I pressed myself against the cold metal door and listened. Pete's voice carried clearly now, thick with the desperation of a cornered animal.

"Shut that baby up, lady, or I'll do it permanent!"

The infant's crying cut off abruptly, replaced by the mother's muffled sobs. My jaw clenched hard enough to crack teeth. Using women and children as shields. That was Pete Kowalski, all right. A yellow-belly who'd burn down a family's home just to cover his escape.

I'd been tracking Pete's network for the better part of six months, watching him slither from Colorado to Wyoming and back again, always one step ahead of the law. Rustling was just the start. His gang had graduated to robbery, kidnapping, and murder. They called him "Knife-Edge" because of what he did to witnesses who tried to identify him later.

The door handle felt ice cold under my palm as I calculated angles, timing, and the dozen things that could go wrong in the next thirty seconds. Pete would be positioned to watch both doors, probably with a clear view of the aisle and at least three hostages within easy reach.

Standard outlaw thinking. Control the space, control the people, control the outcome.

Time to show him how wrong he was.

Lord, guide my aim and keep the innocent safe, I prayed silently, the same words Gray Shaw had taught me before every dangerous job. A man's skill meant nothing without divine guidance, and I'd need both today.

I took one last steadying breath and made my move.

The door flew open under my boot, slamming back against the car wall with a crash that made several passengers scream. But I was already moving, rolling low across the threshold as Pete's shotgun boomed overhead, buckshot splintering the wooden frame above me.

From my position on the car floor, I could see everything with the crystal clarity that came in moments like these. Pete stood halfway down the aisle, one meaty arm wrapped around the throat of a well-dressed businessman while his other hand worked the shotgun's action. Behind him, passengers cowered in their seats. Men, women, and children who'd done nothing wrong except buy a ticket on the wrong train.

Pete's eyes found mine, and his scarred face split into an ugly grin. "Well, well. If it ain't the famous J.J. Westin. Heard you was taller."

"Heard you were smarter," I replied, shifting my weight to get a better angle. "Guess we're both disappointed."

"Smart enough to know you won't risk hurting these good folks." Pete dropped the shotgun and drew his Colt, pressing the barrel against his hostage's temple, and the businessman whimpered. "So here's how this plays out, Westin. You drop that iron and back away, or I start decorating this car with blood."

I stayed low, Remington steady in my grip, reading the situation like words on a page. Pete thought he held all the cards, but desperation made men sloppy. He had positioned himself too close to the seats, giving me limited angles but also restricting his own movement. He had made the smart tactical choice, trading the shotgun's power for the Colt's precision and maneuverability. But it also meant he had to be more careful with his aim.

Most importantly, Pete was talking instead of shooting. That meant he needed something from me, which gave me leverage.

"Funny thing about your operation, Pete," I said conversationally, never taking my eyes off his trigger finger. "Spent considerable time mapping it out these past six months. Amazing how many threads connect back to one ugly spider."

Pete's grin faltered slightly. "Don't know what you're talking about."

"Sure you do. Wyoming, Colorado, that whole network you've been running from Cheyenne to Trinidad. Amazing how far stolen beef travels when you've got the right connections." I shifted another inch to my left, opening up a sliver of clean shooting angle. "Tell me, Pete. How many ranchers did you bleed dry?"

The color drained from Pete's face, confirming what I'd suspected. His rustling operation wasn't just random theft. It was an organized network that had been terrorizing honest folks across two states.

"You don't know nothing," Pete snarled, but his voice carried a tremor that hadn't been there before.

"Know enough to shut down your entire operation." I let that sink in for a heartbeat. "Wyoming's finished, Pete. Colorado's next. 'Course, that assumes you live long enough to see the inside of a courtroom."

Pete's face flushed crimson, rage overriding the fear that had been building in his eyes. His jaw worked like he wanted to spit every curse he knew, but he made the mistake of trying to reach for the dropped shotgun while keeping hold of his hostage. The businessman, terror finally overcoming paralysis, twisted free just as Pete lunged for the weapon.

I put one bullet through his gun hand before he could grip the shotgun. Pete howled, dropping to his knees as he clutched his shattered fingers, blood streaming between them.

I was on him before he could recover, driving my boot into his ribs and sending him sprawling across the aisle. By the time he stopped rolling, my Remington was pressed against his skull.

"Stay down, Pete, or the next one goes between your eyes."

Pete lay gasping, his ruined hand pressed against his chest, eyes blazing with pain and fury. "You broke my shooting hand, you—"

"Could've put that bullet through your heart," I said calmly, keeping the gun steady. "Be grateful I didn't."

Around us, passengers began emerging from their hiding places, some weeping with relief, others staring at the blood-spattered scene with the fascination folks always showed when they witnessed real violence.

"Who are you, mister?" asked a young man with wide, doe-like eyes.

"Westin. J.J. Westin."

The reaction was immediate. Gasps, whispers, a few excited murmurs as word spread through the car. The women tittered behind their hands while the men looked me up and down like they were comparing reality to legend.

"I thought he'd be taller," someone muttered from the back of the car.

The words stung more than they should have. Not every man could be six feet of muscle and menace. Some of us made our reputations through skill and determination rather than size. But I'd learned long ago that living up to the legend was harder than building it.

"The rustler hunter," breathed an elderly woman, clutching her reticule like it might protect her.

That was the truest thing anyone had said all morning. For eight years, I'd made it my business to track down cattle thieves, horse rustlers, and the gangs that preyed on honest ranchers. Hired by cattlemen associations fed up with their losses. Forty men brought to justice by my hand, and Pete would make forty-one.

I hauled Pete to his feet and pressed him against the back of a seat. Blood was still seeping from his shattered fingers, so I yanked his red bandanna loose and wrapped it tight around the wound. Pete hissed through his teeth but didn't pull away. Smart enough to know he needed the bleeding stopped.

"Don't want you bleeding to death before you stand trial," I said, binding his hands with his own belt, careful to keep the injured hand elevated. The shattered fingers were already swelling, but he'd live to see the inside of a courtroom.

"Pete," I mumbled, making sure the passengers couldn't overhear. "That Wyoming operation of yours is finished. Colorado's next. But you're running to Arizona. Why?"

Pete's eyes narrowed, pain and calculation warring in his expression. "You think you know everything, don't you, Westin?"

"Know enough to put you away for twenty years. Question is whether you want to add federal charges to that." I leaned closer. "What's in Arizona?"

Pete was quiet for a long moment, weighing his options. Finally, he spat blood and grinned through gritted teeth. "Opportunity, Westin. The kind you ain't never seen. They got operations down there that make my little Wyoming setup look like a Sunday picnic."

"Who's 'they'?"

"Wouldn't you like to know." Pete's grin turned ugly. "But I'll tell you this much. The Arizona Territory's got plenty of opportunity for men who know how to take it. And plenty of ways to bury folks who get in the way."

The train began slowing, and I could see buildings

through the windows. Raton, New Mexico, if I had my bearings right. Perfect place to hand over a prisoner.

As the train shuddered to a stop, I gathered Pete's weapons and what few possessions he had. Nothing useful—no letters, no maps, no convenient list of accomplices. Professional outlaws rarely carried evidence that could hang them.

My hand found the familiar weight in my vest pocket. Auggie's gold button, worn smooth by fifteen years of worry and guilt. Pete's capture should have felt like victory, but his words about Arizona left me uneasy. The metal felt warm against my palm, a constant reminder that success could turn to tragedy in a heartbeat.

But today, at least, justice had won. Pete Kowalski's Wyoming and Colorado operation was finished, and the rustler himself was headed for prison.

Whatever waited for me in the Arizona Territory, I'd face it when I got there. But first, I had a prisoner to deliver.

———————

WHEN THE TRAIN stopped in Raton, New Mexico, I shoved the outlaw toward the jail. The sheriff took one look at the bloody mess I dragged in and kindly took him off my hands, agreeing to fetch the U.S. Marshal for transport back to Trinidad. I could've seen to it myself, but I was due in Holbrook today. Unlikely I'd make it, especially if I waited to hear about Magnus.

I sent a telegram up to Trinidad to let the Colorado Stock Growers' Association know I got their man. Added a note about Magnus. If they could track him down, I wanted him shipped to Holbrook. Then I wired Burt Mossman, letting him know I had business to wrap up before heading his way.

After slipping on my dark glasses, I stepped into the

afternoon sun. Heat pressed against me like a too-tight shirt. My headache hadn't backed off yet, but I forced it aside. Raton wasn't much to look at with its train stop, sheriff's office, a few saloons, and one sketchy hotel. Not much else.

Hunger clawed at my gut, so I headed toward the hotel, hoping it served lunch. To my delight, it did.

The wretched pounding in my head didn't help my mood. I scarfed down my meal, barely tasting it. Just fuel. When I finished, I trudged upstairs and downed a willow bark tablet, patched my shoulder up, and stretched out on the bed.

The headaches started a few months back, while I worked a job up in Wyoming. At first, I ignored them. Figured it was just long hours and harsh weather. When they stuck around, I paid a visit to a doctor in Denver, who claimed they came from light exposure. His solution? Darkened glasses. Ain't much dignity in admitting I needed them, but the alternative was worse.

Now, here I was, a renowned rustler hunter with a notorious reputation, wearing tinted spectacles like some Eastern businessman. At least the newspapers hadn't gotten wind of it. Yet.

Every man had his weaknesses, I supposed. Some just hid them better than others. The glasses weren't the only weakness I carried.

My fingers found the worn gold button in my vest pocket, rolling it between my thumb and forefinger like a worry stone. Auggie's button. Papa's button, before that. The last piece of a boy who'd trusted his older brother and paid for that trust with his life.

I'd been carrying this guilt for fifteen years, letting it shape every choice, every job, every lonely night in towns whose names I'd forget by morning. Maybe some men deserved forgiveness, deserved peace.

I wasn't one of them.

2 - Testing Mettle

———————

Canyon Diablo, Arizona Territory
January 10, 1898

Hayley

THE BEANS WERE burning.

I'd been so focused on the hushed conversation outside the bunkhouse that I hadn't noticed the acrid scent rising from the cast-iron pot until dark smoke began curling up from the stove in the far corner. Carter and Mac had been discussing something about "moving the stock" and "adjusting the count" in voices meant not to carry, but their words had drifted through the gap in the wallboards. I'd been straining to hear without drawing attention to myself.

My wooden spoon scraped against the bottom of the pot, trying to salvage what I could of tonight's supper, but the damage was already done. The cowboys would taste char with every bite, and in a place like Canyon Diablo, that meant trouble. I prided myself on my cooking—it was one of the few advantages I had in maintaining my cover—and letting a simple pot of beans burn felt like a failure.

"Problems, Miss Hayley?"

Hutch's voice carried a now familiar edge of authority mixed with something darker. He sat at the large wooden table that dominated the center of the room, arms crossed, watching me with the calculating stare of a man who missed nothing. The fireplace crackled behind him, casting dancing shadows across the bunks that lined both sides of the main wall. Everything about him reminded me of my father. The way he commanded a room without raising his voice, the cold intelligence behind his eyes, the sense that violence lurked just beneath his controlled surface.

But unlike my outlawing father, Galen Harper, Hutch seemed to possess something resembling a moral code. Twisted perhaps, but present nonetheless.

"Nothing I can't handle," I replied, dumping the burned beans into the slop bucket and reaching for the spare pot I always kept ready. Years of cooking for demanding men had taught me to plan for disasters. "Supper might be a few minutes late, that's all."

Several cowboys looked up from their bunks along the opposite wall, drawn by the smell of smoke and the promise of drama. The entire bunkhouse felt smaller suddenly, more dangerous, with every eye in the place focused on the cooking area where I worked.

"Funny thing about problems, Miss Hayley," Hutch continued, his voice carrying easily across the open room. "They have a way of showing a person's true character."

I kept my attention on opening a fresh can of beans, but every nerve in my body hummed with awareness. This wasn't a casual conversation. This was an examination, and I had the distinct feeling my life might depend on passing it. Worse, it was happening in front of an audience of rough men who would judge every word, every reaction. No amount of training would ease that fear, though I had perfected the art of appearing calmer than I felt.

Carter entered with Mac and swaggered across the room toward my cooking area, three other cowboys trailing behind him. His eyes held a vicious gleam I'd learned to recognize in men who viewed women as prey. The scent of whiskey and unwashed bodies drifted from the group, making my stomach clench with memories of my father's gang descending on our house like locusts.

"Where's our grub?" Carter demanded, stepping closer than necessary to where I worked at the small wooden table beside the stove. "We been waitin' near an hour."

"It'll be ready when it's ready," I said evenly, continuing to work. Never show fear. Never back down. The lessons Galen Harper had beaten into all his children through neglect and cruelty served me well now, even if I hated owing him anything.

The room had gone quiet except for the crackle of the fireplace. I could feel every man watching, waiting to see how this would play out. In the corner of my vision, I caught sight of my brother Flynn straightening at the wooden table, his hand moving instinctively toward his gun. Apparently, he wasn't picking up my subtle look to stay calm. Our usual uncanny ability to read each other failed me in that moment.

"That ain't good enough." Carter reached across me to grab a piece of cornbread cooling on the small table, his arm deliberately brushing against my shoulder. "Maybe you need some help concentratin' on your duties."

The rage sparked in my chest. Hot, immediate, and liquid. How many times had I watched my father's men take the food they wanted, when they wanted it, while the rest of us went hungry? How many nights had Lilian and Justine locked themselves in the root cellar to escape the attention of drunken outlaws who saw young women as entertainment?

Flynn shot to his feet like an avenging angel, his wild blue eyes locked onto Carter's hand near my shoulder. I watched my brother's face transform into something that would have made Galen Harper proud and terrified. The entire bunkhouse could see the change, the shift from protective brother to something far more sinister.

"Get your hands off my sister." Flynn's voice carried the promise of violence, low and deadly. His right hand hovered near his gun, fingers twitching with barely restrained fury.

The temperature in the room dropped ten degrees. Cowboys on their bunks shifted nervously, some reaching for weapons, others just getting ready to dive for cover. Carter straightened slowly, but his eyes held challenge rather than submission. In a heartbeat, this could explode into a gunfight that left half the bunkhouse bleeding on the floor. And Flynn had started it. Ready to blow up my investigation just two weeks in.

I needed to defuse this fast. My Pinkerton training kicked in, searching for the right pressure point to redirect the confrontation.

"Oh, my stars!" I exclaimed loudly, spinning toward the stove with exaggerated alarm. "The cornbread!"

I grabbed a dish towel and yanked open the oven door, releasing a cloud of steam that wasn't quite smoke but looked alarming enough. "Flynn, help me get this out before it burns completely!"

The sudden shift caught everyone off guard. Flynn blinked, his hand still hovering near his weapon, but the immediate threat of a ruined supper broke the deadly tension like a snapped wire. Cowboys who'd been reaching for guns now groaned in disappointment.

"Aw, come on, Miss Hayley," Derek called out. "Not the cornbread too!"

I pulled out the second batch of golden-brown bread, perfectly fine, and set it on the small wooden table with a relieved sigh. "Just caught it in time. Flynn, would you mind checking the barn? I think I heard one horse acting up earlier."

Flynn's jaw worked silently, his eyes still locked on

Carter, but the moment had passed. Carter stepped back with a smirk, understanding he'd been outmaneuvered but not wanting to push his luck with a room full of armed men who valued their cornbread.

"Sure thing, Hay," Flynn said finally, his voice still tight with barely controlled anger. He shot one last warning glare at Carter before heading for the door.

Hutch had watched the entire exchange with that calculating stare, and now he rose from his chair. "Quick thinking, Miss Hayley. Takes a special kind of woman to keep her head when men start seeing red."

"Just didn't want to see good food go to waste," I replied, cutting the cornbread into squares. "Especially when we're running low on supplies."

"About that," Hutch moved closer to my cooking area. "How are our stores holding up?"

I launched into an assessment of our dwindling supplies, grateful for the mundane topic that let everyone's tempers cool. By the time I finished explaining our need for flour, coffee, and salt pork, the cowboys had settled back into their evening routines.

"Think you and your brother could handle a trip to Holbrook?" Hutch asked. "Pick up what we need and maybe see what news there is from town?"

My pulse quickened. Holbrook meant contact with Mossman and the Pinkerton office, a chance to report what little I'd learned about the rustling operation Allan Pinkerton had sent me to investigate. "We could handle it. When do you need us to go?"

"Tomorrow morning. Take the pack horses and get enough supplies for a month." Hutch turned toward the table, then settled into his usual seat, his ramrod, Ford, to his right.

The conversation was clearly over, and the cowboys began sitting at the table for supper. But I couldn't shake the feeling that everything had just changed.

I finished serving supper while my mind turned over

every word of our conversation. Hutch's comments about keeping my head under pressure, the way he'd watched Flynn's protective instincts. None of it felt random. He was evaluating us, but for what purpose?

The cowboys ate with their usual intensity, discussing the day's work while I listened carefully for useful fragments. References of cattle counts that didn't match official tallies. Mentions of brands that needed adjusting. Casual comments about avoiding certain valleys where complications might arise.

Nothing concrete, but definitely suspicious. Half-heard conversations like these had first alerted Mossman to problems at Canyon Diablo.

After supper, I prepared a plate for Flynn and covered it with a dish towel. "Luciana, would you mind handling the cleanup tonight? I need to check on my brother."

She nodded with understanding, already gathering the empty bowls while the cowboys settled into their evening routines of cards and weapon cleaning.

I slipped outside with Flynn's supper, grateful for the excuse to seek him out. The barn stood dark against the star-filled sky, warm yellow light spilling from the open doorway where Flynn had been working since I'd sent him away during the confrontation.

I found him aggressively brushing his horse, taking out his frustration on the poor animal's already clean coat.

"Brought you some supper," I said, setting the covered plate on a nearby hay bale.

He looked up, his wild blue eyes still blazing with anger. "That piece of trash put his hands on you."

"And you nearly blew our entire operation over it." I stepped closer, keeping my voice low. "Two weeks, Flynn. We've been here two weeks, and you almost threw it all away because Carter brushed against my shoulder."

"He was—"

"He was testing me. Just like Hutch was. Just like they all do." I crossed my arms, studying my brother's face in the lantern light. "This isn't our first assignment. You know better. Though it is our first time working together since I convinced you and Shane to help with this Aztec Land & Cattle Company assignment. Three Harper siblings, three different law agencies, one rustling ring." I paused, thinking of Shane at the eastern bunkhouse, probably dealing with his own set of suspicious cowboys. "Shane positioned us perfectly—you here with me, him twenty miles east gathering intelligence from that end."

Flynn's jaw tightened, but he couldn't argue with the truth. As a Deputy U.S. Marshal, he understood the rules. He'd worked undercover before. Though not with me. And that was the problem entirely.

"I can't stand watching men like that think they can touch you. It reminds me too much of the ones who came around when we were kids. What they did to our older sisters, the way they took our food while we went hungry..."

The pain in his voice cut straight to my heart. "I know. But that's exactly why Allan Pinkerton asked me to involve you. Your protective instincts and my investigation skills." I softened my tone slightly. "But if you can't control your temper, you'll get us both killed."

Flynn set down the brush and leaned against the stall door. "I know you can handle yourself, Hay. It's just..."

He trailed off, but I understood his need to fill that protector role. With Shane investigating at a different bunkhouse, Flynn had picked up the mantle. Shane had been more father than brother to all of us, carrying the weight of keeping us alive when Galen abandoned us. Nearly nine years older than me, he'd been barely more than a child himself when he started hunting to keep us from starving, standing guard through long nights while Flynn, Ike, and I slept.

"Seeing men like these," Flynn continued quietly, "it brings it all back."

His raw honesty reminded me why we were all here.

Only by the grace of God had I been spared the worst of it. That and Flynn teaching me how to fight when I turned twelve and started looking less like a child.

I'd come a long way since then. Twenty-two years old. Several years of Pinkerton service and training had honed me into a stronger woman. More than capable of defending myself. All things not needing said to the brother who knew me better than I knew myself.

"That's exactly why we're here," I said. "Remember what we swore the night we burned down the house?"

Flynn paused mid-bite, his eyes growing distant. "I remember everything about that night. The four of us standing in that circle, watching Galen's house burn. At least Lilian and Justine were already safe by then—Justine with that livestock detective Shane works with now, Lilian with her veterinarian husband. They'd found good men who got them away from all of it."

"We swore we'd be different. That we'd fight for justice instead of running from it. Four siblings making a sacred promise while our father's dilapidated, neglected house burned, choosing law over the lawlessness that had nearly destroyed us." I leaned against the stall beside him. "Shane was the one who suggested we make it official. Said we needed words to bind us together."

"And Ike quoted the verse." Flynn's voice dropped to almost a whisper. "When justice is executed, it is a joy to the righteous but a terror to evildoers."

The words of Proverbs hung between us, sacred as any oath. That January night felt like a lifetime ago, the four of us holding hands while flames consumed the abandoned house where we had suffered so much. We'd dedicated our lives to justice that night, choosing law over the lawlessness our father had embodied.

"We meant it, Flynn. Every word." I placed a hand on his arm. "Shane works with the Livestock Commission now. You serve as a federal marshal. I found my calling at the Pinkertons. Ike's studying the law. We're all keeping that promise."

Flynn took another bite, chewing thoughtfully. "These rustlers are stealing from honest ranchers. Families trying to build something good."

"We can't let our past keep us from stopping them," I agreed.

"I know." Flynn ran a hand through his hair. "It's just harder than I thought it would be, pretending to work alongside men like Hutch."

"Hutch isn't like our father," I said, though I wasn't entirely sure why I felt the need to defend him. "There's something different about him. Maybe not entirely without honor."

Flynn snorted. "Honor among thieves?"

"Maybe. Or maybe he's not what he appears to be." I thought about Hutch's careful questions, his interest in how I handled pressure, the way he'd evaluated Flynn's protective instincts. "Either way, we need to stay focused on our mission."

"You're right." Flynn straightened, some of the tension leaving his shoulders. "I'll do better. Keep my temper in check."

"We leave for Holbrook tomorrow morning. That's our chance to report to Mossman and get new instructions." I headed for the barn door, then paused. "And Flynn? Next time someone tests me, let me handle it. That's what I was trained for."

As I walked back toward the bunkhouse under the star-filled sky, I felt the weight of our mission settling on my shoulders. Tomorrow would bring new challenges, new tests, new opportunities to gather the evidence Mossman and the Pinkerton Agency needed to bring these rustlers to justice.

I just hoped I had played my part convincingly enough. If Hutch suspected what Flynn and I really were, tomorrow's trip to Holbrook might be our last.

3 - Land-sakes

Holbrook, Arizona Territory
January 13, 1898

J.J.

THE TRAIN JOURNEY from Raton to Holbrook had been mercifully short after three days of cooling my heels waiting for word about Magnus. The delay had given me time to think through Mossman's telegram and what lay ahead, but I was eager to get this assignment started. Standing on the platform in Holbrook with the afternoon sun beating down, at least I knew my horse was waiting.

It took longer than I had hoped to confirm Magnus's whereabouts. The station manager in Trinidad shipped him to Holbrook as I asked. Except the man in Holbrook forgot to notify Raton they received him and stabled him at the livery in Holbrook.

I ran a hand through my hair before I plopped my Stetson down on it. Guess cooling my heels in Raton had some benefit. Found time for a bath and a shave. As I rubbed my hand over my smooth face, I held back a groan. It'd grow back soon enough.

"Jay Wagner?" The largest man I'd ever seen asked.

At the sound of my alias, I gave a sharp nod.

He introduced himself as Pearce. Wasn't sure if it was his first name or last name. No matter.

"You got a horse?"

"Waiting at the livery."

Pearce followed behind me. Never before had I felt so small. Sure hoped I wouldn't have to tangle with that one. Would take some real crafty thinking to bring down the beast of a man.

"Mossman is waiting at headquarters."

The livery owner had Magnus saddled and ready to go. I inventoried my things: saddlebags, bedroll, Winchester M97 pump-action shotgun. The pricey gun had been a gift from the Winchester Repeating Arms Company. Being famous was good for something. I rounded to the other side and almost smiled when I saw my Winchester M94 lever-action repeating rifle.

In my line of work, there was no such thing as too many weapons.

Magnus snorted when I eased up into the saddle. That was about as warm a greeting as he doled out. Pearce led the way to headquarters.

"Go on in. I'll care for your horse."

I opened the door of the cabin. Smaller than I expected for the headquarters of the largest cattle company in the Southwest. A man as large as Pearce stood near the door. A jagged scar ran from below his right eye down to his chin. He stopped me.

"Leave the guns."

I gritted my teeth as I slipped my Remington six-shooters from each hip. A man couldn't feel more naked than leaving his guns at the door. Though I held onto the knife concealed in my boot. He didn't ask about it, and I saw no need to enlighten him.

"Take a seat," the man behind the oak desk said. "Winston, leave us."

Something about Winston didn't sit right with me. Maybe it was the way his eyes lingered too long, or how he positioned himself near the door like he was ready to bolt. Eight years of hunting men had taught me to trust my gut, and my gut said Winston bore watching.

The scar-faced man exited the room as I studied the man before me. Must be Mossman. His round face matched the slight roundness of his girth. A bushy brown mustache masked his upper lip. Light-colored eyes narrowed as he glanced at my empty holsters.

As I eased into the chair, he began. "What do you know about the Aztec Land & Cattle Company, Mr. Westin?"

"Best we keep to my alias. Don't know if the walls have ears."

"I trust these men implicitly. They're mine, not part of the Hashknife crew."

I held his gaze for a few seconds before answering his question. Mossman didn't blink, didn't shift in his seat, didn't hesitate, like a man too sure of his own authority.

"Heard it's the largest outfit in the Southwest."

"As the superintendent, I oversee more than one million acres from the New Mexico border all the way to Flagstaff. That's six hundred and fifty miles. There's over eighty cowboys employed by this outfit. Not to mention the groomers, laundresses, cooks, and more. Got bunkhouses every twenty miles. We staff each with about ten cowboys, one groomer or wrangler, and two women to cook and clean. We have over fifty thousand head of cattle. Two thousand horses. All wear the Hashknife brand."

He rattled off statistics like they meant something, like size alone was enough to control men. Maybe he believed his men were loyal. Maybe they weren't. Didn't much matter. Loyalty didn't keep men from cutting throats when money was involved.

A million acres, eighty cowboys, and rustlers living among them. I'd worked smaller operations where one bad apple could spoil the whole bunch. Here, with this much land and this many men, the corruption could run deeper than anyone suspected.

It was larger than I thought. Wasn't sure how I was gonna hunt down a whole gang of outlaws masquerading as cowboys by myself. Wouldn't know where to start.

"My first day on the job, I heard about a gang stealing our cattle. Pearce, Winston, and I found their camp. We arrested three men from this outfit. "So, Wagner, this is why I reached out to you."

Better. At least he was listening to my concerns about keeping my real name quiet. Anyone could be listening.

"Our rustling problem isn't coming from some gang hiding out in canyons and washes. They're living in our bunkhouses, eating our food, and on our payroll. The company has taken steep losses over the last eighteen months. It must end as fast as possible."

Mossman mentioned three men already arrested, but something about his tone suggested there were more. A lot more. And men smart enough to stay hidden this long wouldn't be easy to root out.

"You got any idea which bunkhouse is the worst?"

"I'm sending you to the Canyon Diablo Bunkhouse. Only been on the job for a few weeks myself, but I've heard rumors that Mark Hutchinson might be the leader. He rules that bunkhouse with an iron fist."

Canyon Diablo. My fingers flexed near my empty holsters before I caught myself. Any place named Devil's Canyon was bound to ooze trouble.

The name alone set my teeth on edge. Mossman kept talking, but my mind ran through the places I'd worked before. Tough towns, desperate men, justice hanging by a thread.

Holbrook had been rowdy, sure, but it was civilized compared to what he was describing. Twenty miles south of the railroad, no law, no order, just men who thrived in twenty-four hours of whiskey-soaked debauchery and blood-drenched revelry.

Men working that section were as rough as they came, and I was about to walk straight into their territory. This wasn't just another hunt for a rustler. This was weeding out a crew so tangled in crime, the line between outlaw and cowboy had disappeared completely.

Hardest job I'd ever had. No question about it.

"One woman, Hayley Harper, is here today picking up some supplies. The wrangler at that stable is helping her. He's her brother Flynn. You can ride out with them. You'll be camping overnight for one night."

"How far is Canyon Diablo from here?"

"Almost sixty miles."

We talked for another half hour, solidifying details of how he wanted to receive communication from me. Then I holstered my beloved guns, feeling their familiar weight settle back against my hips where they belonged. The tension sitting between my shoulders loosened just a fraction. A man without his weapons might as well be bare in the desert. This felt right again.

Donned my dark glasses, exited the building. Then stopped short.

My mouth went dry as I took in the sight before me. The loveliest woman I'd ever seen sat atop a silver mare. Her blond hair hung down the center of her back in a braid. A plain white shirt peeked out from the gap in her tan leather duster. A simple brown skirt bunched up and revealed her booted feet as she sat astride. A dark brown cowboy hat perched on her head.

Her eyes. They looked like a dusty gold nugget sparkling in the light.

I'd seen plenty of pretty women in my eight years of hunting rustlers, but none who'd made me forget my own name. This one was different. Dangerous in ways that had nothing to do with weapons.

A smile stretched across her soft, full lips. Her face was as pretty as a painted wagon. It was a face that could make a man want to settle down. And I wasn't a settling-down kinda man.

"If you're done gawking at my sister, we need to head out."

Must be the brother, Flynn.

"Miss Harper." I touched my fingertips to the brim of my hat.

Her laughter floated through the air like a sweet kiss from heaven. That kind of softness didn't belong out here, not in the places I worked, not in the places I lived.

"Mister, in case you haven't noticed, you're about to enter the wildest of the West. Ain't no Miss nuthin' out here. Hayley suits me just fine."

Mmm. I had to agree with that. Didn't mean I was fool enough to entertain thoughts about her.

Flynn nudged his buckskin roan forward. The pack-horses strung out behind him. I squeezed Magnus's side, and he followed, a position he liked about as much as I did. Hayley fell into pace beside me, and I noticed Magnus's ears swivel toward her, more curious than wary. Most horses took time to warm up to strangers, but my mustang seemed drawn to her calm energy.

"What's with the dark glasses?" Hayley asked.

I shrugged. "They diffuse the light."

She cocked an eyebrow. "So you've got sensitive eyes? Didn't peg you as delicate."

My gut squeezed. Wasn't delicate, not by a long shot. But she didn't need to know how much I relied on them.

"Can I see them?"

I scowled. Bold little thing, wasn't she? "Maybe when we stop."

She studied me as if she filed the details away for later. Didn't like that one bit.

"So, you must be Jay Wagner."

"Yup." Chatty little thing.

"Heard you worked up in Colorado. Why'd you leave?"

"Don't like the cold winters."

She snorted. "In case you couldn't tell, it's not much warmer here."

"Don't see no snow."

"Yet. This area gets plenty of it, especially closer to Flagstaff."

"Nothing like the Rockies, I'd wager."

She tilted her head, sizing me up. "You sure talk like a Texas man."

Instead of answering, I shifted the conversation. "Where you from?"

"Yup, Texas alright." She gave me a knowing look. "You remind me of some men I knew from there."

I ignored that.

"Anyway, I'm from Arizona. Born and raised in Congress."

"Where's that?"

"A good day's train ride from here. More central Arizona, between Prescott and Phoenix."

She might as well have said the moon for all I knew of the territory. Probably shoulda studied a map before taking the job.

"Flynn, that's my brother." She pointed ahead. "He's spent some time up in these parts. Knows it better than I do. I just started right after the new year."

"So why'd you leave Colorado?" she pressed again.

I exhaled slowly. Persistent little thing.

"Land-sakes, lady, I prefer the quiet while I ride. If you don't mind."

Without waiting for a response, I nudged Magnus into a trot, moving up the line of packhorses.

Hayley hollered after me, "Aw, c'mon, Texas! You scared I'll out-talk you?"

Lippy. Far too lippy.

A woman in the middle of nowhere. Too pretty, too bold, too reckless. Didn't seem like the kind who'd last long in Canyon Diablo.

My grip tightened on the reins, but I kept my face set in stone. Holbrook had been rough, but Canyon Diablo was where the wolves lived, where the weak didn't make it, and where survival wasn't earned through charm.

And Hayley Harper had all the makings of someone who didn't take kindly to being told how dangerous a place could be.

I nudged Magnus into a trot, putting distance between us. Problem was, I'd be riding straight into that trouble with her.

And something told me she wouldn't go quietly. Wouldn't take a lick of help, a word of warning, or an ounce of caution from me. And when that got her in trouble, because it would, I'd be right there, fixing what she wouldn't let me prevent.

4 - Tight-lipped Cowboy

Hayley

JAY WAGNER WAS about as friendly as a cholla cactus, needle-sharp and impossible to grip without drawing blood. His sudden arrival at the Hashknife Outfit set my nerves on edge. Mossman met with him privately, behind closed doors, no introductions, no explanations. Unusual. Flynn thought so too, which meant I wasn't just imagining it. Mossman wasn't the sort to waste time on unnecessary hires, so why bring in a man who looked like he'd rather be anywhere else?

"Come on, Telli," I whispered to my silver mare. Her full name was Telluride, but I had shortened it to Telli, mostly to annoy Flynn. Best reason to do anything.

"How long did you work in Colorado?" I asked as I met up with Jay.

Though I couldn't quite tell through those dark glasses, his head barely turned toward me with a dismissive glance, like I wasn't worth answering.

"Some time."

Ugh. Tight-lipped cowboy. I'd try again when we stopped. Maybe he'd warm up around a campfire later. I kicked Telli into a trot and caught up with Flynn.

In the ten days I'd been around, I'd already figured Hutch as the leader of anything nefarious. Mark Hutchinson commanded compliance from the men. His size demanded a certain amount of respect. But something else hid beneath the surface. Something the men knew, and I didn't. My job didn't require me to know everything. Just uncover the crimes and provide evidence. Hopefully, even learn about a crime before it happened with enough time to report it back to Mossman.

If Lilian ever discovered I became a Pinkerton agent, she'd be livid. After all the trouble she went through to rescue Justine and me from our father's ranch, she'd say I was walking straight back into danger.

Flynn and I had trained for years, learning how to turn speed into power, precision into survival. Shane had been too busy to teach him, Ike too young. Me, just over a year older than Flynn, built nearly the same until he turned sixteen, had made the best sparring partner.

We mapped out weak spots on a man's body: kidneys, kneecaps, the arch of the foot. Learned the exact amount of force to deliver. Nearly every day from the time I was twelve until I left home at eighteen, Flynn and I fought, practiced, tested each other's strength.

The endurance, the control. It saved me more than once. My sisters feared for me, feared that my golden hair and soft skin made me an easy mark. But I never felt like prey. Because I never was.

Victor Mason learned that firsthand. I smiled at the memory. Fourteen years old, one well-placed stomp to the arch of his foot, and a knife driven deep into his gut. He never tried again.

I could take care of myself. No matter my height, no matter the odds.

My two years as a Pinkerton furthered my knowledge of self-defense and spycraft. Allan Pinkerton himself commended me on the success of my first two assignments. Funny how a deep desire to be the opposite of my father fueled my success as a secret agent of justice. I prayed this assignment would be equally successful.

As the sun lowered in the sky, Flynn picked out a campsite. Same one we used on the way out two days ago. Had the Diablo Bunkhouse not been so far from the railroad, we probably could have traveled by train instead of horse.

After I dismounted Telli, I pestered Jay again. "Let me see those glasses before the sun sets."

He groaned and took them off. My fingers brushed his as I grasped the wire temples. Little tingles ricocheted down my arm. Then I put them on. Sheesh. Practically looked like nighttime in the waning sun. I handed them back to Jay.

"It's a little dark to wear them now," he said as he stowed them in his vest pocket. "But in the bright sun, they keep me from squinting."

It surprised me that it was an issue for him. He already wore a dark hat. Stetson, if I remembered my hat brands correctly.

While he removed his saddle, I studied him. Dark brown must be his favorite color considering the hat, duster, and boots. Even his horse's saddle carried the same shade. Just about everything he owned looked weathered but cared for, like he didn't waste a penny on things that didn't serve a purpose. No embellishments, no signs of comfort, just function.

But his weapons told a different story. His holsters weren't worn raw, not like those of men who scraped by with the same pistol for years. His rifles were top-of-the-line, well-balanced, and expensive. It was the kind you could only get if you were rich. Or had influence. Or a reputation that gun companies wanted attached to their weapons.

And then there was his horse, a mustang. Not a slow, steady ranch pony, but a breed built for endurance, speed, and sheer grit. The kind a man didn't choose unless he cared about outpacing trouble.

Jay Wagner wasn't just some hired cowboy passing through. He was something else. Something faster, smarter. Something dangerous.

Jay was shorter than Flynn by a fair amount, but still several inches taller than me. Hard to tell what was under that dark brown duster. If he was lean or muscled or paunchy.

"Hay." Flynn nodded toward the fire.

Heat warmed my cheeks as I turned my attention to fixing some grub. Once it was ready, I dished up two bowls of the steamy stew. Nice thing about the cold temperatures was that food kept longer even while on the trail.

"I never tire of your cooking," Flynn said as he dished himself a second bowl.

I glanced at Jay. Not even a hint of whether he liked it other than he took seconds.

"That's a fine horse," Flynn said once he finished eating.

"Mustang."

Flynn let out a low whistle. "Barely tame?"

"Something like that."

"Had him for long?"

"A year or so."

Vague. Every tidbit of information from the man slipped through my fingers like water through desert sand. There, but impossible to keep hold of. He answered questions without really answering them, leaving me chasing shadows. My fingers twitched at my side. I wanted to shake him, to drag something solid from him, just one clear truth. Tight-lipped cowboy.

I tossed my saddle near the fire and laid down, weary of pulling words from the man.

Jay Wagner wasn't just tight-lipped. He was impossible. But I had cracked tougher men before. He may be a walking mystery wrapped in a duster, but tomorrow, I'd find the loose thread. I always did.

And once I started pulling, a man's secrets never stayed hidden for long.

———————

I WOKE WITH a start, every nerve bracing for a fight, before my mind caught up. The scent of bay rum flooded my senses, sharp and invasive, followed immediately by pressure, a hand clamped over my mouth, unyielding. Heat pressed against me, searing through my wool blanket, through my clothing, sinking into my skin.

Too close.

My body jolted, instinct roaring to life. I twisted, ready to strike, to lash out, to get free, when a deep voice rumbled near my ear. Not Flynn.

"Stay silent. Someone's watching the camp."

I froze, my pulse pounding against my chest, my breath tangling in my throat. Every muscle locked, not from fear, but from the sheer force of discipline drilling one command into my bones: stay still, assess, react smartly. But his closeness activated every defensive instinct I'd honed over years of unwanted attention. Except this wasn't a threat. This was different. He wasn't trying to trap me. He was protecting me.

That realization unsettled me more than anything.

Slowly, Jay's fingers loosened from my lips, the warmth of his grip fading but leaving its presence behind, a phantom sensation, disturbing and too familiar in ways I didn't care to name. He didn't move right away, not like a man shifting his weight or adjusting his stance. No, he was listening, calculating. I could feel the sharp focus of someone trained to hear what others missed, a tension held in his frame that was controlled and deliberate.

His hand moved to his gun, fingers wrapping around the grip with practiced ease. Whatever he'd heard, it was enough to make him ready for a fight.

Then, in the space of a breath, he was gone. I never even heard him move.

The sudden void sent a shiver down my spine. I slid my hand down to my Colt, easing my fingers over the grip, comforting myself with its solid weight. My heartbeat thudded loudly in my ears, too loud. I willed myself to steady, to listen for whatever had put Jay on edge.

Flynn stood, shifting slowly and deliberately as he looked in the direction Jay had pointed, his expression unreadable in the dim firelight. Jay didn't hesitate. He slipped between the trees with an eerie kind of precision, like a man who'd done this before. Flynn held his palm toward me and gave a sharp motion.

Stay.

I stayed, even though both men faded into the black, swallowed by the night. The fire flickered behind me, offering nothing but a false promise of safety. Minutes stretched like hours. Every shadow seemed to shift, every sound amplified in the darkness. My training told me to stay calm, but my heart hammered against my ribs like a caged bird.

The sound came again, closer this time. The deliberate creak of leather, the soft jingle of spurs muffled by careful movement. Someone was out there, and they were trying hard not to be heard.

Boot leather scuffed against rock in the darkness, so close I could have reached out and touched whoever made the sound. I pressed myself deeper into my bedroll, fighting the urge to grab my knife. Don't move. Don't breathe. Don't give us away.

Canyon Diablo was the kind of place where men didn't go looking for trouble because it found them first. Violent, teeming with outlaws who made their own rules. If someone was watching us, it wasn't by accident.

Flynn and Jay finally returned, slipping back into the firelight as if the dark had never touched them. I let out the breath I'd been holding, my lungs aching from the restraint. But Jay's expression was grim, and that sent ice through my veins.

"Not sure what we heard," Flynn whispered, but his tone suggested otherwise.

"Three horses," Jay corrected quietly, his voice barely audible. "Maybe four. They were positioned to surround us." His jaw tightened. "This wasn't random."

I blinked, studying his shadowed face. "You got all that from a sound?"

Jay's lips pressed into a thin line, like he realized he might have said too much. That told me everything I needed to know.

"They're gone, but they'll be back," Jay added, his voice low and certain. "Someone wanted a real good look at us tonight."

Jay Wagner wasn't just a cowboy. He was something sharper, something trained, something dangerous. And Canyon Diablo had just reminded me that danger never came alone, and neither did men like Jay Wagner.

Whatever we were riding into tomorrow, we weren't making the journey unnoticed.

5 - Stars Rule the Night

J.J.

I COULD HAVE kicked myself all the way to next Sunday for revealing so much. Carelessness. A moment too easy, too comfortable. A slip like that could cost a man everything in the wrong company, and I didn't know if I was in the right company yet.

Hayley's brow arched, sharp with curiosity, before she masked it. That flicker of surprise meant she'd caught it, caught that I was more than what I let on. Everyone wore masks in the West, not letting a soul get too cozy, never knowing if a handshake meant peace or a prelude to a bullet. Despite how comfortable Flynn and Hayley made me feel, comfort didn't mean trust.

Guess I'd find out soon enough whether I'd just given away more than I intended.

I wasn't a fool. But tonight, I'd been careless. Maybe too careless.

A slip like that could cost me more than just the job, more than my cover, more than my life. Men who hunted rustlers didn't die slowly or from old age. And if someone traced my name, my work, or my past, it wouldn't just be me paying the price. It'd be whoever was foolish enough to stand beside me when the bullets started flying.

I shifted slightly, letting my gaze drift past Flynn and Hayley, scanning the dark beyond the firelight. No movement. No glint of steel. No sound of boots shifting in the dirt. Didn't mean nothing was there. Didn't mean my mistake hadn't already set something in motion.

I settled back onto the ground, resting my head on the seat of my saddle. The blanket of stars overhead lit the night sky, not much different from the stars in Texas, Wyoming, Colorado, or New Mexico. Still just as beautiful, regardless of Orion's position.

My mind drifted back to when Auggie and I were teenagers. Not quite children, not quite men. That awkward in-between stage where we pushed boundaries one minute and sought the protection of our stepfather the next. Gray Shaw did his best to teach us how to become men of honor, worthy of respect, worthy of our father's name.

We spent years under the stars crisscrossing the trails, Gray leading wagon train after wagon train through desolate, hostile land. Countless times I watched as doe-eyed hopefuls set out with dreams bigger than their provisions. Fewer arrived than what started. Hope disappeared fast once reality set in.

One night, staring up at the sky after Mama retired, I asked Gray why he kept doing it. Why he kept leading.

"It's my calling, son," he said, steady as the ground beneath us. "God gave me the toughness of a warrior, the heart of a hero, and the desire to help others. I was born for this."

Born for it. Gray didn't hesitate, didn't doubt, didn't carry the weight of mistakes he couldn't undo. He led men to safety while I led them into ambushes, believing I was doing the right thing. He guided families toward new lives while I spent mine tracking men to the gallows, watching justice strip them down to nothing. Gray built futures. I ended them.

A guide knew where he was going. A man like me only ever knew where he'd been.

"Just like these stars guide us along our trail by night and the sun by day, I guide these families," he continued. "But I'm much more than just a guide. I use the knowledge I've gained over the years to lead them the safest way possible. To teach them how to survive on the trail and in their new homes. Some train bosses are running from something. Others seek the thrill and danger of the journey. Me? I am a teacher and a guide. With each group I lead across the wilderness, I pray I leave them with the skills they will need to build a new life."

My eyes darted from Orion to Taurus to Pleiades. Stars that God hung in the sky to guide us. I needed some guidance.

At twenty-seven, I'd only known a nomadic life. I followed Gray all over the West until he settled down with Mama in Texas. Auggie was gone by then. A name carved into memory. A shadow stretched across every fire I sat beside.

Gray believed in redemption. I only ever believed in regret. I hungered for adventure, or maybe I tried to outrun my past. I never sat on the thought long enough to figure it out.

I convinced myself I'd found my calling by hunting down rustlers, sniffing out outlaws, blending in with the worst of men, learning their secrets so I could bring them to justice. A warrior. A protector. A vigilante. And yet, as empty as the day I left Mama's home.

If chasing the wicked was meant to make a man whole, I should have felt something by now. Satisfaction. Fulfillment. Instead, all I ever found were more trails, more enemies, more masks. Whatever I had hoped to gain from this life, I still hadn't found it.

Yet no other path ever seemed to fit. So I kept walking the same one, just like Gray taught me, following justice like a man chasing shadows. Maybe someday I'd discover the other life I was meant to live, if one even existed. Or maybe I'd just keep chasing shadows, pretending they held answers, pretending justice was enough, pretending ghosts didn't follow me, pretending Auggie never did, pretending I wasn't lying to myself with every step.

Somewhere overhead, the stars watched in silence, always knowing more than I ever would.

"GIVE THANKS TO the Lord of lords, for his steadfast love endures forever. To him who made the great lights, the sun to rule over the day, the moon and stars to rule over the night, for his steadfast love endures forever."

As I saddled Magnus, the weight of the words settled into my chest, familiar as the leather beneath my fingertips. A habit drilled into me with every sunrise, every journey, every hard mile that pulled me farther from home. The scent of morning dew clung to the earth, mixing with the musk of horse sweat and worn tack. The creak of tightened straps, the soft snort of Magnus shifting his weight next to me.

A tether to something steady. Something unmoving. Something I hadn't felt in years.

"What's that?"

My arm jerked, a sharp jolt like a misfired reflex. Too close. Too quiet. It bothered me how easily she got near without me noticing, like a shadow slipping between trees. I wasn't used to being caught off guard. Felt like riding blind into a box canyon, just waiting for some outlaw to make me part of the scenery. And not the kind folks admire.

"Nothing," I answered, flattening my tone, forcing the tension from my muscles before sticking my foot in the stirrup and swinging my other leg over Magnus's back.

The saddle shifted beneath me with the familiar pull of worn leather and the steady strength of my horse.

A twinge of guilt gnawed at me. Maybe I should have helped her up first. Then she and Flynn mounted at the same time, smooth, practiced, and effortless. I snorted. Guess she didn't need help after all.

"I grew up on a ranch," Hayley said before turning her horse toward the trail. The crisp morning air carried the scent of dust and sagebrush as her mare's hooves kicked up the earth.

Of course, she did. That explained the easy way she sat her saddle, the confidence in her movements. Most women I'd met were either city-bred or ranch-raised, and there was no mistaking which camp Hayley Harper fell into.

I nudged Magnus forward, following behind as the rising sun stretched long shadows across the land. The rhythm of hoofbeats settled, steady as a heartbeat. But the further we rode, the heavier the silence felt, like something waiting just beyond the horizon.

Diablo Bunkhouse. Even the name carried a warning. I'd worked plenty of rough outfits, but something about this assignment felt different. Maybe it was the way Mossman had looked when he'd given me the job, or the careful way he'd chosen his words. Maybe it was the fact that he'd paired me with the Harper siblings, who carried themselves like they knew more about this territory than they were letting on.

I didn't know yet what I'd find at Diablo, but I knew better than to walk into a place blind. Problem was, walking in with questions might be just as dangerous as walking in ignorant.

The way Hayley rode ahead of me, quiet and measured, like she already knew exactly what I was about to step into, made me wonder if I was more out of my depth than I thought.

I touched the gold button in my vest pocket, feeling its

familiar weight against my chest. *Lord, I'm walking into something here, and I could use Your guidance. Keep me sharp, keep me safe, and help me do what's right when the time comes.*

The prayer came as natural as breathing, a habit Gray Shaw had taught me years ago. Even when I felt far from God, even when the work I did seemed to pull me into darker places, I held on to those morning prayers like a lifeline.

Especially now, riding toward a place called Diablo with a woman whose secrets might be as dangerous as my own.

6 - Diablo Law

J.J.

THE REST OF the ride remained uneventful. We arrived at Diablo Bunkhouse mid-afternoon, and Hayley swung down first, moving with the ease that came from knowing exactly where she stood in a place like this.

I took a little longer, scanning the bunkhouse as I loosened my grip on the reins. The weathered wooden structure looked sturdy enough, but there was something about it that set my teeth on edge.

Hayley approached. "I'll show you to an open bunk."

She handed her reins over to Flynn, and he held out his hand, waiting for mine. I hesitated, not because I didn't trust Flynn, but because turning over my reins felt like giving up a piece of control. And maybe because trust wasn't something I handed off easily these days.

Hayley and Flynn had done nothing to make me doubt them. But doubt wasn't about proof. It was about survival. Still, something about them made it hard to hold on to suspicion.

Reluctantly, I handed over the reins. Magnus turned his head toward Hayley as Flynn gathered both sets of reins, nostrils flaring as if memorizing something important. She reached up to stroke his neck without hesitation. "Easy, boy," she murmured, and the mustang leaned into her touch like he'd known her for years instead of days. Traitor.

I grabbed my saddlebags, bedroll, and arsenal—all the things I didn't plan on letting go of anytime soon. Already I'd revealed too much about my tracking abilities last night. In a place like this, being too competent could be as dangerous as being too weak. Jay Wagner was supposed to be just another drifting cowboy, not a man who'd brought in forty-one rustlers.

Only then did I step inside.

After eight years of hunting rustlers, I'd learned to read a place the way other men read newspapers. The layout told its story immediately. Escape routes blocked by furniture placement. Sleeping arrangements that put the strongest men near the doors. This wasn't sloppy housekeeping. Someone had arranged things this way on purpose.

The bunkhouse air hit me with the familiar cocktail of sweat, smoke, and old leather, scents that lingered long after the men inside had gone. The floorboards creaked beneath my boots, warped from years of restless pacing in the dead of night. Men who didn't sleep easily left their marks on a place.

I breathed deeper, parsing the stale musk that told me half these men probably weren't working steadily. Loungers, drifters, men who knew how to slip through life without breaking a sweat. The kind who made their living in the gray spaces between honest work and outright thievery.

And this place was already whispering secrets I didn't like.

Hayley hurried past me, the door hinges groaning like they'd had enough of carrying the weight of this place's secrets.

"All the best bunks are taken," she said, tossing me a glance over her shoulder. "Hutch has outlined a pecking order. I'm sure as the new cowpoke, you'll be over here. He's the tall hog at the trough, if you know what I mean. If he asks you to move, you better."

I didn't say anything, but I took a good, slow look around. Tall hogs didn't get that way unless the others let them. That told me more about the men here than any introduction ever would.

"Where do you stay?" I asked as I dropped my stuff on the floor in front of the bunk.

"There're living quarters and a washroom on the other side of that wall. Only accessible from outside. We have a stove and fireplace."

I figured the outside door was to deter the men from wandering over there. Smart precaution in a place like this.

"I'll be back in a few minutes to get supper started as soon as I check in with Luciana. That shelf at the foot of the bed is for the bottom bunk. The one at the head is for the top bunk."

I chose the bottom bunk since both were empty. Then I leaned my rifle and shotgun against the side of the shelf. I retrieved my extra set of clothes and grooming kit from my saddlebags and set them on the shelf. When I pulled out the satchel containing my Bible and Auggie's gold button, I stowed it under my bed. It'd be best to feel out the disposition of the crew before setting out the Word.

When Hayley returned, she hummed as she worked over the stove. Like she belonged there. Like the rough edges of the bunkhouse didn't so much as nick her confidence.

Watching her work, humming like she hadn't a care in the world, stirred something in me I had no business feeling. A man in my line of work couldn't afford distractions. But heaven help me, Hayley Harper was becoming exactly that.

I watched her, wondering why such a pretty gal took a job in a dangerous place. Wondering why she wasn't nervous. She could have her pick of men. Instead, she was here. Either she had more guts than sense, or she had a reason.

"What?" she asked as she glanced over her shoulder.

I pointed to my chest and raised an eyebrow.

She snorted. "I can feel your eyes on me."

I wasn't sure what I was looking for, but I was certain I'd find it.

"Sorry." Heat climbed up my neck and settled onto my face.

"Come, sit at the table while I work. Not much else for you to do right now."

After I sat, I cleared my throat. "Why do you work here?"

"Oh, I just started. Wanted to see what it was like."

I scoffed.

"I like to cook. Cleaning, well, no getting around it anywhere I go."

As I crossed my arms over my chest, she dumped a large stack of diced potatoes into a huge pot.

"Seems like there're lots of safer places to cook."

Like for a husband in a secluded little cabin nestled at the foot of a beautiful mountain overlooking a grassy meadow. Or in a quaint house in a quiet, civilized town. I shook my head to dislodge the image from my mind.

She turned around to face me and propped one hand on her hip while punctuating her words by poking the air with the knife in her other hand.

"Now you sound like Flynn. I can take care of myself."

When she turned her attention back to the meal, I asked a few questions.

"What kind of men bunk here?"

She sighed. "Cowboys."

After she glanced over her shoulder at me, I raised an

eyebrow, and she continued.

"Hutch is the foreman for this section, at least by the way he acts."

I hummed low in my throat, filing that away. Men who acted like they ran the show weren't always the ones pulling the strings.

She placed more vegetables and meat into the pot and added some seasoning before she gave it a quick stir. Then she mentioned Ford.

"I think Ford Spencer might be the ramrod. Or maybe he's just worked with Hutch long enough to bend his ear. He doesn't say much, but he doesn't miss much either."

When Hayley mentioned Ford Spencer, something cold settled in my gut. I'd learned to trust that feeling over the years. Quiet men who bent the foreman's ear were often the ones really calling the shots. I'd need to watch Ford Spencer real careful.

I glanced her way, but kept my thoughts to myself. Quiet men didn't always lead, but they always survived. She framed Hutch as the man to obey, the one with a grip on this place, but she wasn't dismissing Ford either. That she'd picked up on it had me wondering about her role in this place again.

I'd seen enough outfits where a loud man held the reins while someone quieter watched his back and whispered in his ear. Best to hold off deciding who really ran this place until I saw them in action.

As Hayley told me about the other men, she moved ingredients to make biscuits to the table and worked the dough.

"Carter makes my skin crawl. He's young, but strong. I try not to be alone with him."

I snorted. Didn't take a genius to figure out what that meant. She said it like a fact, not an opinion, like she'd learned it firsthand. That told me more about this place than anything else she'd said so far. Trouble had a way of making itself comfortable in places where rules only stretched as far as a man's temper.

"Kurt is quiet. Keeps his head down and does what he's told. Glenn's always in the middle of everything, but somehow never really part of it, if that makes sense. Derek Gibson is a blatherskite. I think he's in love with the sound of his own voice. Then there's Mac Burns and Ian Kelly. I know very little about them. They seem polite enough when Luciana or me are around."

"The last one. What's his name again? Oh, right. Howard Stiles. He looks like he's been cowboying longer than I've been alive."

I filed the names away, but I listened more to how she said them than what she said. Kurt was quiet, but quiet could mean smart, could mean dangerous, could mean waiting for an opportunity. Derek talked too much. Sometimes men like that made a lot of noise just to distract from what they didn't want noticed. Her description of Glenn piqued my curiosity. I'd figure out what she meant by it soon enough. Mac Burns and Ian Kelly were polite when the women were around. That meant something, too.

After she rolled out the biscuit dough, she cut out rounds and placed them on a sheet. Then she set them in the oven to bake. By then, the stew filled the place with a delicious aroma that made my stomach growl.

"They'll be here soon, and we'll have supper."

If she hadn't been in the room, I would've spent some time digging through their things, checking for signs of men who knew how to cover their tracks, men who got sloppy, men who didn't plan on staying long. Didn't know when I'd get the chance. And time had a way of closing doors quicker than a man expected.

Lord, keep me sharp and keep her safe, I prayed silently. *And give me wisdom to know when to act and when to wait.*

The door flew open, banging against the wall hard enough to rattle the shelf beside me. A dark-haired man grinned. "Hallelujah! Hayley's back. I thought Carter scared you off, and we'd go back to that miserable gruel Luciana passes off for food."

His voice carried, confident and brash, a man who filled space whether or not folks wanted him to.

Hayley's golden eyes met mine, the corner of her mouth twitching with something unreadable. "That'd be Derek."

I studied him as he took stock of me, sizing me up the way men do when deciding whether to test a new face or leave him be. I could already tell Derek wasn't the testing type. He liked talking too much to waste time picking fights.

"Who we got here?" he asked once he noticed me.

I stood and introduced myself to the men as they filed in. Hayley began setting out bowls, spoons, and the food.

"I could eat a side of beef. I'm so starved!" Derek exclaimed as he took a seat. He offered me the one next to him.

Guess I'd best get ready for an earful of chatter.

The men settled in, dishing up without hesitation, like men used to eating fast and talking faster. Flynn entered and took an empty seat while Hayley reached over Mac's shoulder to set a basket of biscuits on the table.

Then she squeezed between Carter and Kurt with another basket. Carter's hand rested on her backside before the basket even touched the table.

My muscles tensed, slow and tight. Instinct said to haul the hooligan outside, to make sure he thought twice before trying it again. But instinct was dangerous when a man didn't know the room. I hadn't learned enough about these men yet. Didn't know which ones followed Carter's lead and which ones simply tolerated him. And until I knew that, I couldn't afford to act.

I exhaled slowly, forcing my grip to stay loose. Didn't make it sit any easier. Felt like swallowing nails.

As Flynn stood, his chair flew out behind him, legs scraping against the floor loud enough to get everyone's attention. Before he rounded the table, Hayley moved quicker than I'd thought possible, quicker than Carter had, that was certain.

Her fingers locked tight in his hair, dragging his head back as she pressed the nastiest Bowie knife I'd ever seen against his throat.

That blade appeared in her hand like magic, not with the fumbling of an amateur, but with the practiced motion of someone who'd been trained. Trained well. The angle she held it, the controlled pressure against Carter's throat, the way her body stayed balanced and ready. This wasn't just a woman protecting herself. This was someone with professional training.

The room froze. Even Derek, who never missed a chance to talk, kept quiet. Silence hung thick, stretched too long. The kind that meant a line had been crossed, and everyone was waiting to see what happened next.

Who exactly was Hayley Harper?

Maybe she could take care of herself after all. Maybe Carter was a fool to worry about. Then again, he might not be long for this world if the icy glare in Hayley's eyes didn't soften, or if Carter decided to test her patience.

7 - Hands Off

Hayley

THREE SECONDS AFTER Carter rested his hand on me, I made my decision. Show no weakness. Not here. Not ever. These crusty cowboys weren't the type to respect silence, but they understood force. Carter thought he was testing me. He just didn't realize I was testing him right back.

Across the table, Flynn moved with pure instinct. His chair scraped against the floor, his muscles coiling, ready to lunge. Jaw clenched. Eyes locked on Carter like a predator sizing up prey, like he wanted to finish what I hadn't even started yet. His fingers curled into fists, knuckles white, as if he was already imagining the force it would take to break Carter's nose.

I caught his gaze. *Stop.* The word never left my lips, but he heard it anyway. His nostrils flared, his chest rising with a sharp inhale, like a man forcing himself to stand down when every bone in his body screamed to act.

I unsheathed the hidden Bowie knife from my waistline; the blade whispering freely with a sound sharp as a promise. The blade moved with muscle memory drilled into me by Allan Pinkerton's best instructors. Angle, pressure, control—all calculated to subdue without killing unless absolutely necessary.

A fistful of Carter's sandy hair twisted in my grip, his head snapping back with a grunt. The cool steel kissed his throat, not enough to cut, just enough to remind him how easily it could. His breath hitched. Eyes widened around the table.

Flynn exhaled sharply, but I could still feel his tension coiled and waiting.

"You ever heard of Galen Harper?"

Carter grunted, but I felt the shift, the tension rippling through the men like a stone dropped in still water. Using Galen Harper's name left a bitter taste, but it was a tool, one of the few advantages his legacy had ever given me. Let them fear the daughter of the most notorious outlaw in the territory.

"I'm his kin."

The words tasted bitter, but I swallowed them down. Respect or fear, either would do.

"Unless you want to meet your maker," I growled, pressing the blade just enough for him to feel it, "kindly take your hand off my person."

His fingers twitched. Sweat beaded on his temple. Slowly, his hand slid down my leg and back to the table.

I shoved his head forward, the motion sharp and controlled. For good measure, I slapped my palm hard against the back of his skull. He twitched. I let the satisfaction settle while I cataloged the reactions around the table. Who flinched, who leaned back, who looked impressed. Information I'd need later when deciding who could be trusted and who couldn't.

Then, I locked gazes with each man around the table.

"There's no uninvited touching, you hear me?"

Silence. I could feel them weighing the moment, deciding whether to challenge it.

To drive home my point, I stabbed the wooden table

next to Carter's hand with my knife. The blade sank deep, the wood groaning under the force.

"Yes 'um," a few of the men muttered.

I narrowed my eyes. Not good enough.

"I'm sorry, Carter. What was that?" I asked, rocking the knife back and forth.

His throat bobbed. "Yes, ma'am."

When I jerked the blade up, he flinched. Only then did I step away from the table.

Flynn picked up his chair, sitting down with a force that made the legs scrape against the floor, a sharp, grating sound like a blade dragged over stone. Jay's eyes burned a hole in my back as I stowed my knife in its hidden sheath at my waistline. My fingers trembled against the clasp.

With shaky hands, I dished myself a bowl of stew and sat in a chair next to Luciana at a small table near the stove. The warmth of the bowl seeped into my palms, grounding me.

Do not fear, for I am with you; do not be afraid, for I am your God. I will strengthen you; I will help you; I will hold on to you with my righteous right hand.

I recited the words in my mind, adding my own silent prayer. *Lord, You've placed me here for a reason. Help me see what I need to see, learn what I need to learn, and stay strong enough to see justice done.*

Once I plunked down my bowl, I rested my hands in my lap until they stopped shaking. Jay glanced down at them before returning his attention to his meal. His stillness during the confrontation hadn't been fear. It had been an assessment. The way his eyes tracked every movement, every reaction, reminded me of federal agents I'd worked with. Men trained to observe before acting.

Flynn's glare told me he'd have words with me soon. The tension hadn't fully settled.

"Shoot, Carter! She showed you," Derek said.

Carter glowered at him.

Hutch cleared his throat. The sound cut through the

room, drawing every eye. I let out a slow breath. He wasn't just speaking to Carter; he was speaking to all of them.

"Miss Hayley is our pot rustler. Her grub tastes good. She cleans up after you pigs. Remember that the next time you decide to kick up a row."

Hutch narrowed his eyes at Carter. Carter's shoulders slumped forward, and he stared into his bowl.

"Your reward for not knowing dung from honey is to wash the dishes for Miss Hayley tonight."

I straightened in my chair at the unexpected support from Hutch.

Carter slammed his palm on the table, the sound sharp and angry. He started snorting like a bull with a burr on its rump. Ford set his spoon down, leaned forward, and narrowed his eyes. Carter grit his teeth before he relaxed his hand. Once he lifted a spoonful of stew to his mouth, the room relaxed.

The shift was subtle, but it was there. I had just changed the rules.

As the clank of spoons hitting tin bowls faded into conversation, I breathed easier. My stomach settled, and I swallowed down my lukewarm meal.

When I finished, I set the empty bowl in the washbasin, then lifted my duster from the hook and shrugged it on. Flynn appeared at my side, mirroring the motion as he pulled his own coat over his shoulders before he held the door open for me.

When I stepped outside, the chilly air bit at my cheeks, sharp enough to remind me I was still alive. I followed Flynn to the barn, the crunch of our boots against the dirt filling the silence.

He was too quiet. Not the kind of quiet that meant he had nothing to say, the kind that meant he was trying not to say something he'd regret.

Then he spoke.

"Are you off your mental reservation?" His voice was low, edged with something between exasperation and barely contained fury. "That's about the craziest stunt I've ever seen from you."

"I needed to establish I'm tough." I folded my arms across my chest.

"Or a plumb fool."

I huffed. "What would you have me do? Let you defend my honor? Or Jay?"

He turned to face me, the lantern light casting gold highlights over one side of his face while the other remained in shadow. His jaw was tight. Too tight.

"These are rough men, Hay." His voice was clipped, like he was forcing himself to stay calm. He shook his head, then shoved the barn door open, the hinges protesting with a loud groan. He stood there for a second, exhaling like he needed the cold air to cool the fire in his chest.

"And you'd have me do nothing? What happens when you aren't around?"

His nostrils flared. His fingers twitched at his sides, like he needed something to hold on to before he lost it.

"At least they'll think twice about anything now that they know I can defend myself."

Flynn growled. "Or they'll gang up on you."

The words came out rough and sharp, like he was barely keeping them from turning into a shout.

Slowly, I nodded. "They might. But I'm trusting God to protect me. I'm not here by accident, and you know it."

Flynn's frown didn't fully disappear, but after a few seconds, it softened. Not because he believed me. He knew there was nothing he could do to change my mind.

"Just watch yourself. Some men don't like being called out in front of others. Carter just might be of that ilk."

I held his gaze. "Remember, I know exactly what men like this are capable of."

His jaw tightened. Then, without warning, he pulled me into a quick hug, too tight, too fast, like he needed the reassurance more than I did.

"I know," he murmured. "I just... I don't know what I'd do if they hurt you."

I squirmed out of his hold, then fake-punched his arm. "Don't worry. I'll be careful."

When he let out a long breath, it ended in a half laugh, but it wasn't real.

"That's some knife."

I smiled. "You like it? When I was..."

Stanton's smile surfaced in my mind, effortless, charming, so convincing I once believed every word out of his mouth. My stomach twisted, not with fear, but with the sting of a fool's mistake. Stanton had taught me knife work, among other things. The irony wasn't lost on me that his betrayal had made me better at protecting myself from men exactly like Carter.

I cleared my throat, forcing the image away. Not now. Not here.

"When a friend taught me how to use a knife, I picked it out. He thought it was too large for a concealed blade, but we figured out a way to hide it."

Flynn snorted. "You shoulda seen Ian Kelly's eyes. That man probably won't even make eye contact with you now."

I laughed, short and controlled. "See? My approach was effective."

He cleared his throat. The shift was subtle, but I caught it.

"When they were stabling the horses, I heard them say they're gonna stay out a little longer tomorrow. Won't be back until after dark. That'll give you..."

An opportunity to snoop. The words settled heavy between us. Tomorrow's opportunity couldn't come soon enough. The men were getting comfortable around me, which meant they'd start letting their guard down. Time to find out what Hutch and his crew were really up to.

I nodded, finishing the thought in my head for him. Flynn didn't add anything, but I could feel his unease, like he wasn't just handing me an opportunity, but a warning.

"Let me walk you to your room," he said.

I shook my head. "You can watch from here. I think it's better if I go by myself."

He hesitated. A half second too long.

"Be careful." Not a suggestion. A quiet command.

His warning lingered, settling in my chest like an echo I couldn't shake. I exhaled, forcing my shoulders to relax as I turned toward the bunkhouse.

Then I rounded the corner. That's when I saw him.

Jay. Leaning against the wall, out of sight from the barn, but not hidden. Just... waiting.

My breath hitched. Not because I was afraid. Because I wasn't sure I should be.

"Hayley." His voice was steady, familiar, too familiar. Like he already knew how I'd react before I did.

"Jay, you nearly took a year off my life." I forced my words to sound breathy while I placed a hand over my heart.

"You alright?"

I frowned. Something in his tone didn't sit right. Not concern. Not suspicion. Something in between.

"Perfectly fine, thank you."

He nodded, pushing away from the wall with an effortless movement, too calm, like he hadn't just been loitering for no reason. Like he was waiting for me.

"Lock it after I leave."

My fingers tightened around the door latch. Why did it sound more like a quiet demand than a simple suggestion?

I forced my voice to sound bright. "Thanks for the reminder."

When I stepped inside, I nodded to Luciana, then slid the bar in place before pressing my ear against the door. Silence. But it didn't matter. Because I could still feel him on the other side.

It perplexed me. My connection with Flynn felt like

this sometimes. No, not quite the same. Similar. Something I couldn't name yet, but would soon enough.

Shaking my head, I settled into the rocking chair by the fireplace, picked up a book, trying to push it away. Trying to push away the tension from earlier, the unreadable way Jay had watched me tonight.

But my mind kept circling back. Jay's gaze when I sat down to eat. The weight behind it. The unspoken something. He wasn't like the others. There was trust there. And something else. Something I wasn't quite ready to name.

And tomorrow, when they rode out late, I'd have my chance to find out exactly what that something was.

8 - The Outlaw's Invitation

_____

J.J.

THE SCENE FROM supper the night before rolled around in my mind while I readied for a long day in the field. As I walked toward the barn, I replayed it, new details sticking out that I hadn't noticed before.

Hayley had shown tremendous gumption. The size of her blade gave me pause and certainly had the same effect on the other men. But it wasn't just the knife that stuck in my mind.

It was Hutch.

Shielding her. Defending her, as if his authority relied on it. Not what I expected from a band of outlaws. Some men would see protecting a woman as a weakness. But these men hadn't.

That alone told me there was more to this crew than stolen cattle. Be an interesting puzzle to solve for sure.

After I saddled up Magnus, I mounted and waited for the rest of the men. Flynn Harper watched me with steely eyes. Son of Galen Harper. A name that meant nothing to me, but something to a few of the men around the table last night.

The moment Hayley spoke it, Carter backed down. The others straightened.

It stuck with me.

If Galen Harper's name had that kind of power, I needed to know why. And I needed to know how much of that power Flynn carried.

"Morning," Derek greeted me as he led his horse out of the barn. "Guess you're one of the early birds."

I nodded as the other men strode out.

As we rode out to where the cattle grazed, Ford Spencer rode next to me.

"That's an interesting pair of shooting irons," he said.

"Nothing special. Just '75 Remington single-action."

"Outlaw gun," he muttered.

Sure enough, many outlaws preferred the Remington six-shooters over the Colt Peacemaker, even though the Colt was readily available. Though both were fine weapons, the Remington helped me blend in better.

"I bought 'em cause they jam less and have a nice grip," I said.

Ford moderated his tone as he slid his gun from its holster. Held it by the barrel. Angled the handle toward me. Not quite an offer. More like bait.

Like he wanted to see what I'd do.

I didn't move right away. A heartbeat too long. Then I reached steady, controlled. Forcing my fingers to stay loose and the sudden, sharp tension in my ribs to settle.

The air between us thickened. A fraction, barely noticeable, except I noticed it.

Ford watched.

Then, just as my grip was about to meet the handle, he twisted it. A fraction of an inch. Enough to shift it out of reach, enough to make sure I never actually touched it. The metal band caught the light. A deliberate flicker of movement, a message rather than an invitation.

My pulse spiked once, hard, like my lungs tightened for half a breath. I ignored it. Didn't blink. Didn't move.

Didn't let Ford see the moment my instincts told me I was being played.

"I prefer the ivory handle myself."

As Ford holstered his weapon, he gestured toward the cattle scattered across the valley. "Carter, take the north flank. We'll work them south toward the main herd."

I caught Carter's quick glance toward Hutch before he acknowledged the order, but something in his expression suggested he was measuring Ford's reaction too.

At Ford.

Something about the way the other men moved around Ford struck me as odd. They didn't just respect him. They watched him. Waited for his approval.

I pointed to my hat and duster. "As you can see, I'm partial to brown."

Ford let out a loud, derisive snort, the sound echoing harshly. "So I noticed."

I exhaled, slow and measured. Not relief. Just calculation. He wanted a reaction. He didn't get one. But my chest felt tight, just for a second, a reminder that my body hadn't quite caught up to my mind yet.

I forced it down.

Then the shift.

"How do things work here?" I asked, hoping to build on the conversation.

He didn't answer right away. Not out of hesitation. Out of strategy. Sizing me up. Deciding what would make me talk.

"Hutch gives our assignments. He wants you to ride flank with me today."

I dipped my head. A test. Not an invitation.

Ford studied me for a beat longer. Like he wasn't just deciding if I belonged, but if I could be trusted.

Then the first real push.

"What's with the dark glasses?"

I held back a sigh. "Doc recommended them to prevent eyestrain."

Ford snorted. "Don't like not being able to look you in the eye."

The words were casual. His tone wasn't. Testing me again.

I flexed my fingers briefly, then forced them still. Not too fast. Not too obvious. No tells. No giveaways.

"Whatcha need to look me in the eye for?" I asked as I removed the glasses and slid them into my leather vest.

"You a longrider?" He wanted answers. He wasn't asking. He was digging.

A sharp shake of my head didn't seem to satisfy the man, so I explained I wasn't on the run from the law.

"Best I can tell, none of my misdeeds have ever been discovered."

Ford narrowed his eyes. Held my gaze. Measured it. Waited.

I kept my expression neutral, though my pulse did a slow, deliberate kick in my neck. It wasn't nerves. Not really. It was instinct. What he wanted to see versus what I let him see.

"You ever kill a man?"

Something in his tone made my gut tighten. Ford asked questions like a man who already had half the answers.

I exhaled slowly. Not too slow, not too careful.

"Is that a requirement of the job?"

Ford snorted. "You have."

I held still. Let the silence stretch just enough to make Ford second-guess what he thought he saw. Then I leaned back just slightly, giving the impression of ease without actually feeling it.

"What makes you say that?"

Ford watched me. "In my experience, those who haven't are eager to boast. Those that have dodge the answer. Though a few, like Hutch, readily admit it with a stony stare."

That odd conversation stuck with me as I watched Ford wheel his horse toward Hutch. They chewed the fat for a good fifteen minutes before Ford took his place near me. Every time my gaze flicked his direction under the cover of my dark glasses, I caught him studying me.

Eyes fixed, assessing. Not just idle curiosity. Intentional analysis.

No doubt he tried to riddle out my character.

When I first started working undercover, such scrutiny had made me twitchier than a lady standing on a fire ant hill. I was better at hiding it now. But it didn't mean I didn't feel it in every strained breath and ticking heartbeat.

In more recent years, not having the number one or number two man boring holes through my skull with their eyes made me even more nervous. I expected it. And I found the calmer I remained, the quicker I received an invitation to whatever diablerie was afoot.

Late in the afternoon, a young steer with a strange brand ambled in front of me. Not the Hashknife brand of the Aztec Land & Cattle Company.

The Hashknife brand looked more like a flattened omega topping an upside-down T. The brand on the steer looked more like a hanging R. A half-circle attached to the top of an R.

No way to burn that over the Hashknife or vice versa.

I forced my face to remain unreadable.

Mixed herds happened. But not like this. Not this many. And not this deep on Hashknife land.

The longer the day stretched, the more brands I spotted. Not just one or two strays, but a pattern. A deliberate, orchestrated pattern.

Mossman's gut instinct had been dead on.

This wasn't suspicion. This wasn't theory. This was an operation. And I was in the middle of it.

At the end of the day, Hutch sent Ian Kelly and Kurt Fleming back to the bunkhouse. The rest of the crew nudged their horses in Hutch's direction. I followed closely behind.

"Tonight we go to town, boys!" Hutch exclaimed.

The hair on my neck stood on end. Not from excitement. From the way the men nodded. Slow, solemn, like an agreement had already been made and Hutch was just speaking it aloud.

Not a celebration. Not downtime.

This was something else. Something I wasn't prepared for.

"What's the job?" Derek asked.

Hutch's mouth split into a cocky grin. "Mercantile."

Derek blurted, "Yer bristles still up over the—"

"Shut your beak," Glenn snapped as he jerked his head toward me.

A warning. A reminder. I wasn't in their inner circle yet.

I kept my face neutral, but my ribs felt tight. They weren't just testing me. They were deciding what they could trust me with. And whether I'd walk away from it.

"Hey, no reason to be as techy as a teased snake."

"Wagner!" Hutch bellowed.

"You keep an eye on the horses when we get to town."

I answered with a sharp nod before Hutch spurred his horse to a gallop.

No one explained what we were about to do. Or where other than the mercantile. This band was more cautious than most.

Figured they were testing me. Or pulling me in.

Either way, I aimed to earn their trust. Because that was the job. Mossman sent me here to do exactly this. Get in, get trusted, get answers.

And now, I was exactly where I needed to be.

So, I nudged Magnus to keep pace with the outlaw gang.

9 – Incognito

Hayley

"EVENING, MISS HAYLEY," Kurt said as he set his hat on its hook.

As I leaned to the side to look around him, I frowned. "Just you and Ian?"

"Yes 'um. Hutch said the rest won't be back tonight. Don't hold supper for them."

A loud sigh escaped my lips, not for the wasted meal, but for the lost time. For the gap Hutch had just created, one I needed to fill before it closed completely.

"Sorry, Miss Hayley," Ian Kelly said. "Sure must be exasperating to plan a hearty meal and only have two cow-pokes show up."

I offered the shy cowboy a half-smile. "It'll keep for tomorrow."

Of course, I'd have to lug the pot down to the root cellar. None of that was the source of my frustration, though. I needed to get to town as soon as possible to find out what they were up to. Eight men riding together meant something bigger than cattle rustling. In my experience, gangs only moved in full force for three reasons: a major robbery, a territorial dispute, or revenge.

"Luciana, I'm feeling a mite peaked. Can you take over?"

"Si."

I stuffed a roll in my pocket and hurried toward the barn, my boots scuffing against the packed dirt. Flynn met me halfway. His brow quirked, but his eyes were sharp, already reading my urgency.

I kept my voice low. "Hutch kept everyone out except for Ian and Kurt."

Flynn's jaw ticked, barely, but enough to catch. "What do you know?"

"Not much. They went to town. I need to go."

His expression hardened. "Hay, wait a few minutes for me to eat some grub. I'll go with you."

I shook my head. "No. I have a perfect disguise. No one will even know it's me."

Flynn shifted, not just a step, but deliberately, blocking the direct path to the barn. "At least take the roan. Not Telluride."

I nodded, barely stopping. "Of course. I know what I'm doing. Been on several assignments without my little brother tagging along."

His snort wasn't amused, it was knowing, resigned. Still, his hand shot out, not rough or forceful, but firm enough to catch my arm for half a second before I pulled away.

"I'll keep Ian and Kurt occupied so you don't have to worry about them seeing you from the window."

I squeezed his wrist briefly in thanks before I scurried to the barn, where I kept a crate of costumes hidden under Flynn's bed. I pulled the pre-positioned disguise kit from its hiding place, a habit drilled into me during Pinkerton training. Always have an escape, Allan had said. Always have a backup identity ready.

I donned a pair of trousers, wrapping my chest to flatten it as best I could before yanking a flowing, black cotton shirt over my head. Then came the hardest part, becoming someone else. Pinning my hair tight to my scalp. Securing the short, dark wig. Erasing Hayley in favor of someone unrecognizable.

Topping it with a newsboy cap, I studied myself for a breath. Different. Not perfect. But enough. It had to be enough.

After retrieving the roan Flynn mentioned, I picked one of the plain saddles and adjusted the straps for my short stature. Then I walked the horse away from the barn to the nearby forest, stashed my duster, and swung up into the saddle.

I pressed the roan for speed along the back trail to town, confident that Hutch and his men would stick to the main trail. Though I doubted I would arrive before they did, they'd be easy to spot if they rode together.

On the outskirts of town, I headed to the laundry building. Having scouted the town with Flynn early last week, I knew it was the perfect place to hide my horse. A gang of outlaws would never look behind a laundry. Nothing exciting there.

Once I dismounted, I stuck to the shadows in the alley closest to the main street of town. Sure enough, I spotted Hutch and his men clustered together riding on the back streets. Even in the fading light, I counted all eight men. They said nothing as they continued toward the main part of town. The music from the dance hall drowned out any sound their leather saddles and horse hooves made. Clearly, they did not want to be discovered.

As I kept to the shadows, I thought through what their purpose could be. Most of the men limited their conversation around me and Luciana to everyday topics. How the beeves looked. When they'd get time off again. Who wanted to play cards that night. Anyone has any tobacco left. How good the grub tasted.

Only Derek gabbed a lot. Stories and tall tales from his few years as a cowboy.

Derek's words from that second day came flooding back with crystal clarity. A Pinkerton agent learned to file away every detail, every casual comment that might later prove crucial.

"Elmer took the big jump," Derek had said.

"He was between hay and grass," Kurt had replied. "Barely out of short pants. Only sixteen."

Ian had shaken his head. "Such a shame."

"Hutch's little brother, too." Derek said. "Won't be long before Hutch avenges his death. Wouldn't want to be the mercantile owner. Looking over my shoulder every day, waiting for the reaper to show."

The pieces clicked together with sickening clarity. I sucked in a sharp breath.

The mercantile owner had killed Hutch's younger brother. No idea why. But it didn't matter. Hutch was riding into town for blood. And now, I was riding straight into the middle of it.

I glanced down the alleyway. Jay slowed his horse. Crud. He had to have seen me.

I darted across the alley, boots scraping against the uneven ground, heart hammering against my ribs. I had barely rounded the next building before skidding to a stop, palms catching against the rough wooden wall. My chest heaved, muscles burning.

I forced myself still, pressing into the shadows, hands flat, legs tense. The last thing I needed was for my panting to give me away. I swallowed, trying to level my breath. Too loud. Too fast.

Jay's horse had slowed further. I could feel it, even if I couldn't hear it. I strained my ears. Nothing. That was worse.

I darted around the building. The scent hit first—bay rum, sharp, distinct, familiar. Then came the impact.

I ran straight into Jay's chest, solid, unmoving, an unyielding wall of muscle and bad timing. Drat.

I ducked my head, turning sharply, instinct screaming

at me to get away, to move, to vanish. Avoidance was survival. Even though I doubted he'd recognize me in my getup, I couldn't take any chances. Best not to make direct eye contact.

But his grip was already there, fast, unhesitating, fingers locking around my arms like he already knew I was running. The way he moved, silent and controlled, wasn't the gait of a simple cowboy. I'd seen federal marshals move like that. Pinkerton agents. Men trained to hunt other men.

My head snapped up. His eyes flickered. Suspicion. A fraction of recognition. A moment I couldn't afford.

Even through my disguise, Jay had recognized something. The way he'd moved to intercept me, the certainty in his grip, he hadn't stumbled into me by accident. He'd been hunting me. Was he hunting Hayley Harper, or hunting a suspicious figure in the shadows?

I stomped hard on the arch of his foot. The breath hitched in his throat, a grunt, not pain, more surprise. His grip loosened, but not enough. His other hand clamped tighter around my arm, firm, unrelenting. Trouble. Deep trouble.

I thrust my fist into his gut, using the upward motion to leave him winded, buying much-needed time. I used every trick Stanton had taught me, from misdirection to pressure points to exploiting momentary advantage. For all his betrayals, the man had been an excellent teacher in the art of escape and evasion.

Jay's hold faltered, only for a second. A second was all I needed.

Maybe I should have waited for Flynn after all, I thought, before I whipped away, sprinting hard, feet pounding against the dirt, cutting through the next alley like a shadow that wasn't supposed to exist.

10 - Some Pot Rustler

———

J.J.

ONCE IN TOWN, the noise slammed into me, louder than Holbrook, sharper, raw. Voices tangled in shouting, laughing, arguing, men barking over the off-key twang of a piano that barely held its tune. Boots thudded against the packed earth, some quick and purposeful, others dragging slow and aimless. The air carried too many smells, layered and thick. Sweat, whiskey, tobacco, blood. Something rancid baked in the heat, settling in the alleys like it had nowhere else to go.

Canyon Diablo had a pulse, but it wasn't steady. It was erratic. Like something waiting to crack.

We wove through the back streets, where shadows stretched long, pooling in uneven patches against warped wooden walls. Some alleys gaped too wide, meant for wagons and movement. Others ran too narrow, as if they existed only to swallow men whole. A figure hovered on the edge of one, half-hidden, watching, waiting.

My fingers tightened on Magnus's reins as I slowed him, the hair on the back of my neck standing on end. My eyes darted toward the alleyway.

The brim of a newsboy cap flashed from the edge of a building, then disappeared as a slim figure cut across the far end of the alley.

Ford caught the movement, too. "What'd you see?"

"Someone's watching."

I dismounted Magnus and handed Ford the reins. "Be along in a minute."

Ford nudged his mount forward, letting me disappear into the shadows. I eased toward the end of the alley, breath steady, muscles coiled. A pebble clunked against the wall, small but sharp enough to make me shift. Then movement. A flash of dark fabric topped with a newsboy cap lurched into the dim light from a nearby window.

Not just a shadow. Deliberate. Watching. Running.

I scurried after the boy. Had to be a boy. Had to be. Not a full-grown man yet. But when he cut down another alley, I pivoted, circling the building to meet him in the back. Or lose him if my gut was wrong. It rarely was.

As I rounded the corner, the boy ran straight into my chest. Hard. Solid. And then gold. Dusty gold-nugget eyes flashed in the light from a window. Eyes I'd recognize anywhere. Eyes that had occupied more of my thoughts than they ought.

Eyes that narrowed just before a boot smashed down on mine.

"Ow," I moaned softly, white-hot pain pulsing through tendon, through bone.

I grabbed her arm just as knuckles slammed into my gut, forcing everything to collapse. Breath, control, air. She broke free before I could react, but there was something too practiced about the way she moved. Too controlled. Like someone who'd been trained to fight.

Fool woman was gonna get herself killed. Or worse.

I sucked in a deep breath and ran after her, ignoring the searing ache in my ribs. Then I dove, knocking her to the ground. She twisted, kicked hard, rolling over, trying to break loose. Every movement was calculated, efficient.

Not the flailing of someone panicked, but the deliberate actions of someone who knew exactly how to escape a hold.

I tightened my grip on her wrists, my body weight pinning her down, pressing her into the dust. Not that I wanted to. But she left me no choice. The moment registered. Softness beneath me, curves she'd fought hard to hide. Curves I couldn't ignore now.

Not ideal timing.

"Ugh." She groaned, wriggling free just enough to slam her palm against my chin. My teeth jarred. I rolled to the side, shaking off the pain, just as she launched another attack. She brought her knee up sharply. I angled fast, avoiding disaster, though my hip throbbed from the blow.

"Stop fighting," I growled, jumping to my feet.

She scrambled backward, then flipped onto all fours, quick, like an animal bolting free before launching to her feet. I chased. Turned toward her last position and caught a plank of wood slamming hard against my arm.

"Thunderation!" I barely blocked the second swing, knocking the weapon from her hand. Then I circled my arms around her, locking her tight in place.

She squirmed, frantic, but I was stronger. Her breath hitched, body tensed, and for half a second, just half a second, I had half a mind to kiss her, hoping the shock would still her. Unfortunately, she tried to bite my arm instead.

No way, no how was Hayley Harper some pot rustler. But now, I had to decide what that meant. What on earth was she really doing here? And how much trouble had she just stepped into?

"Would you stop? I don't want to hurt you."

"Then let me go."

"Not until you tell me what you're doing in town."

Canyon Diablo was no place for her. Not even disguised as a boy. She was lucky it was me who found her. Had it been Hutch, I couldn't say for sure what he would've done. But I knew it wouldn't have been pleasant.

This place had a way of swallowing people whole, especially those who didn't belong.

She drew a breath sharply, her muscles tensing beneath my grip. My pulse kicked in warning. I released her long enough to clamp one hand over her mouth before she could scream.

"Hayley, stop it!" I hissed. "I'm not gonna hurt you."

Her body stilled. Her breathing slowed, controlled, careful. I braced myself for another beating. At least she hadn't unsheathed that wicked Bowie knife.

11 - Uninvited Protection

Hayley

The moment Jay said my name, I froze. His voice was low, dense with certainty, pressing against me like it already had hold of the truth.

I weighed my options. Clearly, my disguise hadn't fooled him for a second. I could try to deny it. Deflect. But he had already spoken my name, and there was no unhearing it now.

"Can I trust you?" he asked.

Though his breath warmed my neck, a shiver crept along my spine—sharp, involuntary. The real question was, could I trust him?

After a second, I nodded.

His fingers loosened their grip, first over my mouth, then from my waist, slowly, like he wanted me to feel the choice he was making. Then he flattened against the building, his posture tense, listening as he glanced back the way we had come.

The man was as fierce as a mountain lion. All corded sinew, unreadable intent, patience that felt more like stalking than waiting.

"Thanks, mister," I said, forcing my voice into something rougher, thinner. Less me.

"What're you doing here, Hayley?"

I frowned, stuffing my hands into my pockets. Almost propped them on my hips. Almost, but that would be too much like me.

This cowboy was getting on my nerves. And under my skin.

A noise rattled further down the alley, sharp enough to send Jay's head snapping toward the sound. Before I could react, his grip caught my arm, firm, unhesitating, as he dragged me deeper into the shadows. A finger pressed lightly against my lips, sending a wave of tingles down my arms, through my ribs, and pooling in my gut.

I held my breath, aware of nothing but the scent of bay rum, horse, and sweat. Him. The noise faded. Only then did he drop his hands to his sides.

"Well?"

I cleared my throat. "Mister, I don't know who you think I am."

"Cut the act. I ain't no featherhead."

No flicker of doubt in his tone. No chance of escape through lies. When I figured he wouldn't budge, I forced my shoulders to relax.

"How'd you know it was me?"

He snorted. "No one else with eyes like yours, sweetheart."

I hated that word. Sweetheart. Hated the way Stanton had twisted it into something else, something unclean.

I stiffened. My chin lifted. My spine straightened. He leaned on the walnut handles of his guns, watching me, not in a relaxed way, but assessing and analyzing me.

"Fine," I finally said. "I got wind something might be up."

"Best leave it alone."

"Are you part of it? You an outlaw, too?"

"Might be. Might not be. Don't see how it's your

concern."

I studied his face in the dim light, searching for anything. Not trust, but proof. His eyes held a hard edge. Narrowed. Yet there was something about Jay Wagner that left me wanting to trust him.

I had no reason to. Only known him for a handful of days. Not to mention he was in Canyon Diablo. With Hutch's gang. He hadn't been sent back to the bunkhouse. Which meant Hutch trusted him enough to involve him.

That, more than anything, should have been enough to tell me Jay Wagner was trouble.

"Don't let them kill the mercantile owner."

Jay leaned forward, the shift subtle, yet heavy, as if my words had landed harder than he expected.

"What's he got to do with anything?"

I snorted. "You don't even know why you're here."

His eyes locked onto mine, not that I could see them in the near dark. But I felt it. The weight of his stare. The pressure in his silence.

"He killed Hutch's younger brother not long before Flynn and I arrived. Pretty certain tonight's mission is retribution."

A flicker. Not hesitation, not shock, but something guarded. Something watchful.

"Wagner!" A harsh whisper snapped from the end of the alley.

Jay's body shifted before I could react, moving in front of me, blocking any view of where I stood. Covering me without a second thought.

"Get outta here if you know what's good for you." No pause. No explanation. He stepped toward the voice, calm and natural, like the moment had never happened.

"You catch him?" Ford asked.

"Just some errand boy for one saloon. He didn't know nuthin'."

I stayed still, pressing against the wood, listening as their voices faded. Jay's protection lingered longer than it should have. Longer than I wanted it to.

He hadn't hesitated, hadn't weighed the risk. He had moved. Covered me. Like instinct. Like second nature. But that didn't mean I trusted him. Didn't mean I should.

I eased around the side of the building, waiting until the men's voices disappeared into the hum of Canyon Diablo. My breath came evenly and slowly, but my hands shook.

Flynn had warned me not to go alone, said it'd be too dangerous. I laughed off his concerns. I was a Pinkerton. Master of disguise. Confident. Reckless.

No. Stupid.

Lord, forgive my pride, I prayed silently. *Help me use the wisdom You've given me instead of rushing headlong into danger.* Flynn had been right to worry. I'd let my confidence override good sense, and that wasn't being professional. It was being foolish with the life God had entrusted to me.

But not entirely foolish, I reminded myself, thinking back to Jay's keen observations when we camped on the way back from Mossman's headquarters. His ability to sense movement, pinpoint details, and read the surrounding air rivaled even the best agents I'd worked with.

So what was he doing here? Why had Hutch trusted him enough to bring him along? And why had he shielded me without hesitation?

There was something about Jay Wagner that didn't fit the mold of a typical outlaw. Something in the way he carried himself, the way he'd protected me just now. *Give me discernment, Lord. Help me see the truth about this man.*

I considered the possibilities as I crept back to my horse. My cover had been blown. I couldn't afford to linger. I didn't trust Jay enough to risk staying, but something about him made me hesitate.

As I climbed onto the borrowed roan's back, I pointed her toward a slow walk out of town. When I passed the mercantile, I spotted Jay on a side street, holding the reins of several horses.

He jerked his chin sharply toward the outskirts. Not just a warning. A directive.

I pressed my heels into the mare's sides, and she answered with a trot. Something was about to happen. I could feel it in my gut, in the heavy silence just beyond the lights of town. And I was missing it.

I forced down my frustration. There would be other chances to uncover the illegal dealings of Hutch's gang. And when I did, every last one of them would pay. Even Jay, if he was mixed up in it.

Whatever he was doing here, it wasn't for a cowboy job.

Near the bunkhouse, I dismounted and tied the roan to a tree where Flynn would find her. My fingers felt clumsy as I removed my hat, shaking out my long blond locks before retrieving my duster from its hiding place.

I slipped it on and strolled back toward my quarters, waiting in the shadows until Luciana left for the outhouse before slipping inside. Quickly, I changed into my nightgown and burrowed under the covers just before she returned.

Despite the soreness in my muscles and the bruises to my pride, sleep came fast. Jay's presence lingered in the warmth of his breath against my neck, in the rough press of his fingers when he silenced me, in the sharp way his eyes had held mine even in the dark.

Whatever game he was playing, he was good at it. But so was I.

12 - A Bad Box

_____

J.J.

When I followed Ford back to my mount, I thanked God for watching over Hayley. Good thing I'd caught her in town and not one of the others. Didn't want to think about what would have happened to her, especially if Hutch figured out she wasn't just another saddle bum.

The hair on the back of my neck stood on end as we dismounted behind the mercantile. Why had she told me that tidbit about the owner? Not just a warning. Something more. Had she come into town just for that? Had she meant to tip the man off, maybe light a shuck before it all went sideways?

I held back a frown, keeping my features stoic and unreadable as I gathered the reins for the horses. Glenn led the way toward the back door while I stood watch, scanning the alley, searching the shadows, waiting for trouble like a man already caught in a bad box.

As Hayley rode by, I frowned and nodded sharply toward the edge of town. Fool woman should've chosen another route, especially since she knew Hutch would be here. She kicked her horse into a trot, and I breathed a little easier. If only for a second.

I looked over my shoulder, slow, deliberate. None of the gang were in sight. Good. None of them had seen Hayley dressed up as a boy. And I had to admit, it was a mighty fine disguise. If I hadn't seen her eyes in the light from that window, or tackled her, I might have been as blind as a snubbing post.

Which brought me back to my quandary. Why was Hayley Harper pretending to be a boy? And why was she sneaking around the dark alleys of Canyon Diablo? Could she be part of the gang?

I shook my head. Not a chance. She'd asked me to keep them from killing the mercantile owner. Blood rushed from my head as the most unlikely, impossible reason came to mind.

She was undercover. For Mossman. Too.

My grip tightened on the collection of reins, my eyes darting back and forth down the alley. No movement. No sign of anyone lurking outside. How could Mossman have put her in a bad box like this? And more importantly, was Flynn part of it, too? Had his presence eased Mossman's conscience, made it feel less like sending Hayley straight to a bone orchard?

The thought settled like lead in my gut. Next time I saw the manager, I'd nail him to the counter and dig into it. Hard.

For now, I tried to push down the roiling questions, shove aside the unwanted thoughts of what would happen if anyone at Diablo Bunkhouse discovered her true purpose. Right now, I had to focus. Because tonight, everything was about to boil over fast.

Gunfire ripped through the night. Bullets whistled past my ear. Winchester rifles barked and snapped, mixing with the deeper boom of shotguns. This had gone sideways faster than a bronc with a burr under its saddle. Either someone had tipped off the mercantile owner, or we'd walked straight into a trap. Either way, staying meant dying.

I spun, instinct taking over, catching sight of Derek and Mac running like the devil was burning the breeze behind them.

"Ready the horses!" No hesitation. I dropped the reins for theirs, then Howard's, as he vaulted onto his horse from the back. A crazy stunt, but we didn't have time to be careful.

Ford and Carter staggered forward, an arm each hauling Glenn, who looked one breath from his final sunset. Not good. I rushed toward them, grabbing Glenn, hauling him onto his horse, forcing his weight to settle despite his sagging frame. The bullet had caught him high in the shoulder, missing the major arteries but tearing muscle. I'd seen enough gunshot wounds to know he'd live if we could stop the bleeding and get him to proper care.

We had to get out of here. A shotgun blast flashed through the nearby window, both barrels of what sounded like a Parker side-by-side letting loose at once. The double-ought buckshot splintered wood where my head had been a second before. I could hear the distinctive *click-click* as the shooter broke open the breech to reload. Curses ripped through the air, wild and raw, men barking like they were fit to be tied.

"Go!" Hutch snatched his reins from my hand, swinging into the saddle.

A bullet whispered past my head, close enough to sting the air. I mounted Magnus fast, barely spurring his sides before he lurched forward. Magnus's ears pinned back at the gunfire, but his stride never faltered. The last year of chasing outlaws had taught him the difference between thunder and trouble, and he knew which one meant we needed to run.

Wind tore at me. Dust whipped against my face, clinging to sweat, to the remnants of a scrape that could still bury us. My breath came fast, ragged, deafening in my ears as I leaned low, spurring Magnus for more speed.

Then Glenn's horse faltered. The rest of us slowed, barely pulling back. A wounded man couldn't stay in the saddle much longer, not with the way he was swaying.

"Hutch!" Ford hollered, pointing toward Glenn.

Hutch veered toward him, catching him as he listed sideways, his body moments from slamming into the ground. Magnus snorted, sensing the tension, the need for movement. I steered him closer, assessing the injury despite no one asking.

"We need to staunch the bleeding."

"Carter! Derek!" Hutch snapped the order. "Help him down!"

I dismounted fast, Ford grabbing my reins as I ripped open my saddlebags, clawing for clean rags, anything to stop Glenn from crossing over to the big jump. I pressed hard against the wound, knowing it would hurt, knowing it had to. *Lord, help him hold on,* I prayed silently. *Don't let this be his time.* He grunted, weak, barely hanging on. Then his body went limp.

"I don't think we should move him," I said, voice tight. "Riding might just send him to glory."

Hutch wasted no time. "Howard!" he barked. "Ride back for a wagon!"

The crusty cowboy spurred his horse, kicking up dust as he hightailed it toward the bunkhouse. The wait stretched, each second heavier than the last, Glenn's breathing thin, rattling, fading.

Half an hour later, Flynn arrived with the wagon, the quarter moon barely casting light over the mess we'd become.

"Help me," I said, voice rough. I looped my forearms under Glenn's armpits, lifting him, hauling his dead weight toward the wagon as Flynn caught his legs, guiding him in slow, steady. Flynn handled it like he'd done this before. No hesitation, no squeamishness. Just the calm competence of a man who understood that sometimes saving a life meant getting your hands dirty.

As soon as Glenn was settled, Flynn climbed onto the seat, slapped the reins down, sending the wagon lurching forward. The rest of us spread out, riding close, watching the shadows, half-expecting another shot to chase us down. Standard formation for men who knew pursuit might come hard and fast.

My pulse finally settled when the barn rose ahead, rising from the dark like a beacon in a storm.

"I'll go get Hayley," I said, tying Magnus off, dragging a hand over my sweat-streaked face, trying to shake off the remnants of what we'd just walked through.

Mac muttered something about handling the horses, but I barely heard him. I rounded the corner of the bunkhouse, exhaling slowly, forcing my grip to loosen.

That had been closer than I liked. A quick inventory. Sore, bruised, torn up, but no bullet wounds. I ran a hand over my face, feeling the grit, the dried sweat, the tension still locked in my muscles.

Hadn't been hit. Hadn't been caught. But it wasn't luck. Luck didn't exist, not in Canyon Diablo, not in the bunkhouse, not in life. It was God. Even if I didn't always feel Him near, even if my faith felt thin, stretched at the edges, the truth still held.

Gray had taught me that. Drilled it into me, let it settle deep, woven through my thinking even when I wasn't looking for it. And somehow, even running with men I had no business trusting, even with bullets slicing through the surrounding air, I knew. God had been watching over us tonight.

I reached the door and pounded hard, my voice rougher than before. "Hayley!"

Hopefully, she could patch Glenn up before it was too late.

13 - Midnight Caller

Hayley

THROUGHOUT THE NIGHT, I woke with every little sound, every shift in the wind, every creak of the bunkhouse settling. Sleep came in restless fragments, never long enough to drown out my racing thoughts.

The horses in the yard. Boots on the ground. Muffled voices. The gang had arrived.

I barely breathed as I listened, waiting, tense. Then a pounding at the door. Sharp, urgent.

"Hayley! Come quick."

Jay.

The last threads of exhaustion vanished. I threw back the covers, my pulse slamming against my ribs as I snatched my work dress from the chair and pulled it over my shift. My fingers fumbled with the ties, all thumbs in my hurry. Not enough time to fully wake, just react.

I grabbed my medicine kit from the shelf and hauled the door open, breath still uneven.

Jay stood there, face drawn tight, posture rigid. "It's Glenn. He's been shot."

I frowned. Not a question, just instinct. I opened my

mouth, words forming, pressing forward, but Jay shook his head before I could ask.

"Best you don't ask questions. Just patch him up. The less you know, the safer you'll be."

Safer. The word wrapped around my ribs like a vise. Safer for me. Not for Glenn. Not for anyone else tangled up in this mess.

Jay spoke cautiously, warning in directives that made too much sense. But concern didn't fit a man like him. Not here. Not now. Not when he was supposed to be one of them.

I hesitated, but only for a breath, only for the smallest crack of doubt before survival pushed me forward.

He waited for me to round the corner of the building, then he fell into step behind me.

Every lamp in the bunkhouse blazed, throwing stark light across the room. Glenn lay twisting on the table, his shirt stained deep, the fabric clinging to the wound that had stolen his strength. Ford leaned in, pressing his shoulders down, keeping him from thrashing as the pain surged through him.

The bitter iron scent of blood saturated the air, thick enough to turn my stomach. I forced it down, squared my shoulders, and stepped closer.

"What happened?"

Jay's eyes flicked wide for a brief second. A warning. I caught the silent message and amended my question. "What can I do?"

"Caught a bullet in his shoulder," Hutch said. "Can you stitch him up?"

"Is the bullet still in him?"

"Don't think so."

"Carter, go get Flynn," I ordered.

Minutes dragged as I waited, the heaviness in the room bunching my neck muscles. *Lord, give me steady hands and clear thinking,* I prayed silently. *Let me use the skills You've given me to help this man.*

When Flynn finally arrived, he moved fast, steady hands working alongside mine as I reached for the whiskey and poured a generous amount over the wound. The Pinkerton training had included field medicine. Bullet wounds, knife cuts, broken bones. Allan had insisted his agents know how to patch themselves up and others when doctors weren't available.

Glenn flinched, body tensing, then his muscles slackened as consciousness slipped from his grasp. Flynn gently eased him onto his side. An exit wound. No bullet lodged inside.

"Good." I breathed out the single word, already shifting toward the next step.

I pulled my Bowie knife from my belt, turning it in my palm before handing it to Jay. "Heat this up."

His brows lifted, not just a flicker of unease, but full of hesitation. For a second, he looked ready to ask why. Then he thought better of it, jaw tightening as he strode toward the fireplace. He stabbed the blade into the coals, letting the heat lick across the steel.

A minute passed. Then another.

"Bring it back."

He did, though there was a tightness in his grip, as if he wasn't sure what I was about to do.

I didn't hesitate. Pressing the flat side of the blade against Glenn's back, I let the heat sear into the wound, sealing what thread and whiskey alone couldn't. The technique had saved more than one agent's life in the field.

Glenn's body jerked violently. "Hold him down!"

Ford braced him as Glenn fought against the pain, his gasping breath shallow, strained. His fists clenched, grasping for anything solid, anything steady. His pulse beat wildly beneath my hands. I swallowed hard, ignoring the tremor in his limbs, ignoring my own unease.

One last pass. Front side now. Quick. Efficient.

I barely had time to pull back before Glenn threw himself upright, wild-eyed and ragged. His chest rose and fell fast and unevenly. Then, with one staggering step, his knees buckled.

Ford and Carter caught him before he hit the ground, dragging him toward his bunk, their movements careful, controlled.

I hadn't realized Flynn had stepped next to me. He took the knife from my grasp. Not a word, not a flicker of hesitation. Wiped it clean, handed it back.

The job was done. Nothing left but the aftermath. I exhaled, dragging my gaze across the blood-drenched table, the grime, the remnants of a job I hadn't asked for but had done anyway.

For a beat, I stood there, pulse still too fast, hands stiff at my sides. *Thank You, Lord, for letting me help him. For the training that made it possible.*

"I'll help," Jay said finally, glancing at me once before adding, "After I see her safely back to her room."

Flynn studied Jay, his expression unreadable. Then his gaze met mine. He knew me well enough to see my answer without words.

We stepped outside, the cool air wrapping around me, cutting through the lingering heat of tension still coiled in my muscles. We hadn't made it far before Jay stopped.

"Flynn know you were out tonight?"

I raised my chin, kept walking.

"I see."

I turned, locking eyes with him. "What exactly do you think you see?"

Jay's mouth twitched, something unreadable, something knowing, but not pushing.

"Get some rest, Hayley. Sun will be up soon enough."

Not an answer. Not a challenge. Just the promise that he'd be watching.

He held the door open, waiting until I stepped inside before shutting it behind me. I dropped the bar in place, listening as his boots thudded down the steps.

Then, finally, I sank onto the bed, tension sinking deep into my bones.

For the first time since taking the assignment, I wondered if I had made a mistake. The way Jay had looked at me tonight, the careful way he'd spoken, the protection he'd offered without being asked. Either he was the finest actor I'd ever encountered, or there was more to Jay Wagner than met the eye.

I wanted the outlaws to pay for their misdeeds. But maybe, just maybe, I was in over my head. The thought should have frightened me. Instead, it made me more determined than ever to see this through.

Even with Flynn watching my back, even with whatever game Jay was playing, I had a job to finish. And Harper women didn't quit when things got difficult.

14 - Clean Up Crew

J.J.

I RAN A hand through my hair as I set my hat on its hook by the door. The entire night had been a hog-killin' mess, one close call after another. I'd learned more about Hutch's gang than I ever wanted to. For now, I was one of them, as much as I hated it.

The Lord knew my heart. He had equipped me for jobs like this one. He would be with me. But tonight had worn me thin as a fiddle string.

If I made it through this, maybe I ought to go back to Texas. Take a long break. Spend time with Mama and Gray, get back to something real, something good. Between the headaches, the light sensitivity, and the danger, maybe it was time for a new life.

An image rose fast and clear. Hayley, standing on the porch of a quaint cabin.

I shook my head, trying to dislodge the thought before it settled too deep. She was the daughter of an outlaw. I hunted men like her father, brought them to justice. She'd never be interested in a two-faced man like me.

I pivoted toward the stove, catching sight of the pot

of warmed water waiting on the iron top. Flynn poured it into a bucket with a few shavings of soap, and I rolled up my sleeves, grabbing a pile of rags already worn thin from too much scrubbing.

The two of us spent the better part of an hour working the stains out of the table, scrubbing hard, pushing past the stench of blood and sweat clinging to the wood. Scrubbing this mess out felt like trying to clean up a butcher's block with a lick and a promise, like the grime might stay long after the water ran clear.

Flynn finished first, heading back to his room in the barn. Ford lingered near the clean table.

"You did good out there tonight," he said. A rare thing, praise from a man like him. "Might have saved Glenn's life."

He held out a small pouch, heavier than I expected. I worked hard to maintain my calm demeanor, despite the unease snaking through my gut. They had stolen from the man they had murdered.

"Hutch says this is your cut. You earned it."

The words landed in my chest like prairie coal—rough, dark, staining everything they touched. Blood money. The bile climbed the back of my throat, and I forced it down.

Lord, forgive me. Show me the path through this darkness. Help me use this evil for good.

I took the pouch, not for myself, not for what they'd meant it to be, but for the dead man's family. Someday, when this job was done, it would go to them. It wouldn't make up for their loss. Nothing ever could.

I was riding the fence between right and wrong, and the barbed wire was cutting deep. Times like this made me want to quit this nasty business for good. Even pretending to be alright with their actions sickened me.

After I turned down the last lamp, I toed off my boots, stretching out on my bunk, willing the images from the night to fade into something quieter. But my mind didn't settle in the direction I wanted.

Memories of my encounter with Hayley in town rolled through my thoughts, drawing closer, sharper, unwilling to be ignored. If her eyes hadn't given her away, her fragrance did. Apples. Honey. No boy would be caught dead smelling like that. And no outlaw should be caught thinking about it, either.

Something stirred deep in my soul as I thought about her. Silky blond hair. Dusty gold nugget eyes that made my pulse throb and my heart warm. She was one sweet calico with more grit than a Texas butter biscuit.

Grit. Courage. Disguises. That crazy Bowie knife. And then those full pink lips. I wondered if they tasted like honey.

The thought scared me. I never spent time thinking about the cooks or laundresses at a bunkhouse. Never once had I pondered kissing a woman before even meeting her properly.

Yeah, well, I'd never met one quite like Hayley Harper before.

The thought lingered longer than it should have, settling deep in my chest as the days stretched on. But I had no time for distractions. No time for wondering. Every sunrise pulled me deeper into the gang, deeper into their trust. And the deeper I got, the more I saw, the more I couldn't ignore.

Over the next few days, I became a trusted member of the gang. Saving Glenn's life, something I would have done for any shot-up man, earned me everyone's respect.

My focus had to remain on riddling out all the gang's illegal activities. As more brands appeared mixed in the herd, I knew they continued to steal cattle. I just couldn't figure out who and when.

"Wagner!" Ford motioned for me to join him and Hutch.

"You any good with that fancy rifle and shotgun?" Hutch asked.

"They ain't for show."

Hutch narrowed his eyes. Then he reached for his shotgun. I unsheathed mine fast, pumped a cartridge into the chamber, and leveled it at him before he even pointed his. His hands shot up, that cocky grin stretching wide.

"That's the shotgun," Hutch said. "How about the rifle?"

"Can you shoot a thin branch off that tree?" Ford asked.

I stowed my shotgun, retrieved my Winchester Model 94, and circled Magnus once to settle my stance. I sighted the first thin limb, one hundred yards out, and cracked a shot clean through. Levered another round, fired again. The third shot came just as crisp, the brass cartridge expelled fast, glinting in the sunlight.

"Not bad," Hutch muttered.

"Better'n most of the crew," Ford said, leather creaking as he leaned forward in his saddle.

"Ever shoot at a fast-moving target?" Hutch asked.

"Like?"

"Say, a fast-moving mode of transportation?"

My gut tightened hard, coiling like a rattler ready to strike. Had to mean a stage. Train was impossible, but either way, it meant trouble. Hutch filed my answer away, slow and deliberate, like a man setting a trap and waiting for the right moment to spring it.

"A time or two."

"Good to know."

Ford cleared his throat. "You and Derek need to round up all the beeves without the Hashknife brand. Then take Mac and head out."

I blinked at him, uncertain why we needed to round 'em up. "Today," Hutch added with a wave of his hand.

Glenn moved slower than usual as we saddled up, favoring his wounded side. When the others were busy with their horses, he stepped closer to me. "Wagner," he whispered, his voice still rough. He paused, as if the words weren't coming easily. "What you did the other day..." Another pause. He met my eyes directly. "I don't forget." That was all he said, but the way he gripped my shoulder briefly before riding away told me everything. Glenn wasn't the type for flowery speeches, but his word was his bond.

I rode off toward Derek and relayed our orders. The others helped us round up the stolen cattle. I counted nearly thirty head of cattle from six different brands. Then I rode out with Derek and Mac. At least Derek seemed to know exactly where to drive the cattle.

A few hours before dark, we arrived at a corral near the railroad tracks, but far away from any signs of a station. In the distance, a whistle blew. Then the iron beast came into view, slowing as she approached. When it stopped, a man in all black opened the stock car and dropped the ramp down. We ushered the beeves in.

After exchanging a few words with the man in black, Mac joined us. He patted his vest pocket. "Payday, boys!"

"'Bout time," Derek said. "I was wondering if we were gonna hold 'em till Easter."

Mac snorted. "Hutch knows we'd revolt long before then."

Then Mac withdrew an envelope from his vest. "Wagner, you make sure this gets back to Hutch. Ford can give it to him. I'll see you back at the bunkhouse tomorrow morning."

"Where you going?" I asked.

"Like I said, it's payday. Diablo ain't the only mouths to feed."

"Come on, Wagner. If we get back soon enough, Hutch might let us head into town for some entertainment."

Though I wanted to follow Mac to determine who else was involved, I decided there would be time for that later. I kicked Magnus into a canter.

As Derek and I rode back to the bunkhouse, I asked

about Galen Harper as it had been nagging at the back of my mind for days. "He is so crooked, he could swallow nails and spit out corkscrews. Several years back, he finally got caught rustling. Had been up for murder too, but there wasn't enough evidence to convict him for that. The man they convicted swung from a rope."

"Where is he now?"

"Last I heard, he's in the territorial prison down in Yuma."

"You think Flynn and Hayley were part of his gang?"

Derek rubbed a hand over his beard. "Don't rightly know. They seem a little young to have been involved when Harper was at his peak. Could be they grew up used to having things and turned bad to keep a leisurely life-style."

If Hayley had been flush with coin, I doubted she'd be playing housekeeper for this sorry lot.

"Hutch ain't too sure about Flynn. Can't get a good read on him. Not like you. He likes you."

A good thing, but also a dangerous thing. Trust was worth a plugged nickel in a place like this. And Flynn? Flynn didn't sit right in the story, not yet. Something was missing with the Harper siblings, something that didn't add up.

We arrived back at the bunkhouse as dusk fell. Most of the boys guzzled down their supper. Ford waited until Flynn, Hayley, and Luciana left before he divvied up the earnings. Then Hutch said anyone who wanted to head into town could. I stayed behind. So did Ian Kelly. The rest couldn't mount their horses fast enough.

As I sat on the rocker, watching dusk settle heavy over the bunkhouse, I ran through everything I knew. The gang, along with some unknown players, ran a rustling ring against smaller ranches. They murdered. They stole. And now they needed someone to shoot a moving target accurately.

Sounded like a whole lot more than just rustling happening at the Canyon Diablo Bunkhouse.

Despite my progress, the old familiar restlessness gnawed at me, same as it always did. I wanted the assignment completed, done, wrapped up tight, but something about this job felt different.

Something about Hayley felt different.

I'd spent years drifting, chasing justice, never looking back. But for the first time, I wondered if I did look back, would she be there?

15 - Full House

Hayley

THE SMELL OF stale whiskey, sweat, and smoke clung thickly to the air, pressing against my senses as I stepped inside the bunkhouse several weeks later.

Bottles littered the table and floor, some cracked, others drained dry. Shot glasses lay tipped over, sticky with last night's liquor. Half the boys snored louder than a steam engine, arms flung over their eyes, boots still on, shirts untucked and wrinkled from sleep.

A deck of cards sat askew at one end of the table, scattered from careless hands. The ones face up showed a full house. Someone had won big. Someone had won more than just coin last night.

Clearly, I had missed something.

"Morning."

I flinched at the whisper, sharp enough to draw breath fast, heart kicking against my ribs. Jay stood behind me, coffee in hand, gaze steady, like he'd been waiting for me to notice him.

"Care for some coffee?"

I blinked. Did he just offer me coffee? Wasn't that

my job?

"Sure."

The mug felt warm in my grip, and I took a sip, eyes drifting across the mess again. Jay was the only hand awake. The rest were scattered, half-dressed, nearly dead to the world.

"Payday."

I frowned. "No, it wasn't. That's not until this afternoon when Pearce arrives."

Jay's gray eyes locked onto mine, unreadable, his sip slow and measured. I tried to read the message there, but couldn't make sense of it. My gaze flicked away. Back to the wreckage of the night before.

"Should I even make breakfast?"

"I'd surely like some of your fine vittles."

I sighed, downed half the coffee before setting the mug aside. Luciana's gasp came from behind me, the sudden intake of breath confirming she saw the mess too.

I asked her to clean while I moved toward the stove. To my surprise, Jay stepped in without being told, gathering empty bottles into a waste bucket, hauling them outside. He straightened chairs, while Luciana wiped down sticky cards and scrubbed at the grime covering the table.

The bacon in the frying pan popped, pulling my focus back. I cracked two dozen eggs into a bowl, whisking fast, steady, then poured them into the waiting skillet. The rich scent of fresh biscuits wafted through the room, stirring the first groggy movements from the bunks.

Not that it answered anything about what had happened last night.

"What time is it?" Derek moaned.

"Not quite lunchtime," I replied. He shot me a cheeky smile, barely awake but already back to his usual self. I pointed at the clock. Seven o'clock sharp.

After snapping his suspenders in place, he stumbled toward the door, yawning as he left. A few other cowpokes dragged themselves after him, their sluggish movements proving whatever had gone down last night had been one for the books.

Ian held the door open as Flynn stepped inside. He took one long look at the half-dressed, half-hungover men, then raised a brow.

"Is it a holiday?"

I shrugged, grabbed a dishcloth, and wiped my hands clean. "Jay said it was payday. Yet my reticule sure doesn't feel any heavier."

Flynn's expression sharpened, his gaze sliding to Jay, who sat at the far end of the table, coffee mug in hand, watching but not talking. The silence stretched. Wordless. Calculated.

He knew something we didn't. And that was dangerous.

Flynn glowered at Jay, but Jay didn't flinch. Just sipped slowly, unreadable as ever. Not good. Two undercover agents, completely in the dark.

Flynn's gaze held steady, his voice measured. "You want to help saddle up the horses?"

Jay slowly and deliberately shrugged his shoulder, then rose and followed Flynn out the door.

A few minutes later, the rest of the men stumbled back in, hair wet, smelling marginally better, but still dragging from whatever had drained them last night. I pressed my lips together, resisting the urge to ask again. Jay had already made it clear he wasn't going to answer.

As soon as Hutch sat down, I set out the food, moving with quiet precision, my gaze flicking between the groggy cowpokes slouched around the room. At the smaller table, I sat beside Luciana. Jay and Flynn returned and took the far end, both sharper, more alert than the others, but still unreadable.

No one said much. Kurt looked peaked, despite the morning light filtering in. Derek rested his head on his palm, barely lifting his fork, still half-lost in whatever had drained the men last night. Only Jay, Glenn, and Flynn looked human.

Glenn should have been just as rough as the others, but his caution had grown since returning to the saddle days ago. Maybe drinking hadn't seemed worth the risk.

"Need a volunteer to stay back to help unload supplies," Hutch said, his voice cutting through the sluggish quiet.

Half of the men raised their hands, eager to opt out of riding today. Jay didn't. Didn't stir, didn't glance up, didn't react.

"Wagner, you think you can handle it?"

He gave his usual curt nod, wordless, final.

I swallowed hard, glancing at Jay as he took another slow sip of coffee. He knew something. My stomach twisted with anticipation, knowing this was my chance. Maybe, just maybe, I could pry something out of him today.

But the morning passed without an opening, Jay staying just out of reach, his silence pressing deeper into the unknown.

By afternoon, Pearce arrived with several wagons loaded with supplies. The other two drivers washed up, and I offered them sandwiches in the bunkhouse while Jay and Flynn unloaded the crates.

Supply days caused additional work for me and Luciana. We cataloged the supplies and directed the men where to store things. Some ended up down in the root cellar. Others in the barn. Some in the kitchen.

I fell into step beside Jay as he hauled a crate toward the bunkhouse, his movements steady.

"What happened last night?"

He didn't slow. Didn't glance my way. "I wouldn't worry your pretty head about it."

The words rolled off him too easily, and before I could press further, he dropped the crate onto the floor with a solid thud, pivoting out the door before I could stop him.

I jogged to catch up. "The place was a disaster this

morning."

"I told you. The boys said it was payday."

"You expect me to believe they were suddenly flush a day before Pearce arrived with the payroll?"

Jay halted so fast I almost collided with him. Before I could step back, his fingers locked around my arm, firm, controlled.

"You as shy of brains as a terrapin is of feathers?"

Heat flared up my spine at the insult.

"You keep poking around Hutch's business, you'll get yourself killed."

"I can take care of myself."

Jay rubbed a hand over his stomach, his gaze flicking toward the grove of trees near the barn, as if seeing something I didn't. "Yeah, I recall. You know I could've stopped you with a bullet that night."

The words hung heavy between us, something unspoken pushing against the air. I held my ground. Refused to waver.

"And why didn't you?"

His jaw tightened, eyes shadowed with something unreadable. A growl rumbled low in his throat before he turned sharply, muttering under his breath. "Fool woman."

When all the crates stood stacked in the bunkhouse, I enlisted Jay to pry off the tops. Each motion was restrained, like he was keeping his thoughts locked beneath the surface.

Luciana and I worked through the pantry, stocking supplies, while Jay hauled the crates of salt pork and bacon down to the root cellar. I followed.

"Look," I said, my voice measured. "I know there are illegal dealings going on here."

Jay's grip on the crate tightened, knuckles flexing before he set it down. "Best you keep your mouth shut. I ain't gonna tattle on you, but most everyone else will."

"I know. That's why I'm asking you what happened yesterday."

He turned toward me fast, closer now, the space between us too thin. Before I could move, his hands locked onto my upper arms.

"Hutch is mean enough to steal the coins off a dead man's eyes." His gaze flicked toward the corner of the room, shadowed, distant, before muttering, "Already did."

A chill crawled up my spine. When his eyes found mine again, his expression had softened, edged with something else.

"You seem real nice, Hayley. The kind of gal who ought to find a husband and settle down in a quiet town."

The shift was too sudden, too precise, like he was testing the response it got from me.

"Why do you keep poking around here?" he asked. "What's your angle?"

"I just want to know if I'm in danger."

He exhaled loudly. "You are." His voice dropped lower. "And that's all you need to know."

Then he thumped up the stairs, leaving me there with nothing but the weight of his warning sitting in my stomach like a stone.

Lord, give me wisdom to see clearly, I prayed silently as I stood in the dim cellar. *My training tells me not to trust him, but my heart says something different. Help me know which voice to follow.*

The evidence pointed in one direction. Jay was with Hutch's gang. He'd been trusted enough to participate in whatever happened last night. He spoke of stolen money and dead men as if he'd been there. But my instincts, the same ones that had kept me alive through two years of Pinkerton work, whispered something else entirely.

Sometimes the most dangerous thing an agent could do was ignore their gut feelings in favor of what seemed logical on the surface.

Once the crates were emptied, I asked Flynn to stow the wagons while I wrapped up sandwiches for Pearce and the drivers. As I stepped away, I noticed Jay heading toward Pearce, empty-handed, moving with a quiet purpose.

I circled toward the side of the barn, keeping my steps light. His voice was too soft, too quiet against the wind.

"...murdered. This... his family."

A few coins clanked together. My throat tightened. Was he giving Pearce money? That didn't track. Pearce was too loyal to Mossman to be paid off.

"...Delivered cattle... money... sharpshooter."

I held back a groan. His voice was too low, the wind carrying pieces away. I needed to get closer.

As I inched along the edge of the barn, Jay rounded the corner. "Hear anything interesting?"

My face heated instantly. How had he known I was there?

"You're not as stealthy as you think."

"Humph."

I marched past him, refusing to acknowledge the victory in his tone, even as his laughter echoed across the yard. Figures. He sure enjoyed needling me.

But as I walked away, one thought kept circling through my mind. If Jay was truly an outlaw, why had his conversation with Pearce sounded like a report rather than a bribe?

16 - Sweet Calico

J.J.

A FEW DAYS later, Hutch sent me back to the bunk-house early. Too early. No explanation, no warning, just a clipped command and a watchful glance before he rode off, like a man sending a hound after something he didn't want to catch himself.

Last time he sent a man back early, it had been the day he murdered the mercantile owner in Canyon Diablo. That thought sat wrong, like a hornet's nest hanging low over the trail. Someone was playing a game, and I wasn't sure whose side I was on.

The unease lingered as I reined in Magnus near the barn, scanning the yard. Flynn stepped forward, offering to care for him, his movements too swift, like he'd expected me sooner.

I snagged my saddlebags and headed for the bunk-house. Luciana pulled laundry from the line, working quickly and focused, as if she had no time to talk. No Hayley. She always handled the laundry with Luciana.

Something was off. The skin at the back of my neck tightened, that old, familiar warning whispering through my senses, too quiet to ignore.

After pocketing my spectacles, I reached for the door latch, but didn't lift it right away. I waited. Listened. The bunkhouse had a feel to it—stretched silence, something held too still, too carefully.

I lifted the latch, slow and deliberate, and pushed the door open.

Hayley squeaked, whirling around faster than a jackrabbit dodgin' a coyote. I caught the wildness in her eyes, like a horse that knew it was fixin' to be saddled, but wasn't keen on the idea. Her hands darted behind her back, holding something, standing right in front of my bunk.

Mine.

My jaw tensed as I stepped inside, letting the door swing shut behind me. I tossed my saddlebags over the back of a chair, closing the space between us swiftly, purposefully, testing the air between us.

"What're you doing?" I asked, my voice low and edged.

She blinked fast, color rushing to her cheeks, gaze refusing to hold mine. "Nothing. Not a thing."

Liar. As plain as sunrise on the prairie.

I reached behind her, but she twisted fast, keeping whatever she held just out of reach. Too practiced to be accidental. I tried again, my arms circling her, but the scent of her—apples, honey, the faintest trace of dust from the day's work—stole my focus before I could stop it.

I froze, breath lodging hard in my throat, warning me I was too close, too aware. She had a certain sass and defiance about her, the kind that men knew to steer clear of, but always found hard to resist.

Slowly, she lowered her lids, then lifted her chin before revealing those mesmerizing, hypnotic eyes, sharp enough to unravel the smartest man into reckless decisions. My mouth went dry, my resolve slipping. The bag. I reminded myself to focus, to remember why I'd stepped closer in the first place, as my gaze dropped to her lips, then back. Dangerous territory.

I took a step forward. Too close. Close enough that the length of her pressed into mine, warm, solid, and simmering like a teakettle. Nothing but breath between us. Not the smartest idea I'd ever had.

I hoped the nearness would unnerve her, make her step away, give me a reason to stop. Except she didn't flinch. Didn't pull back. And unfortunately, all rational thought fled my mind entirely.

Bag forgotten. Choice forgotten. Everything forgotten. She was one sweet calico, too captivating, too impossible to resist.

I slid my hand to her low back, anchoring her against me, already lost, already reckless. A noise came from the doorway, cutting through the moment to remind me I wasn't alone. I registered it and knew better than to ignore it. Didn't care.

Instead, I rested my other hand on her soft neck, drawing her closer, closer, too close to turn back now. Her breath caught, her pulse racing beneath my fingertips, faster than I had time to process. Her hands rose slowly, tracing a burning trail up my chest, settling behind my neck, fingers curling in my hair, testing, teasing, but sealing my fate.

I lowered my lips to hers, already knowing there was no stopping it now. She leaned in. I warned myself to pull back, to be smarter, to remember that I had a job to do. Terrible idea. Kissing her like this, like I'd waited my entire life for her. It was reckless, irresponsible, and every kind of foolish I had sworn to avoid.

But kissing her felt like coming home after years of drifting, like finding something I hadn't even known I was searching for. For a man who'd spent his life chasing shadows, Hayley Harper was sunlight.

A rough hand clamped down hard on my shoulder, yanking me away so fast my boots barely scraped the floor before I lost my footing. Then, searing pain exploded in my gut, stealing what breath I had left. I barely had time to process the first hit before another one landed.

"What are you doing with my sister?"

Flynn looked at me like he was fixin' to dig my grave before I even took my last breath. Another fist slammed into my ribs, tearing through muscle, ripping the last ounce of oxygen from my lungs. Good hit.

Before I even touched the ground, my instincts took over, and I braced myself for the next blow. Wasn't gonna swing back at Flynn. Didn't blame him. He was as wild as a wolf backed into a corner, and Hayley was his to protect, no matter what it cost me.

"Flynn, stop!" Hayley's voice cut through the chaos, firm and commanding.

I peeled my eyes open in time to see Flynn hesitate, just barely, but enough. He stepped away, breath ragged, fists still clenched, rage simmering beneath his skin like dynamite waiting for the next spark.

"Did he... Did he hurt you?"

I sat up, ribs aching, lungs burning, the fight still ringing through my bones, watching as a slow, soft smile tugged at Hayley's lips. Her fingers brushed against them, light, and lingered, like she could still feel the imprint of mine there, like the memory of the kiss hadn't left her yet.

Her breath hitched, just slightly, before she locked her dusty gold nugget eyes with mine, unwavering and unreadable. Except I could feel the truth in them, thick as smoke in the air between us. I wasn't the only one who had felt it, wanted it, reveled in it. Wasn't the only one who had enjoyed that kiss.

Her gaze flickered away, and just like that, the moment broke, sense filtering back in.

Then the truth hit me like a bucket of cold water. I looked back at my bunk, everything appearing normal until it wasn't. My satchel had been moved, just slightly, one edge now showing beneath the bed where before it had been completely concealed.

She had been rifling through my things.

Terror clawed up my throat like ice water. Auggie's button. Had she seen it? That tarnished piece of metal would look like worthless junk to anyone else, something to be thrown away or swept up with the dust. She couldn't know it was all I had left of Papa and Auggie. What if she'd already tossed it aside? What if the last connection to the two people who'd meant everything to me was already gone forever, discarded like trash?

My hands trembled as panic flooded through me. I wanted to tear through that satchel right now, to feel the familiar weight of the button in my palm, to know it was still safe. But I couldn't. Not with Flynn standing there. The helplessness crushed down on me like a landslide. All I could do was sit here, not knowing if the most precious thing in my world still existed.

Lord, please let it still be there. Please don't let her have thrown it away.

Heat rushed up my spine, my pulse slamming hard. She had done it before the kiss, before that moment, the one that made me forget reason, made me want more. But it didn't matter. The betrayal burrowed deep, like a rattler's fangs sinking into flesh, venom spreading, heat turning to ice.

I climbed to my feet, body still shaking from Flynn's attack, but now there was something else ripping through me, something colder. Whatever warmth Hayley had left in me, whatever fire that kiss had ignited, drained out like venom hitting blood.

Barely steady before Flynn stepped into my view again, blocking out everything else, shutting out every thought but the rage still burning beneath his skin.

"Keep your hands off my sister." His blue eyes weren't just warning me. They were a blade at my throat, daring me to test him, daring me to be reckless again.

"What's going on here?"

A harsh voice broke the tension. A scar-faced man stepped through the doorway, moving with deliberate slowness, his eyes taking inventory of everything and everyone, like he was deciding who mattered and who didn't.

Hayley slipped around me quickly, keeping her voice level despite the nervous energy in her movements. "I best get supper started."

My eyes tracked her as she scurried to the other side of the room, a feeling I couldn't name settling deep in my ribs.

Then I turned toward the interloper, Mossman's scar-faced enforcer. "Winston, was it?"

I kept my tone even, my grip on my control tight, though the weight in my gut told me I was already on unstable ground.

The large man crossed his arms, unmoved, his stare piercing me like he was waiting for an excuse. "Mossman wants to see you."

I held back a frown. Too soon for another check-in. Winston showing up instead of Pearce—and only a few days after Pearce had been here—set every instinct I had on high alert. In my line of work, when the usual contact changed without warning, it meant either the operation was blown or someone was about to be.

"And her."

Hayley swung around fast, brows pinched in confusion, the unease creeping into her stance. "Me? Whatever for?"

Winston shrugged. "Get what you need for a few days, then meet me at the barn."

Cold suspicion sank its claws in deep. This wasn't routine. This wasn't normal. Suddenly, I was as worried as the mama of a newborn standing in a pit of snakes. One wrong move, one misstep, and it was all over.

Pearce was my primary contact. Not Winston. And what did Hayley have to do with any of this? The hair on the back of my neck stood on end, warning me before I could even figure out what I was supposed to be bracing for.

I grabbed my saddlebags off the chair, every instinct screaming at me to check for Auggie's button. My fingers itched to tear through that satchel, to find that worn piece of my past, to know it was still safe. But Winston was watching, Flynn was glowering, and Hayley left to gather her things. No time. No privacy. The helplessness twisted in my gut like a knife.

Then I snagged more ammo and checked my guns before heading out to the barn, the uncertainty eating at me with every step.

Why me and Hayley? It wasn't about the kiss. Wasn't about Flynn and Hayley, like the day I met them, hauling supplies back to the bunkhouse. So what was Mossman up to?

Winston eyed me warily as he swung into his saddle, his stare lingering, like he was expecting trouble. I eased onto my horse, which Flynn had already saddled, his movements stiff and tight, like every muscle in his body was wound too hard.

Hayley's silver mare stood patiently, unaware of the tension thick enough to snap between me and her brother. Flynn glared at me, eyes fierce, unforgiving, his fists clenching like he was resisting the urge to land another blow.

"You better not lay a hand on her again, Wagner."

I exhaled slowly, steadily. Wouldn't be a problem.

He stormed into the barn, his departure like a slammed door, rattling in my chest even after he disappeared.

I could keep my hands to myself. Keep my mind on my job. At least, that's what I thought.

Until she bounded toward us, her energy unchecked, flashing me a sweet, knowing smile. Before I could stop it, my grip tightened on the reins, my fingers aching from the force, my chest pulling tight in an instant.

I clenched my jaw. I was in as much trouble as an injured calf in the middle of a pack of wolves, no way out, no chance to run.

17 - Outlaw Who Prays

Hayley

HEAVEN HELP ME. That kiss from Jay left me breathless, addle-brained, stuck in place, and unable to think past the way he had felt against me.

It wasn't just the way his lips had moved against mine. It was the way the world had stopped, the way everything else had faded, leaving nothing but the two of us. Took me a solid minute before I could move, before Flynn's attack registered, before logic could claw its way back in, forcing reality into the space Jay had momentarily stolen.

The feel of Jay's warm mouth on mine lingered, even as the room shifted around me, even as footsteps, voices, and movement pulled at the edges of my awareness.

Stanton never kissed me like that. And I thought I loved him. Now, after Jay's kiss, I wasn't sure of anything.

I blinked, mind racing, pulse still unsteady, chest still tight in a way I couldn't quite ignore. Supper. I should start supper. My voice came out scattered, unfocused, muttering something before I crossed the room, trying to force my body into motion, trying to break free from the moment that still gripped me.

A large man filled the doorway, his presence sinking into the room like a weight too heavy to shake. Winston. I recognized him from my last meeting with Mossman. Cold stare, patient movements, too smooth to trust, too practiced to ignore.

He didn't just enter. He owned the space, standing there as if he were already in charge, like whatever happened next was already decided. Something about Winston made my skin crawl. The way his gaze swept the room, taking inventory, noting vulnerabilities. He had the look of a man with too many secrets.

He looked at Jay. "Wagner, you're coming with me."

I frowned, my stomach tightening, the wrongness sitting heavy in my ribs. Me and Flynn made sense. We were both undercover. But Jay?

After I turned supper preparation over to Luciana, I hurried back to my room, gathering what I needed fast, my thoughts still spiraling, my hands trembling slightly as I packed.

Then I met Winston and Jay at the barn. I secured my saddlebags before mounting Telli, schooling my expression to be calm as I caught Jay's reaction. His face reddened when I flashed him a sweet smile, the impact of that kiss clearly still rattling him, too.

I shook off the thought, forcing it down, refusing to let it pull at me now. I tried to project indifference, to ignore the way my stomach tightened, knotted up in ways I couldn't quite shake, couldn't quite reason away.

I couldn't think of one good reason Mossman wanted to see the two of us. Nothing made sense. And if it didn't make sense to me, it sure as anything wouldn't to Jay. Or Flynn. Or Hutch, when he found out.

I swallowed hard, pushing against the worry that Mossman had just blown my cover entirely, that something I hadn't prepared for was already unfolding in front of me. Two years of training, and I'd walked blind into whatever this was.

"Wagner, you lead. I'll bring up the rear," Winston said.

The way he said it bothered me. Not a suggestion or coordination, but a command. Like he was used to being in control. Winston watched us like a hawk circling prey, his attention too intent. Every instinct told me to keep my distance from that one.

Jay guided his horse down the trail with calm confidence, as if none of this troubled him in the least. I nudged Telli behind him, forcing my focus on the road ahead, though my mind tangled with too many unanswered questions.

Once my horse moved forward, I pulled my hat lower on my head, shielding my expression. Jay wasn't all that he appeared to be. The contents of his bag perplexed me, stuck with me longer than I wanted to admit.

A gold button from a Union uniform. Just one. No uniform. Not that Jay struck me as the military type, far too much of a lone wolf for that. But it wasn't just the button.

The more confounding possession was a well-worn Bible, the family tree page ripped out, no way to identify the owner, no name, no lineage. Yet, the spine bore the familiar signs of frequent use, thumbing through pages, worn edges, not just carried, but read. A few verses in the Psalms had been underlined thoughtfully. One about stars came to mind.

To him who made the great lights, the sun to rule over the day, the moon and stars to rule over the night, for his steadfast love endures forever.

I blinked. Jay had recited it on the way back from Holbrook, the day after I met him. Those words flowed from him with natural ease, as if they were second nature, almost like a lived experience.

Lord, give me wisdom to see clearly, I prayed silently. *Help me understand what You're showing me about this man.*

Could Jay Wagner be devout? A Christian? Could I trust him? My brow furrowed as I studied his back.

He carried a rifle, shotgun, and a pair of six-shooters, the kind of firepower that spoke of experience, preparation, and caution. That day last month, when he caught me spying in town, he had followed me, tracked me, tackled me like a man accustomed to pursuit. When I had punched him in the gut, he barely reacted. Like someone used to taking hits, someone who had been in more fights than he cared to admit.

Yet he recited Psalms. Yet he defended me. Yet he watched out for me, walking me to and from my room more than once. Yet he hid his Bible. Hid the gold button.

Why one gold button? What did it mean? Could he really be Army? Cavalry?

I shook my head. It just didn't fit. Christian? Maybe in secret. Cowboy? Yeah. But outlaw? A man like my father? No.

Galen Harper had been rotten to the core, not a hint of love for any of his six children. Wasn't even sure if he had loved Mama, or if she had loved him. Never once did I hear him speak a kind word, never acted in the best interest of another soul. He had been the only important person, the center of everything.

I sniffed, the memories pressing in. The times he left us alone for days at a time, no food in the house, nothing but hunger and desperation. Mama had passed on, leaving Shane and Lilian, the two oldest, to figure out how to feed the rest of us.

Then the brute would show up with his gang, eating what little food we had left. Ordering us girls to wash their filthy, blood-stained clothes. Clobbering Lilian or Justine when they couldn't figure out how to get blood out of his favorite shirt.

That was how an outlaw acted. Galen. Hutch. Ford. Hard, harsh men.

Jay was nothing like them. He might put on a tough

front, carry a fierce scowl, but an outlaw, one rotten deep in his soul, didn't kiss a woman like Jay had kissed me. An outlaw didn't walk the housekeeper to her cabin just to see her safely home.

No way Jay was really an outlaw. Deep down, his heart was pure. I was sure of it.

As the trail widened, Jay slowed his horse, letting me catch up to him, though his smirk said he'd been waiting for me to say something first.

"Run out of words?"

I snorted, shaking my head. He raised an eyebrow. Though I couldn't see those heavenly gray eyes behind his darkened glasses, I knew he studied me.

"Who are you?" I blurted out.

"Jay Wagner."

I shook my head, unconvinced. A slow smile stretched across his lips, deliberate, knowing.

"Come on, Hayley. Still tongue-tied from that kiss?"

Heat warmed my cheeks, creeping up despite my better judgment. Thinking about that kiss was the last thing I ought to do. Each time I did, I let down a little more of my guard, and I couldn't afford to do so until I knew for certain I could trust him.

"And just why did you kiss me?"

His cheeks reddened, his gaze dropping away before he squeezed his horse's sides and moved into the lead again. For a split second, I thought he might say something. Might explain. But he didn't.

Well, I had one answer. He hadn't planned on kissing me. His impulsiveness bothered him. And he enjoyed that kiss. Probably as much as I did. No outlaw acted like that. Right?

As the sun lowered in the sky, Winston asked us to make camp. Something slithery in the way he moved made me uneasy. When he thought I wasn't watching, I caught him studying both of us with an intensity that raised my hackles. Like he was measuring us for weaknesses rather than just escorting us.

"We'll camp cold tonight," Winston announced, scanning the canyon walls with those calculating eyes. "No fire."

The directive felt wrong somehow. Too careful for a routine trip, too paranoid for men supposedly on the same side. Another piece that didn't fit the picture Winston was painting. Too careful for a routine trip, too paranoid for men supposedly on the same side. Another piece that didn't fit the picture of Winston as Mossman's loyal right-hand man.

Maintaining my calm exterior, I passed around some biscuits and jerky I'd packed, both men thanking me. Winston with a nod, Jay with direct eye contact and words. See, things like that made me think Jay was an upright man. It fit with the well-worn Bible, the protective nature, and that kiss.

Jay frowned. "Any particular reason?"

"Pearce got careless a few days back," Winston said, his tone matter-of-fact but with something underneath it that didn't sit right. "Built a fire on his way back from Diablo. Could be seen for miles in these canyons. That's how they got the drop on him."

My contact. The one Mossman asked to pass messages to.

But Jay's reaction—tight, immediate—told me something I hadn't expected.

The news meant something to him too.

I didn't say anything, but my mind spun. Had Jay worked with Pearce before? Had Pearce told him things he hadn't told me?

I kept my expression neutral, passing the last biscuit like nothing had shifted.

I wasn't sure what unsettled me more—Pearce's mistake, or Jay's reaction.

Jay didn't speak right away. Just sat there, brows drawn, the firelight catching the edge of something unreadable in his expression.

Then he turned to me.

"Will you be alright without a fire?" Jay asked me, concern evident in his voice.

I rested my hand on the hilt of my knife, studying him before answering. "Why, you offering to keep me warm?"

He chuckled, backing away with raised hands, palms facing me. "I'll take that as a 'yes'."

The air grew chilly once the sun set, but Winston's explanation about Pearce nagged at me. It made sense on the surface, but something in his tone suggested he knew more about Pearce's attack than he should. How would Winston know exactly what mistake Pearce had made unless he'd been there?

I should have been more worried about my safety. Except I knew Winston had worked with Mossman long before coming to the Aztec Land & Cattle Company. He, Mossman, and Pearce all knew my secret. Knew Flynn's.

Secret. The word hit hard, piercing, cold, unraveling something deep inside me. I laid down, pulling the blanket up to my chin, feeling the weight of it settle into my ribs.

Could Jay be harboring a secret, too? One that Mossman already knew?

And if so, what did that mean for all of us?

18 - Desert Hare or Coyote

J.J.

THE NEXT MORNING, we broke camp at the earliest sign of light, but the sense of trouble brewing hadn't left me. The request for me and Hayley to travel to Holbrook still bugged me. Urgently, too. We could have waited until this morning to leave the bunkhouse. No need to cut out in the middle of the afternoon like we had. Still didn't sit right.

My hand drifted unconsciously to my vest pocket, searching for the familiar comfort of Auggie's button. Empty. The weight of uncertainty pressed against my ribs. Was it still there in my satchel? Had Hayley thrown it away, thinking it was worthless? The not knowing gnawed at me worse than physical pain.

Hutch and Ford would think it as odd as a coyote snuggling up to a desert hare that me and Hayley were gone. At least Flynn and Luciana were the only ones who knew Winston had showed up, and I didn't think either of them would volunteer anything. If Mossman hadn't considered how we'd explain the sudden trip, I'd better have a credible story ready to satisfy Hutch's questions. Last thing

I needed was for him or Ford to doubt me. I'd barely made inroads into the gang.

Once the sun rose, we pushed our horses hard at Winston's direction. He seemed eager to deliver us to Mossman as early in the day as possible. Something about Winston's easy command of the routes bothered me. Too familiar, like he'd traveled these trails more than his official duties would require.

We rode side by side except where the trail narrowed. Then Winston rode out front, followed by Hayley, with me bringing up the rear.

On one such stretch, I allowed myself to study Hayley. Her golden hair whipped in the wind behind her, her movements a fluid extension of her horse's, like any expert horsewoman. The image of Hayley on the front porch of a cabin came to mind again. She smiled like she had after that kiss, eyes full of peace and awe. I handed her a coffee after she took a seat in a rocking chair. She rested her hand on her belly.

An ache as deep as the ocean started in the pit of my stomach and threaded through my heart. It was a wonderful picture. Homey. Comforting.

I blinked several times, forcing the fantasy away. For that's what it was, pure fantasy. Fiction. Nothing about my future involved a wife or a child. It was futile to dream of such things.

The Rustler Hunter, J.J. Westin. That was who I was. A hired investigator and enforcer. Not the sort of man to settle down, marry, and raise a family.

No matter how impossible it seemed, I wanted it. I wanted a place to call home. To stop drifting. To put down roots. Start a family. To kiss Hayley again.

Auggie's fear-filled eyes flashed across my vision the day he slipped from this mortal coil. The memory struck viciously, tightening around my ribs, pressing into my lungs. I didn't deserve to dream about a home, a family, or even a wife. It was my fault Auggie never had a wife or children of his own. My penance was to give up my life for a just cause. An important cause.

Please, Lord, let that button still be there. Don't let me have lost the last piece of him too.

The trail widened, and I dropped my heels into Magnus's sides, urging him forward. He lunged ahead, muscles cording, hooves hammering the earth, sending up a spray of dust and loose rock.

Cold air slashed across my face, biting at my skin, tearing at my lungs. My eyes watered from the sting, letting myself believe that was the reason. Not the truth. Never the truth.

Magnus stretched out, his powerful strides eating up the ground, the rhythmic pounding vibrating through my bones. If only I could outrun the pain snaking around my heart and lungs, squeezing so tight I could hardly breathe.

Then a flash of movement in my peripheral. Golden hair. Silver mare. Hayley.

She matched my mount stride for stride, her body low over her horse's neck, hand gripping her hat against the wind.

"Yaw!" Her voice cut through the rush of air, loud and authoritative.

To my complete shock, she overtook us, her mare surging ahead, hooves kicking up dirt that pelted my face.

I gritted my teeth, yanking back on my reins as she pulled up a few horse-lengths ahead. Magnus snorted, tossing his head, frustrated at the abrupt stop.

"What the—" She gulped a deep breath, her chest rising and falling fast. "Was that?"

Her eyes sparked fire, burning straight through me. No way, no how was I gonna reveal the turmoil clawing at my insides. Not now. Not ever. That angst drove me to take risks, kept me razor sharp, and gave me an edge over the outlaws I hunted. I couldn't lose that.

Her mare danced beneath her, nostrils flaring, hooves shifting restlessly, mirroring her frustration.

"What is wrong with you?"

I snorted and swung down from Magnus's back, boots hitting the dirt hard. She did the same, her breath still uneven, her pulse visible at the base of her throat.

Then she stepped close, jabbing a finger into my chest, her touch firm, unyielding. "You studying to be a half-wit or something?"

I caught her wrist, my fingers wrapping around the delicate bones, holding her hand against my chest. Her pulse hammered beneath my thumb, fast and furious, matching the fire in her eyes.

"Careful, darlin'," I said, my voice rougher than I intended. "Keep poking me like that, and I might think you're worried about me."

Her breath stuttered, but she didn't pull away. "Worried? About a fool cowboy with a death wish?"

"Is that what I am?" I stepped closer, close enough to see the flecks of gold in her fierce eyes, close enough to smell apples and honey beneath the trail dust. "Just a fool cowboy?"

For a heartbeat, something flickered in her expression. The anger was still there, but underneath it was something else. Something that made my chest tight and my resolve waver.

Then she yanked her hand free and stepped back. "You're something alright. Question is, what?"

I grunted, reaching for my canteen, the cool metal grounding me for half a second.

Winston rode up, his horse's hooves crunching against the dry earth. "We'll rest here for a bit," he said.

"We wouldn't have to if this idiot hadn't ridden like he was trying to catch a train."

Hayley growled, spun on her heel, and stalked away, her boots kicking up dust in her wake.

Winston narrowed his eyes at me, but I didn't meet his gaze. The way he watched us wasn't quite protective. More like he was measuring something.

I walked away from the two of them, my thoughts gnawing at me like a dog on a bone.

Auggie would have been twenty-five. He could have been married by now, maybe with a few young 'uns running around a ranch or a farm. He would have grown into a decent man, obedient, compassionate, more like our mama.

I had been the restless troublemaker, always ready for a scrap or an adventure. Just like Papa, according to Mama.

I sighed heavily, the weight pressing into my ribs. Nothing good ever came from daydreaming or traveling over those old memories. Best to leave the past in the past.

After twenty minutes, Hayley sniped at me as she mounted her horse, her tone edgy but not quite biting. "Ain't a race, Wagner. Let's just get there, killing no one or nothin'."

I motioned for her to lead, nudging Magnus to follow behind.

About an hour later, we arrived at Mossman's office.

"Miss Hayley, you go on in. There's a washroom around the corner if you want to freshen up first," Winston said. "West—er—Wagner and me will see to the horses."

"Thanks, Winston."

Hayley grinned as she skipped up the porch stairs, her energy upbeat now that we'd arrived.

I snorted under my breath, watching her go. "You always this chipper after nearly riding a man into the ground?"

She paused at the top step, throwing a glance over her shoulder. "Only when the man deserves it."

I gritted my teeth, leading Magnus and Telluride to the barn, stripping off their tack, letting the routine settle my thoughts.

As I worked, I inquired about Pearce. "Got jumped by someone on the way back from the Diablo Bunkhouse the other day. Bullet grazed his leg. He ain't healed enough

131

for a long ride."

Winston's explanation about Pearce getting jumped felt too convenient. Too neat. If I were Hutch looking to place a man inside Mossman's operation, I'd want someone who could create opportunities, eliminate threats, and control information flow. Someone exactly like Winston. That scar across his face suggested a violent past he kept quiet about.

No wonder Winston hadn't wanted a fire last night. He suspected someone was watching the comings and goings of Diablo. Or maybe he was the one doing the watching.

Once I finished brushing down Magnus, Winston told me to head on up to see Mossman while he took care of Telluride.

I stopped by the trough to rinse off some of the trail dust, letting the cool water settle me before I strolled toward Mossman's office.

Pearce opened the door, his slight hobble noticeable as he motioned toward a chair. Clearly, he was in no shape to ride, just like Winston had said.

A squeal came from behind me, causing my nerves to fire like black powder tossed in flames. "Grady Thatcher!" Hayley exclaimed.

I turned in time to see her launch herself into a man's arms. A very handsome man. A twinge of jealousy pinched my gut, tightening before I could shove it aside.

The hug lasted too long. When he finally released her, I glared at him, my jaw stiff.

"Didn't take you for the swooning type," I muttered.

Hayley whipped around, eyes flashing. "Didn't take you for the jealous type."

I grunted, crossing my arms, but the tension didn't ease. "Jealous?" I scoffed. "Darlin', you flatter yourself. I've seen polecats fight over scraps with less fuss."

Her eyes narrowed, but a smirk tugged at the corner of her lips.

"How's my sister? And baby Amy?"

"Just fine. Can't hardly believe how big my daughter has grown in a few months."

At last, I released my breath; the tension draining as realization settled in. Brother-in-law. That's who Thatcher was to my Hayley.

"Grady, come meet Jay—"

"J.J. Westin."

Thatcher said my real name as he extended his hand, his grip steady. My stomach clenched tightly as I shook his hand, the weight of it pressing into my ribs.

"Pleasure to meet you," Thatcher said. "I've brought some news you'll both want to hear."

I turned toward Hayley, holding back a cringe as her emotions marched across her features. Curiosity. Confusion. Hurt. Then rage. The kind that could curdle fresh milk and send a rattlesnake slithering for cover.

Guess that meant she'd heard of me.

After a minute, she crossed her arms over her chest, her stance unyielding. Then she spat the words I most hated.

"I thought you'd be taller."

I exhaled slowly, forcing my shoulders to stay loose. Well, at least she didn't jab her wicked Bowie knife in my gut. Yet.

I wasn't sure if Hayley was as soft as a desert hare or ready to chew my flesh to the bone like a coyote. The woman could flip from one to the other faster than a rattler striking in the dark, and I wasn't fool enough to think I'd seen the worst of her bite.

19 - Not-so-secret Identity

Hayley

J.J. WESTIN?

The name slammed into my chest like a runaway stagecoach, rattling every nerve in my body. Jay Wagner was none other than the famous rustler hunter, J.J. Westin.

I blinked, my breath tight, uneven, as a thousand thoughts careened through my mind. J.J. Westin. *The* J.J. Westin. And he had kissed me.

My lips tingled at the memory, a twitch of a smile threatening at the corner of my mouth. What a kiss it had been. Then, the almost-smile vanished, scorched away by the heat rising in my chest.

How many women had he kissed? Had he turned their hearts upside down, too? Had he left them spinning like a dust devil, only to move on like it was nothing?

My blood boiled hotter than a branding iron. Rage twisted to fury, and I spat out the only words I could think of.

"I thought you'd be taller."

His eyes narrowed, sharp as a freshly honed blade. Good. Served him right, the lying coyote.

If my brother-in-law hadn't been ushering me to a chair, I'd have half a mind to knock Jay—ugh, J.J.—flat on his back with my expert training. Just for the satisfaction. Petty? Sure. But it'd feel mighty fine.

"Take a seat, Westin," Mossman barked the order. He nodded to Pearce, who made himself scarce.

J.J. shifted stiffly, lowering himself into the chair as Grady took the seat next to me.

"What game are you playing, Mossman?" J.J.—ugh, J.J.—gritted out.

"Sit, and I'll explain why I called you both here." Mossman's gaze swept over us, his tone even. "The Livestock Commission brought an opportunity to us. That's why Thatcher is here."

J.J.'s brow furrowed. "What's that have to do with Hayley?"

I narrowed my eyes, crossing my arms tightly over my chest.

"She's a Pinkerton."

My head whipped toward Mossman. "I thought we weren't letting anyone besides Flynn and Shane know!"

J.J.'s booted foot bobbed up and down, his spurs jangling a steady rhythm. "Who's Shane?" he growled, glaring at me.

"My other brother," I sneered. "And Grady's partner."

I waited, watching as J.J. Westin—really? Westin?—connected the dots, slow as molasses on a cold morning. His jaw locked tight, his knuckles turning white against the arm of the chair.

"So, Shane works for the Livestock Commission."

"Yup," Grady said easily. "Flynn is a Deputy U.S. Marshal. And Hayley is a Pinkerton. All hired by Mossman to root out the rustlers."

I leaned forward, my voice dripping with mock sweetness. "And I suppose you, Mr. Famous Rustler Hunter, are here to do the same?"

J.J. snorted, eyes flashing with annoyance. "Little slow to catch up, Miss Pinkerton?"

I huffed, flicking a hand in dismissal. "Pfft."

Mossman held up a hand, tone firm. "Lady, gentlemen. Let's put the barbs aside and get to the reason you're both here."

J.J. gave a sharp nod, stiff as if bracing for impact. I folded my hands in my lap, lifted my chin, and met Mossman's gaze head-on. He eyed me for a few more seconds, like he was trying to measure whether I'd let my irritation get in the way of business.

"Go ahead, Thatcher."

"Thanks." Grady adjusted in his chair, settling into explanation mode. "My boss got wind of an unplanned Wells Fargo stage heading through Canyon Diablo in two weeks. When I wired Mossman, he asked me to meet here today. I know the shotgun rider, Xavier Mack. He used to work with me at the Livestock Commission, back before Lilian and Deacon married."

I nodded, vaguely recalling meeting Mack years ago.

"Anyway, he and his partner have agreed to be decoys for the real shipment. We, me, Shane, and Mossman convinced them to let us hatch a plan that might help your mission." Grady waggled a finger between me and J.J.

Mossman leaned forward, hands clasped on the desk. "So, I brought you both in. Hayley, you can bring Flynn up to speed. Shane is already aware of the plan and is ready to help if the outlaws at his bunkhouse get involved."

I could feel my thoughts trying to veer off toward Jay—no, J.J.—and his true identity, but I reined them in. I needed to focus on the mission, on ensnaring Hutch and his gang.

J.J. cleared his throat as if shaking off whatever thoughts he had brewing. "What's the plan?"

Grady described how rumors would circulate that the stage held an unusually large stash of gold bars. They'd use a six-team of horses and gold-painted lead bars to bolster the ruse.

"Hayley, if they want an inside person as a passenger, you need to volunteer."

J.J. stiffened, his head snapping toward Grady. "Not a chance," he said, voice taut. "Hutch isn't a man to be trifled with."

I sat up straighter, unsheathing my Bowie knife with deliberate ease, letting the light catch the blade. "Need I remind you, Jaaay Jaaay, that I can take care of myself?"

J.J. exhaled sharply, almost as if he was biting back something stronger than irritation. "You got a death wish or something?"

I tilted my head, letting my smirk stretch a little slower than necessary, daring him to argue. "No. But I'm trained in subterfuge. I can warm up to Hutch, convince him I have a dark side, like my outlaw father."

J.J. shook his head in disgust. "Fool woman."

Grady laughed outright. I turned wide eyes toward him, incredulous. He shook his head, clearly enjoying himself. "Hay, you are something else. Got this one wrapped around your little finger already."

My jaw slackened.

"You two will pose as lovers," Mossman said matter-of-factly. "Obviously, there are plenty of sparks flying already. Won't be much of a stretch."

"No way!" I said.

"No how!" J.J. said at the same time, voice rigid as a drawn bowstring.

Mossman laughed, shaking his head at our immediate protest, clearly entertained. "That will be a suitable cover for why the two of you up and disappeared for a few days."

I narrowed my eyes at J.J., catching the flicker of something unreadable before his jaw locked tight again.

After Mossman dismissed us, Grady followed me as I stalked outside.

"All joking aside, be careful. I know you can take care

of yourself. And that Flynn will have your back."

"I will. Just don't tell Justine about any of this."

"Are you kidding? She'd never let me out of the house if she knew how dangerous my job was. Your secret is safe with me."

"Good."

Lord, help me make sense of all this, I prayed silently as the shock finally began to settle. *I've been deceiving J.J., and he's been deceiving me. But we're on the same side. Help me see Your will in this tangled mess and give me wisdom to work with him despite everything.*

J.J. came up next to me, his usual smirk settling into place. "Well, sweetheart, what do you say us lovebirds head back?"

I raised my chin, refusing to give him the satisfaction of a reaction. "I prefer 'darling'."

"Darlin'." His eyes glinted. Then he laughed outright and headed toward the barn.

"Just what's so funny?" I asked, trailing behind.

"Pinkerton, huh?"

Beyond annoyed, I circled my foot toward his leg, swiping it out from under him just as he placed his weight on it. His balance wobbled, just enough for me to take satisfaction, but then his hand shot out, grabbing my waist.

I landed on top of him, tangled, breath stolen. The solid warmth of him beneath me sent an unwelcome flutter through my stomach. Even knowing who he really was, even with all the lies between us, my body still reacted to his nearness.

I huffed, shoving myself off him. His chuckle rang in my ears all the way to the barn. "Pinkerton! Ha!"

When I opened Telli's stall, J.J. caught up to me, still grinning. "Mossman's right about one thing."

"Yeah?"

"Plenty of sparks flying here."

I growled and reached for him, but he darted away, quick as a fox. The nerve of the rustler hunter! He sure seemed to enjoy riling me.

I ignored his not-so-covert glances and tightened Telli's cinch with a little extra force. This was my biggest win yet, and I wasn't about to let it slip through my fingers. No way was I gonna play it safe.

I'd be right there in the middle of the action when it all went down, come fire or flood. And if that meant working alongside the infamous J.J. Westin, pretending to be his lover while catching the very outlaws he'd been hunting, so be it.

At least now I knew why that kiss had felt so different from Stanton's. J.J. Westin might be a deceiver, but he wasn't a married man playing games with a naïve girl's heart. He was a professional, just like me.

That realization should have made things simpler. Instead, it only made them more complicated.

20 – Darlin'

J.J.

I WONDERED AT the wisdom of pretending to be the Pinkerton's beau. The thought hit my gut hard. Much as I'd enjoy calling Hayley Harper my darlin', she was nobody's gentle sweetheart. On the ride back to Canyon Diablo, I half-expected she might stab me in my sleep and leave me as coyote food.

Winston chaperoned us overnight, but headed back to Holbrook as soon as dawn lit the sky. Hayley barely said a word to me yesterday. Seemed this morning wasn't gonna be much better.

I eased Magnus up next to her, letting the quiet stretch just long enough to get under my skin. My mustang's ears flicked forward, then back, sensing the tension between us. Even the horses knew something was off.

"If we're gonna play the role of sweethearts, you're gonna have to speak to me."

"Humph."

"Maybe we ought to get to know each other a bit."

She snorted, tossing me a sideways glance. "Oh, wouldn't you like that, Mr. Famous I-kiss-all-the-girls Rustler Hunter?"

A smile tugged at the corner of my mouth. She thought I had left a trail of broken hearts in the dust. I couldn't decide if I wanted her to know she'd been the only one.

"Don't worry, you were the best kisser of them all. Your Pinkerton training teach you that?"

When red bloomed on her cheeks, I grinned, satisfied. Good to know she didn't throw herself at many men.

Then her shoulders sagged, the fire in her eyes dimming. "You have no idea." Her voice carried something heavier, something deeper. Regret crept at the edge of my grin. There were layers beneath that comment, and for the first time, teasing didn't feel right.

I softened my tone, easy. "Darlin', you can tell me anything."

She angled in her saddle, flashing those gold nugget eyes at me. Her scowl softened just enough to show the hesitation beneath it.

"His name was Stanton." Whoa. Didn't expect a confession right then. "He was a Pinkerton too. My partner."

I knew the Pinkertons had a reputation for discipline, discouraging distractions. Especially of a personal nature. Somehow, I had a hard time picturing Hayley breaking that rule.

"He trained me. Allan saw the chemistry between us and thought we could..." She paused, choosing her words careful-like. "We were convincing as a couple in love."

Hayley faced forward again, letting out a loud breath. "Wasn't hard to believe, because we were in love. At least I was with him. I didn't know..." She shook her head. "He kissed me like he loved me. Talked about loving me when no one else was around."

Her hand shot up too fast, swiping at her face before the emotion could settle. "He talked about marriage. At least, that's what I thought he meant when he said he couldn't live without me. Looking back, I realize he only implied a permanent relationship. Never used the word 'marriage.'" Her voice dipped hollow now, like the truth had finally settled in after years of denial. "That had just been the foolish notion of a naïve, junior agent."

I exhaled slowly, gripping my reins. My heartbeat pressed against my ribs like a caged animal wanting free.

A sardonic laugh escaped her lips, brittle at the edges. "He pushed things too far. I let him, thinking he would marry me when the assignment was over." Hayley glanced over at me, her eyes fierce but rimmed red. "It's really sad. All those years worrying about protecting my virtue from outlaws on my father's ranch, and I willingly gave it up to a married man."

Her gaze flickered downward, shoulders hunched in a way I hadn't seen before. She was hardy, resilient, but this had cut her deeper than anything else.

"So, Jay, whatever you do to me, don't take my heart with you."

Words jammed up in my throat, stuck like grit in a desert wind. I'd never take advantage of her. Not like the rake Stanton. But I couldn't promise not to steal her heart. Because suddenly, I wanted it. Her heart. Her love. A foolish notion.

Maybe I'd spent too much time picturing her on that front porch. In that cabin, sipping coffee, warmth in her eyes. The fictional image of something that could never be. Except now I wanted it to be real. With her.

"Yaw!"

Hayley kicked her mare into a canter, dust rising in her wake. I let her set the pace, hanging back just far enough not to choke on the dust. Close enough to watch her ride, though. The way she moved with Telluride, like they were one creature. Natural grace from years in the saddle.

I scarcely believed she'd shown me her deepest pain. And not for one second did I doubt the truth of it.

When the Diablo Bunkhouse loomed in the distance,

I caught up with her. "Hayley, we need to get our story straight before we just show up after two and a half days."

Thankfully, she reined in her silver mare, dismounting near an ironwood tree. The location gave us decent cover from the bunkhouse while still offering multiple escape routes if needed. Then she tied her horse to it.

I did the same, positioning Magnus where he could move quickly if trouble found us. Old habits.

"You're right. Lover's tryst?"

I shook my head, jaw tightening. "Don't want to damage your reputation. Or encourage Carter."

She huffed, flicking a glance at me. "What if I received word from my other brother about the Wells Fargo stage?"

I nodded, agreeing immediately. "Ah, I like it. I rode with you to hear the news firsthand and bring it back to Hutch."

"And on the trip, we grew closer." Her tone was smooth, almost too casual. "That will give you an excuse to be seen with me from time to time. Say that you're sweet on me."

My pulse throbbed. No acting needed. I was sweet on my darlin' already.

"Do you think we need to practice kissing?" I asked, winking at her.

The daggers in her eyes told me exactly what she thought about that.

"Just checking. Wouldn't want it to look contrived."

Hayley snorted, flipping a loose strand of hair behind her ear. "Don't think it will."

"You need me to talk to Flynn?"

"No. I will." She smirked, the teasing already settling in. "And don't worry, I'll tell him to get riled up any time he sees you with me. Like an overprotective brother would be."

I shook my head at her amusement, but before I could fire back, something rustled in the dense brush nearby. Instinct snapped through me, my muscles tightening. The sound was wrong. Too deliberate. Too careful for an animal.

Someone was watching.

I pulled Hayley against me, voice low. "Someone's watching."

She narrowed her eyes, but before she could react, I captured her lips, pressing in just enough to make the moment believable. Maybe just a little more than necessary.

She melted against me, hesitation gone. In that breath of time, I wondered how much of her response was truth versus acting. I sure hoped she enjoyed the kiss as much as I did.

When I finally ended the kiss, she smiled up at me, eyes glinting with something unreadable. "I thought we weren't practicing."

I grinned, slow and certain. "Darlin', did that feel like practice to you?"

A sweet purr bubbled up from her throat, soft, rich. Then Hayley turned and mounted her horse, leaving me watching her with too many thoughts tangled in my head.

I climbed into my saddle, unable to shake the feeling sinking deep into my bones. I sure wouldn't mind finding more opportunities to work closely with my darlin'.

21 - Rattlesnake Egg Shells

Hayley

"WHERE IN THE Sam Hill have you been?" Flynn growled as I reined in Telli by the barn. "Hutch is madder than a rabid dog, and I've been worried sick."

"All is well, little brother." I flashed him a sassy grin, sliding from Telli's back. "I just ran away with Jay."

Flynn darted toward Jay, still on his mustang, fists clenching at his sides. I laughed outright, shaking my head. "I'm just joshing you. I got wind of a lucrative opportunity." I chose my wording carefully, scanning our surroundings in case anyone was hanging around to overhear. "Jay came with me to assess the worthiness of the information before we bring it to Hutch."

As soon as I finished tying Telli to the hitching post, Flynn grabbed my arm, ushering me into the barn. He kept moving until we were safely behind the closed door of his room.

"Cut the act, Hay." His voice was low, edged with something raw. "I was seriously worried about you being gone with Wagner. Especially since the last time I saw you, he... He..."

"Kissed me?"

Flynn narrowed his eyes, fists planting on each hip. Yeah, I struck a nerve. "Wanna hear the full story?"

Slowly, he dipped his head, reluctant but listening.

"Grady met with us. And you'll never believe this," I lowered my voice, letting the tension build. "Jay is none other than J.J. Westin."

"What?!" Flynn reeled back, eyes wide, shoulders rigid.

"Oh, it gets better, little brother." I leaned in, voice hushed. "He and I are to play the part of sweethearts while we reel in Hutch." I kept my voice just above a whisper, relaying the entire plan. "Shane is in on it, too."

Flynn scrubbed a hand over his jaw, frustration radiating off him. "I don't like it."

"What's not to like?" I tilted my head, feigning ease. "Grady, Shane, you, me, and 'Jay' are all on the same side. There's safety in numbers."

Flynn's shoulders dropped slightly, but the tension didn't fully ease. "I don't like you spending so much time with Jay." His voice dipped, almost hesitant. "He's gonna break your heart."

Even though J.J. thrilled me with his kisses, I wouldn't give him my heart. We were like burrs that rubbed each other the wrong way. Nothing genuine would ever come out of it. I hoped.

My brows drew together, and for the smallest fraction of a second, doubt flickered. I pushed it aside. "I know what I'm doing."

A knock sounded at the door. "Darlin', Hutch wants to see us."

Flynn frowned, jaw tightening. "Be careful."

I rolled my eyes, pushing past him to open the door.

J.J. offered a winsome smile as I rested my hand in the crook of his arm.

"How much did you tell Hutch?" I asked, keeping my voice low.

"Just that you discovered something he would want to know. Figured we'd best stick close to keep our story straight."

Hutch and Ford sat in the rocking chairs on the porch of the bunkhouse. I took a steadying breath, my fingers curling slightly against J.J.'s sleeve. It all came down to the next few minutes. I prayed my Pinkerton training wouldn't fail me now.

J.J.'s arm was solid under my hand as we stepped onto the porch, but I wasn't foolish enough to think of it as steadying. I had been trained for moments like this. To stand my ground, control my breath, and never let unease slip. Even so, I felt the weight of Hutch's gaze before I even met it. He sat back in his rocking chair, boot planted against the railing, watching us like we owed him an explanation. Ford barely shifted beside him, yet his presence coiled through the space like a tightening noose. Silent, unreadable, but unrelenting.

"Took your sweet time getting back," Hutch said, tapping a slow rhythm against the arm of his chair.

"Had to make sure the information was worth bringing to you," I said, keeping my tone casual. I held his steely gaze, letting my chin lift just slightly. Confidence without arrogance.

His eyes narrowed, slicing through me. "Information?"

J.J. stepped in smoothly. "About the Wells Fargo stage." He kept his voice even, as if there wasn't a single reason to question us. "She caught wind of it from her brother and rode out to confirm. I went along to make sure it was something worth your attention."

Hutch leaned back, exhaling through his nose as he considered that. Ford didn't say a word, but his boot scuffed against the porch rail. Watching. Waiting. Calculating.

"And? Was it?"

J.J. nodded once. "Enough to warrant planning

ahead."

Hutch dragged his thumb across his jaw, gaze flicking between us now. "And what about the two of you?" His tone had changed. Not suspicious, just curious. "Hearing rumors and verifying information... is that all you did out there?"

I tightened my grip on J.J.'s sleeve, just slightly. Enough for him to notice, enough so that I could ease whatever tension might slip through. I let the corner of my lips curl, something subtle, something that hinted at things Hutch might fill in for himself. "I'd say we got better acquainted, wouldn't you, Jay?"

J.J. exhaled like a man caught in something pleasant, shaking his head with mock amusement. "Seems so."

Ford's eyes didn't leave J.J.

"Fine," Hutch finally said, sitting forward. "I want details. Soon."

J.J. dipped his head, all ease and control. "You'll have them."

Hutch turned toward Ford. "Take him out with the others tomorrow. He'll ride with you." Ford barely nodded, but his stare stayed locked on J.J.

I kept my breath steady, my expression smooth, but as we turned away from the porch, the weight of Ford's attention felt like a thousand cuts down my back. He was watching too closely.

J.J.'s voice slipped low beside me. "We need to be more vigilant than ever. Ford's watching."

I swallowed hard, already knowing that with one misstep, this whole thing could come crumbling down.

22 - The Test

———————

J.J.

THE SUN HADN'T even cleared the horizon when Ford Spencer kicked my bunk hard enough to rattle my teeth.

"Wagner! Hutch wants to see you earn your keep."

I peeled my eyes open, squinting against the dim light filtering through the bunkhouse windows. Ford stood over me, hat pulled low, his expression unreadable as carved stone.

"What time is it?" Derek groaned from the bunk above mine.

"Time for you to keep sleepin'," Ford growled. "This ain't your dance."

I sat up, muscles protesting the early hour, and reached for my boots. Whatever Ford had planned, it wasn't going to be a Sunday picnic. The man had been watching me like a hawk ever since Hayley and I returned from our trip to Holbrook.

"Coffee?" I asked, hoping to buy myself a few minutes to wake up properly.

"You can drink coffee when you're dead." Ford's

spurs jingled as he headed for the door. "Five minutes, Wagner. Don't keep me waitin'."

I pulled on my boots and grabbed my gun belt, checking that both Remingtons sat snug in their holsters. The familiar weight settled against my hips like an old friend. Whatever test Ford had cooked up, I had a feeling I'd need more than charm to pass it.

Outside, the air carried a bite that promised a winter storm soon. Ford stood by the horses, already saddled and ready. My mustang Magnus snorted when he saw me, ears pricked forward. I ran my hand along his neck, checking the Winchester in its saddle scabbard. Thirty-thirty cartridges, good for anything up to two hundred yards if a man knew his business.

"Where we headed?" I asked, swinging into the saddle.

Ford didn't answer right away. He just spurred his horse toward the eastern trail, the one that led deeper into the badlands. I followed, keeping pace as we rode through the gray half-light of dawn.

After an hour of hard riding, Ford finally spoke. "Hutch thinks you're solid. Says you handled yourself real good during that business in Canyon Diablo."

I kept my face neutral, though my gut clenched tight as a fist. The business he was talking about was murder. Cold-blooded murder of the mercantile owner who'd killed Hutch's brother.

"Man does what he has to," I said.

"That's what Hutch is countin' on."

We crested a ridge, and Ford pointed toward a small valley below. Through the morning mist, I could make out a herd of cattle, maybe forty head, grazing near a stream. But these weren't Hashknife cattle. Even at this distance, I could see the brands were all wrong.

"Those belong to the Double Bar T," Ford said, settling back in his saddle. "Tom Brennan's spread, about twenty miles north of here."

My throat went dry. "And?"

Ford's smile was about as warm as a January morning. "And Hutch says they're gonna belong to us by sundown."

The bottom dropped out of my stomach like I'd been gut-shot. Rustling. Not just finding stolen cattle or looking the other way but active, deliberate theft. The kind that could get a man strung up from the nearest cottonwood.

"That's a fair piece of rustlin'," I said, fighting to keep my voice steady.

"You gettin' cold feet, Wagner?" Ford's eyes were sharp as broken glass, watching for any sign of weakness. This was it. The test I'd been dreading. The moment where I'd have to cross a line I'd spent eight years hunting other men for crossing.

Lord, forgive me.

"No, sir. Just wonderin' about the plan."

Ford's tension eased a fraction. "Smart man asks questions. Stupid men just follow orders blind."

He laid out the operation with military precision. We'd drive the cattle south through Dead Horse Canyon, where Mac Burns waited with two other men I didn't recognize. From there, they'd push the herd to the railroad junction where the man in black would load them onto stock cars.

"What about the Double Bar T riders?" I asked.

"Brennan's got most of his men drivin' a herd to market in Flagstaff. Left behind two old-timers to watch his home range." Ford's smile turned ugly. "Hutch says they won't be watchin' much longer."

Ice water flooded my veins. "You aim to kill them?"

"Hutch aims to do whatever it takes to get those cattle. Whether that includes killin' depends on how cooperative they feel."

I forced myself to nod, even as every instinct screamed against what I was about to do. Eight years of hunting rustlers, and now I was about to become one. But that was the job. Get in deep enough to expose the whole operation. Sometimes, the only way to catch a wolf is to run with the pack.

We rode down into the valley as the sun climbed higher. The cattle were prime beef, fat and healthy, the kind that would bring top dollar at market. No wonder Ford had his eye on them.

"You take the left flank," Ford ordered as we approached the herd. "I'll circle right. We'll bunch them up and start them moving south."

I heeled Magnus toward the left side of the herd, pulling my rope free of the saddle. The cattle looked up as I approached, but didn't spook. They were used to riders. That made it worse somehow. These animals trusted men on horseback. Trusted them enough to let us get close before we stole them from their rightful owner.

A shout echoed across the valley, harsh, angry. "Hey! What in the Sam Hill do you think you're doing?"

An old cowboy rode hard toward us from the direction of a line shack I hadn't noticed before. Gray-haired and weathered, he sat his horse as if he'd been born in the saddle. His right hand rested on the butt of his pistol.

Ford wheeled his mount to face the approaching rider, his own gun clearing leather smooth as silk. "Mornin', old-timer. Just gatherin' up some strays that wandered onto our range."

"Like blazes you are!" The old cowboy's voice cracked with outrage. "These are Double Bar T cattle, and you know it!"

"That so?" Ford's tone was conversational, but his gun never wavered. "Well, I reckon possession is nine-tenths of the law."

The old man's hand twitched toward his weapon. "You thievin' varmints—"

Ford's pistol bucked once.

The cowboy tumbled from his saddle like a sack of grain, hitting the ground hard and still. His horse shied away, reins trailing. My blood turned to ice water. Ford had gunned down an unarmed man in cold blood. Murdered him for the crime of trying to protect his employer's property.

"Where's his partner?" Ford asked, scanning the valley with deadly focus.

Before I could answer, a rifle cracked from the direction of the line shack. The bullet whined past Ford's ear, close enough to part his hair.

"There," I said, pointing toward a wisp of gun smoke.

Ford spurred his horse toward cover behind a boulder. "Take him, Wagner!"

My mouth went cotton-dry. "What?"

"You heard me! That old fool's got us pinned down. Put a bullet in him!"

I looked toward the line shack, where the second cowboy had fortified himself. Probably an old-timer like his partner, just trying to do his job. A decent man who didn't deserve to die for Hutch's greed. But if I refused, my cover was blown. Months of work gone. The whole rustling operation would slip through our fingers.

Sometimes you have to let one fish go to catch the whole school.

I unsheathed my Winchester, lever-actioning a round into the chamber. The rifle felt heavier than usual, the familiar weight now tainted by what I was about to do. I estimated the range at seventy yards, an easy shot with the thirty-thirty. No wind to speak of, clear sight picture.

Another shot from the line shack. This one kicked up dirt near Ford's position.

I brought the rifle to my shoulder, settling into my shooting stance. Controlled breathing, just like Gray had taught me. In through the nose, half exhale, hold. My finger found the trigger, smooth and familiar. I sighted down the barrel, centering the front bead on the small window where the muzzle flash had appeared.

God forgive me.

I squeezed the trigger, but at the last instant shifted my aim six inches left. The Winchester bucked against my shoulder, the sharp crack echoing off the valley walls. Through the powder smoke, I saw the window frame splinter where my bullet had struck.

"Tarnation!" I hollered loud enough for Ford to hear. "Missed him!"

Ford's head snapped toward me. "What kind of sharpshooter are you?"

I worked the lever, the smooth action ejecting the spent cartridge and chambering another round. "Give me another shot!" This time I aimed deliberately high, sending the bullet into the roof of the shack. Wood chips rained down, but no cry of pain followed.

"Son of a buck is dug in tight," I called to Ford. "Can't get a clean shot from this angle."

Ford's face was dark as a thundercloud. He'd seen me shoot. Knew I could put three bullets through a playing card at a hundred yards. Missing twice wasn't like me. Hutch wouldn't be pleased with sloppy work. But before Ford could voice his suspicions, the rifle fire from the shack ceased.

We waited, breath held, ears straining for any sound. Nothing.

Ford rose from cover, pistol ready. "Think you got him?"

"Maybe. Or maybe he's playing possum."

We approached the line shack cautious-like, weapons drawn. The door hung open, creaking in the breeze. Inside, we found the second cowboy slumped over his rifle, a red stain spreading across his shirt. But he was breathing.

My bullet had caught him in the shoulder. Painful but not fatal. With proper doctoring, he'd live to see another sunrise.

"Well, I'll be hornswoggled," Ford muttered. "Looks like you winged him good."

The wounded man's eyes fluttered open. Old and

pain-filled, but alive with defiance. "Go to blazes," he growled.

Ford raised his pistol, aiming at the old man's head.

"Wait," I said quickly. "He's no threat now. Bleeding bad. Won't last long anyway."

Ford hesitated, finger on the trigger.

"Besides," I added, "gunshots carry. You want half the territory knowing we were here?"

That argument struck home. Ford holstered his weapon with visible reluctance. "You're right. Let the buzzards have him."

We left the wounded cowboy in the shack and returned to the cattle. The old man might live, might die, but at least I hadn't put a bullet through his heart. Small comfort, but it was all I had.

The rest of the day passed in a blur of dust and cattle. We drove the stolen herd south through Dead Horse Canyon, where Mac Burns and two hard-faced men I'd never seen before took over. Mac counted out my share of the profits. More money than most cowboys saw in six months.

Blood money. Same as the coins from Canyon Diablo.

As the sun set behind the mountains, painting the sky the color of spilled blood, I found myself alone with Ford Spencer. The cattle were gone, loaded onto a train bound for markets where no questions would be asked.

"You did good today, Wagner," Ford said, offering me a cigarette. "Showed real sand."

I accepted the smoke with steady hands, though my guts churned like a butter churn. "Just doin' what needed done."

"That's what I like to hear." Ford struck a match, the flame dancing between us. "Too many men these days got soft bellies. No stomach for the hard choices."

"Hard choices?"

Ford's eyes glittered in the matchlight. "Like killin'

when killin's called for. Like takin' what you need instead of beggin' for scraps." The match burned down to his fingers. He dropped it, grinding it under his boot heel.

"This little operation today? That was just the appetizer. Hutch has got a big feast comin' soon."

"The Wells Fargo stage?"

"Among other things." Ford's smile was all teeth, no warmth. "See, Wagner, Hutch says rustlin' cattle is small potatoes. Real money's in bigger game." He climbed into his saddle, gathering his reins. "Banks. Trains. Government payrolls." He touched his hat brim. "Stick with Hutch and you'll never want for anything again."

As Ford rode away into the gathering darkness, I sat on my horse in the canyon, surrounded by the ghosts of my choices. The wounded cowboy's blood was on my hands now. Maybe not directly, but I'd been part of it.

The things we do for justice, I thought bitterly.

But justice felt mighty far away just then. All I could feel was the weight of those stolen coins in my pocket and the memory of an old man's defiant eyes. Somewhere in the distance, a coyote howled. Lonesome and wild, like the sound of a soul crying out in the darkness.

I knew exactly how it felt.

23 - The Newspaper

Hayley

I'D BEEN WATCHING Carter for the better part of a week, and something had shifted in his behavior. The way he lingered near the kitchen when I worked, not with his usual crude leering, but with calculating attention. A hunter sizing up his quarry. His eyes tracked my movements, cataloging details, filing away information.

Today had proved my suspicions right.

"Hayley," he called as I stepped outside to hang laundry with Luciana. "Got a minute?"

Luciana shot me a warning glance, her dark eyes flashing with concern. She'd seen enough of Carter's behavior to know he meant trouble. But I nodded toward the clothesline. "Go ahead. I'll catch up."

Carter approached with that swagger of his, but there was tension beneath it now. A man trying too hard to appear casual while his mind worked on something else entirely. "Been thinkin' about what you said that night. About your daddy."

I kept my expression neutral, continuing to fold the shirt in my hands with deliberate care. Every Pinkerton instinct I possessed screamed danger, but I forced my voice to remain steady. "What about him?"

"Galen Harper." He rolled the name around like he was tasting it, savoring each syllable. "Heard he was quite the legend in his day."

My fingers stilled on the fabric for just a moment before resuming their work. "Legend's one word for it."

Carter stepped closer, close enough that I caught the scent of tobacco and unwashed clothes, close enough to violate the careful distance I'd maintained. "Funny thing, though. Been askin' around about the Harper family. You and Flynn seem awfully... civilized for children of such a notorious outlaw."

Heat prickled up my spine like a warning, but I forced my voice to stay steady. Years of training kicked in. Never let them see they've rattled you. "Prison'll do that to a man's kin. We learned real quick that his reputation brought us nothing but trouble."

"Mmm." Carter's eyes narrowed, studying my face with an intensity that made my skin crawl. "Still, seems strange. Flynn's got the mannerisms of a lawman, not an outlaw's son. The way he stands, the way he watches people. And you..." He paused, his gaze raked over me with a new assessment. "You got the bearing of someone who's been trained. Real trained."

I met his gaze head-on, letting just enough steel into my voice to remind him what happened the last time he pushed too far. My hand hovered near my waistline, ensuring I could reach for my concealed knife if needed. "What exactly are you gettin' at, Carter?"

He held up his hands in mock surrender, but his smirk said he wasn't backing down. If anything, my reaction seemed to confirm whatever suspicions he'd been harboring. "Just curious is all. Man likes to know who he's ridin' with."

"Well, now you do."

I turned to walk away, but his next words stopped me

cold, hitting like a physical blow. "Saw something interesting in town yesterday. Newspaper from Colorado. Had a real fascinating article about a certain rustler hunter."

My blood turned to ice water, but I kept walking, forcing my steps to remain steady and unhurried. "Don't much care for newspapers myself. Too much gossip, not enough truth."

Carter's laughter followed me to the clothesline, rough and knowing. "Said this Westin fellow was known for wearing dark spectacles. Something about sensitive eyes. Ain't that peculiar? 'Bout as peculiar as a certain cowboy who showed up here wearing the exact same pair of glasses."

The words hit me like a physical blow, but I forced myself to keep moving, to appear unaffected even as my heart hammered against my ribs hard enough to crack bone. "Ain't that the truth," I managed, my voice steadier than I felt.

I busied myself hanging wet clothes on the line, my hands working automatically while my mind raced. Carter knew. Or at least suspected enough to be dangerous. Every pin I clipped to the rope felt like I was marking time until everything unraveled. When I finally looked up from the laundry basket, Flynn stood beside me, his expression dark as a storm cloud.

"Well?" he demanded.

"Carter's suspicious about me and you. Says we're too civilized for outlaw children." I kept folding laundry, trying to appear calm while my hands trembled slightly against the fabric. "And he mentioned seeing something interesting in a newspaper from Colorado."

Flynn cursed under his breath. "About J.J.?"

"Most likely." I glanced around to make sure we were alone, scanning the barn, the bunkhouse windows, and the areas where someone might lurk within earshot. "We need to be more careful."

"What we need is to get you out of here."

I dropped the shirt I was holding and turned to face him fully. "Absolutely not."

"Hayley—"

"No, Flynn. We're too close to bail out now. One suspicious cowboy will not scare me off." My voice carried more conviction than I felt, but I'd learned long ago that projecting confidence was half the battle in this business.

Flynn's hands clenched into fists, the knuckles white with tension. "It's not just Carter anymore. Ford's been watching J.J. like a hawk ever since you two got back. Something's brewing, and I don't like the feel of it."

"All the more reason to see this through. We can't let Hutch's gang slip away because we got spooked." The words hung between us, sharp and raw. Flynn's breathing was controlled, but I could see the tension in every line of his body. His shoulders held rigid, with a slight tremor in his jaw. He wanted to act, wanted to protect me, and my refusal was eating at him like acid.

"I'm not being stubborn," I said, softening my tone just enough to show I understood his concern. "I'm being professional."

Flynn laughed, but there was no humor in it. The sound came out bitter, edged with frustration. "Professional? Hay, you're playing house with a notorious rustler hunter while hiding behind Galen Harper's reputation. There's nothing professional about this whole mess."

He wasn't wrong, but that didn't make his interference any more welcome. The irony wasn't lost on me either. Here I was, trained by Allan Pinkerton himself, reduced to washing clothes and cooking meals while trying to expose a criminal network. "I know what I'm doing."

"Do you? Because from where I'm standing, it looks like you're so caught up in whatever's happening between you and J.J. that you're not seeing the bigger picture." Flynn stepped closer, his voice dropping to a dangerous whisper. "You think I haven't noticed the way you look at him? How you light up when he's around?"

Heat flooded my cheeks. "This isn't about J.J."

"Isn't it?" He studied my face, seeing straight through every defense I tried to raise.

"Flynn—"

"He's going to break your heart, Hay. And when he does, I'll be the one picking up the pieces. Again."

The reference to Stanton hit like a physical blow, stealing the breath from my lungs. Flynn had been there during the aftermath of that disaster, had seen me at my lowest point. Sobbing into my pillow, questioning every decision I'd ever made, wondering if I was fit for this work at all. That he was throwing it in my face now told me just how worried he really was.

"This is different," I said, though even as the words left my mouth, I wondered if I was lying to myself.

"Is it? Because it looks exactly the same from here."

Then he stormed off, muttering to himself. I picked up the basket and headed inside, trying not to let doubt take root.

I threw myself into my usual tasks, but Flynn's words echoed in my mind with every dish I washed and every meal I prepared. The rest of the morning crept by like molasses in January. Every glance from Carter felt like a loaded gun pointed at my back, every casual comment weighted with hidden meaning. I cataloged escape routes, checked the position of my weapons, running through contingency plans Allan Pinkerton had drilled into every agent.

The sound of approaching horses drew my attention to the window. When Ford returned from his ride with the men, I watched him from the kitchen window, my trained eye picking up details others might miss. Something in his posture had changed, too. The easy confidence was still there, but underneath it sat a coiled tension. A rattlesnake that had caught the scent of prey and was preparing to strike.

He spoke quietly with Carter near the barn, their

heads bent close together in conversation that never boded well for people like me. Then Ford's gaze found the bunkhouse window where I stood, and for a moment, our eyes locked across the distance. He touched the brim of his hat in what might have looked like a polite greeting to anyone else.

To me, it felt like a threat. A promise of things to come.

When J.J. returned with the others, I was setting out the noon meal, my hands steady despite the turmoil in my chest. Our eyes met across the room, and I saw him register the tension in my stance immediately. Always too perceptive for his own good, reading the subtle signs of distress that most men would miss entirely.

Ford took his usual seat at the head of the table, but his attention kept drifting to J.J. throughout the meal. Not obvious. Ford was too smart for that. But I caught the subtle glances, the way he seemed to weigh every word J.J. spoke, every gesture, every reaction.

"Wagner," Ford said as the men finished eating. "Stick around after the others head out. Got something I want to discuss with you."

J.J. nodded, casual as you please, but I saw his jaw tighten just slightly. A tell that only someone who'd studied him would notice. "Sure thing."

As the other men filed out, I busied myself clearing plates, my ears tuned to every word while I tried to appear focused solely on my work. "That newspaper from Colorado," Ford began, voice conversational. "The one with the story about J.J. Westin taking down that rustler on a train up in Trinidad."

My hands stilled on the stack of plates, every muscle in my body coiling with tension. J.J. said nothing, but the silence stretched thin as a wire, crackling with unspoken danger.

"Interesting reading," Ford continued, settling back in his chair like a man who held all the cards. "Especially the description of the man. Dark hair, gray eyes, about five foot eight. Favors dark clothing. Rides a flaxen chestnut mustang."

"Lot of men fit that description," J.J. said finally, his voice carefully neutral.

"True enough." Ford leaned back in his chair, studying J.J. with patience. A cat watching a mouse. "But not many have the particular skills described in that article. Dead shot with a rifle. Fast draw. Able to track a man across two states without losing the trail."

J.J. shrugged, the gesture perfectly calculated to appear indifferent. "Like you said, interesting read."

"Mmm." Ford's gaze sharpened, boring into J.J. with renewed intensity. "'Course, newspapers ain't always accurate. Sometimes they get details wrong. Change names to protect the innocent... or the guilty."

The threat hung in the air like thick smoke from a dying fire, acrid and choking. I forced myself to keep moving, to appear busy, while my heart hammered against my ribs loud enough that I was certain everyone in the room could hear it.

"Wagner," Ford said softly, the quiet tone somehow more menacing than a shout. "We're gonna take a little ride this afternoon. Just you and me. Got some things I want to show you."

"Looking forward to it."

But J.J.'s voice held a note I'd learned to recognize. A man preparing for trouble, checking his weapons and calculating odds.

As soon as Ford left, J.J. approached the kitchen area where I was washing dishes. He stood close enough that his voice wouldn't carry, but not so close as to draw attention from Luciana, who was sweeping the floor nearby.

"We got a problem," he murmured.

"I know." I scrubbed at a plate with more force than necessary, channeling my anxiety into the familiar motion. "Carter's been asking questions about me and Flynn. Too many questions."

"Ford knows who I am. Not for certain, maybe, but he suspects." I glanced toward the window where Ford was saddling his horse, moving with deliberate precision. A man preparing for something important. "What are you gonna do?"

"Play along. See what he wants to show me." J.J.'s voice was grim, edged with resignation. A man who'd faced similar situations before. "But if something goes sideways—"

"I can take care of myself," I said.

"I know you can." His fingers brushed mine, fleeting, before he reached for his hat. The brief contact sent warmth shooting up my arm. "But promise me you'll be careful. Both of you."

"You too, Jay."

For a moment, something passed between us. An understanding deeper than words, a connection that had nothing to do with our covers or our mission. Then he was gone, following Ford toward the horses, and I was left with the cold certainty that our carefully constructed identities were beginning to crack.

And when they finally shattered, we'd better be ready for what came next.

The afternoon stretched endlessly as I waited for J.J.'s return. That evening, as the sun painted the sky in shades of blood and gold, I stood at the kitchen window watching the horizon. J.J. and Ford had been gone for hours, and with each passing minute, the knot in my stomach grew tighter, threatening to strangle me from the inside.

Flynn appeared at my side, his presence solid and reassuring, though I could still feel the tension from our earlier argument radiating off him like heat from a forge. "Any word?" he asked, voice low.

I shook my head. "Nothing."

"He'll be alright, Hay. He didn't earn his reputation by being careless." The grudging respect in Flynn's voice surprised me. Despite his concerns about J.J. personally, he recognized the man's skill, his ability to survive in situations that would break lesser men.

"It's not carelessness I'm worried about." I turned from the window to face my brother, letting him see the genuine fear in my eyes. "It's Ford. There's something about him that doesn't sit right."

"Agreed."

"He's too observant. Too careful. Like he's always watching, always calculating three moves ahead." I rubbed my arms, trying to chase away the chill that had nothing to do with the evening air. "And Carter's been poking around, too. Asking questions about Galen, about our past."

Flynn's expression darkened, his jaw tightening with anger that made smart men step carefully around him. "I told you that was going to be a problem."

"You did. And I told you I could handle it."

"Can you?" His blue eyes held mine steadily, searching for any hint of doubt or uncertainty. "Because if your cover's blown, if they figure out who you really are..."

He didn't need to finish the thought. We both knew what happened to spies who got caught. It wasn't pretty, and it wasn't quick. "My cover's solid," I said, though even as the words left my mouth, I wondered if they were true.

Flynn was quiet for a moment, both of us lost in our own thoughts, understanding what the other was thinking with no need to voice it. Our mission was balanced on a knife's edge, and one wrong move could send us all tumbling into a pit we might not climb out of.

"Maybe it's time to signal Mossman," Flynn said finally. "Pull back before this gets any worse."

I turned to stare at him, genuinely shocked by the suggestion. "Are you serious?"

"Dead serious. This whole operation is falling apart, Hay. Carter's suspicious, Ford's onto J.J., and we're walking around with targets painted on our backs." Flynn's voice carried the weight of genuine fear. Not for himself, but for me.

"All the more reason to see it through. We're close, Flynn. Closer than we've ever been to exposing the whole network."

"And what if that closeness gets you killed?"

There it was again. That overprotective streak had been driving me crazy since we were children. Flynn meant well, but he couldn't seem to accept that I could take care of myself, that I'd been trained precisely for this work.

"I won't let that happen."

"You might not be able to stop it."

The sound of hoofbeats broke the quiet, and I pressed close to the window, my breath fogging the glass. Two riders approached through the gathering dusk. Ford and J.J., both upright in their saddles, appeared unharmed. But when they dismounted near the barn, I caught sight of J.J.'s face in the lamplight, and my heart clenched.

Whatever Ford had shown him, whatever had passed between them during those long hours, it had left its mark. J.J. looked like a man carrying a heavier burden than when he'd left, his shoulders set in lines of grim determination.

And I had the sinking feeling that our real troubles were just beginning.

Later that night, after the bunkhouse had settled into its usual symphony of snores and restless dreams, I slipped outside to check on the horses. It was a routine I'd established early on. A way to move around the property without drawing suspicion, while also giving me opportunities to observe and gather intelligence.

J.J. was waiting in the shadows near the barn, his presence barely visible against the weathered wood. Even though I was expecting him, I almost missed him entirely. The man could blend into the shadows as if he was born to it.

"Couldn't sleep either?" I whispered.

"Not likely." He stepped closer, and I could see the

tension written in every line of his body. The rigid set of his shoulders, the way his hands rested near his weapons, the constant surveillance of our surroundings. "Ford's got his suspicions about me."

My breath caught in my throat. "How bad?"

"Bad enough. He showed me some of their other operations. Cattle being moved through different routes, coordination with other groups, money changing hands." His voice was carefully controlled, but I could hear the undercurrent of worry. "But he was watching me the whole time. Testing my reactions."

"What sort of test?"

"The sort where a man has to prove how far he'll go for the gang." J.J. paused, his jaw tight with whatever memories Ford's test had stirred up. "He's planning something bigger than just rustling, Hayley. I can feel it. But he's not showing me everything yet."

The way he said "yet" made my stomach clench with dread. "And you still think Hutch is running things?"

"Far as I can tell. But Ford..." J.J. shook his head, frustration evident in the gesture. "There's more to him than meets the eye. Way more."

We stood there in the darkness, the weight of our situation settling around us like a suffocating blanket. Our covers were holding, but barely. Like walking a narrow trail above a deadly canyon, one false step from careening over the edge. Ford was suspicious, Carter was asking questions, and somewhere in the shadows, plans were being made that we weren't fully privy to yet.

"We're walking a tightrope," I said finally.

"I know."

"So, what do we do?"

J.J. was quiet for a long moment, his gaze fixed on something I couldn't see in the darkness. When he spoke, his voice held resolve. A man who'd made peace with whatever price he might have to pay.

"We keep playing our parts. And we pray we're ready

when the real show starts."

"Even if it means crossing lines we never wanted to cross?"

He looked at me then, really looked at me, and in his eyes I saw something that made my heart skip a beat. Not fear, but determination mixed with something deeper, something that looked suspiciously like the emotion I'd been trying so hard to deny.

"Especially then, darlin'. Because some things are worth the risk."

As I slipped back to my quarters, his words echoed in my mind like a prayer and a promise combined. Some things were worth the risk. Were we about to find out just how much we were willing to sacrifice for justice?

And for each other?

24 - Wash of Guilt

J.J.

THE MORNING AIR bit at my face as we rode toward Shepherd's Wash, the dry creek bed where Hutch planned our practice run. A small freight wagon would head through, carrying supplies to an outlying ranch. Nothing as valuable as the Wells Fargo stage we'd hit later, but Hutch wanted to test our timing, our coordination.

Most importantly, he wanted to test me.

I adjusted my dark glasses, the familiar weight settling against my nose. The headache had been building since dawn, a dull throb behind my eyes that promised to get worse before it got better. My Winchester sat snug in its scabbard, thirty-thirty cartridges loaded and ready, though every instinct rebelled against what I might have to do with it.

"Remember, Wagner," Hutch called out as we took our positions along the ridge. "When that shotgun rider goes for his weapon, you drop him clean. No hesitation."

Ford rode up beside Hutch, his voice low but carrying in the morning air. "Might want to see how steady his hand is first. Man's got a reputation, but reputations don't always match reality."

Hutch nodded, his eyes fixed on me. "True enough. Wagner, you hearing this? Ford's got a point. This is your chance to show us what all the fuss is about."

I nodded, checking my rifle for the third time. The Winchester felt solid in my hands, familiar as breathing. The lever action worked smooth as silk, chambering rounds with practiced precision. Problem was, I'd never used it to shoot an innocent man. Even in practice.

Glenn rode up beside me, his face still pale from the bullet wound he'd taken in Canyon Diablo. "First time's always the hardest," he whispered. "After that, it gets easier."

That's what I was afraid of.

I thought of Auggie, of the promise I'd made to Gray Shaw about using my skills for good. How far could a man bend before he broke entirely? The gold button pressed against my ribs, a constant reminder of what happened when I failed to protect someone I cared about.

Below us, dust rose on the horizon. The wagon was coming.

"Positions!" Hutch barked, his voice carrying the authority of a man accustomed to being obeyed.

Hutch had it figured out down to the last detail. He'd sent Derek and Mac to block the road while Carter flanked from the south. Glenn would handle the horses while Hutch kept watch for any complications. Standard ambush formation, the kind that had worked for outlaws since the first coach rolled through hostile territory.

Ford positioned himself where he could observe everything, especially me.

My job was to eliminate the shotgun rider if he didn't surrender immediately.

Lord, I need wisdom here. Show me a way through this that doesn't cost an innocent man his life.

The wagon rolled closer, a weathered freight hauler pulled by a team of six mules. Two men sat on the driver's bench. An older man with graying whiskers handling the reins, and a younger fellow with a shotgun across his knees. Both looked like honest working men just trying to make a living.

My finger found the trigger, but I couldn't make myself settle into the shot. Something wasn't sitting right about this whole situation. Ford had been watching me too closely since we got back from Holbrook. Little comments, testing questions, the way his eyes lingered when he thought I wasn't looking.

And now this. A practice run that felt more like an examination.

"Hold steady, Wagner," Hutch called out. "You know what needs doing. You hit a bottle good enough. But can you hit a man?"

Ford's voice drifted over, casual but pointed. "Curious to see that legendary marksmanship in action."

The wagon hit the ambush point. Derek and Mac rode out, guns drawn, shouting for the driver to stop. The older man hauled back on the reins, his mules snorting and stamping as the wagon lurched to a halt.

The shotgun rider's hands tightened on his weapon.

This was it. The moment they were all waiting for. I brought the Winchester to my shoulder, settling into my shooting stance. Range sixty yards, slight crosswind from the left, clear sight picture. The front bead centered on the young man's chest.

But something made me hesitate.

The young man's hands were shaking as he raised the shotgun. Not the steady movements of an experienced guard, but the trembling of someone scared out of his wits. His face was pale, eyes wide with terror.

He wasn't reaching for his gun to fight. He was reaching for it because he was afraid.

I shifted my aim slightly, just a hair to the left. Controlled breathing, just like Gray had taught me. When the young man raised the shotgun toward Derek, I squeezed the trigger, but at the last instant adjusted my point of aim.

The rifle cracked, echoing off the canyon walls.

The shotgun spun from the young man's hands. The stock splintered where my bullet had struck. He yelped and fell sideways off the wagon, more from shock than injury.

"What in the blazes?" Hutch's voice cut through the air like a whip.

I worked the lever, the smooth action ejecting the spent cartridge and chambering another round. Kept the rifle trained on the scene below, selling the illusion that I was still engaged. "Shot went wide," I called back. "Sun got in my eyes."

It wasn't entirely a lie. I blinked hard, trying to clear the tears that had gathered at the corners of my eyes. The pounding behind my temples had gotten worse as the morning sun climbed higher, and even with the dark glasses, the bright light reflecting off the canyon walls felt like needles stabbing into my skull.

Hutch spurred his horse down toward the wagon, his face dark with anger. The rest of the gang rounded up the two freight handlers, who were now standing with their hands raised. The older man tried to calm his terrified partner.

Ford remained on the ridge, his gaze fixed on me with the intensity of a man studying a puzzle.

I stayed on the ridge, rifle ready, watching the scene below. This had been a test, all right. The question was whether I'd passed or failed.

When Hutch rode back up the slope, Ford was already there beside him. Hutch's expression was thunderous. "Mighty convenient, that shot going wide."

"Sometimes it happens," I said, meeting his stare steadily. "Even the best marksmen have off days."

Ford's voice was quiet, almost conversational. "Funny thing about legendary shooters. Don't usually have off days when it matters."

Hutch's eyes narrowed. "Ford's got a point. Tell me,

Wagner, how many men you killed?"

The question came out of nowhere, sharp and prob-ing. I kept my face neutral, though my gut tightened like a fist. "Why?"

"Because," Hutch said, leaning forward in his saddle, "a man with your reputation ought to have quite a tally. And men who've killed before rarely get squeamish about one more."

I thought about the forty-one rustlers I'd brought in over the years. Some had danced at the end of a rope, oth-ers rotting in territorial prisons. I'd never pulled the trigger myself, but their fates had been sealed the moment I'd caught them.

"Enough," I said finally.

Ford nodded slowly, like my answer confirmed some-thing he'd already suspected. "See, Hutch, that's what I was thinking. Different philosophies, maybe."

Hutch gestured toward the wagon below, where the gang was already loading the supplies onto our own pack animals. "Take today, for instance. The boy with the shot-gun was fixing to shoot Derek. I saw it in his eyes, clear as day."

"Maybe."

"No maybe about it." Hutch's hand drifted to his gun, the gesture casual but unmistakable. "In this business, hesitation gets you killed. And men who hesitate..." He glanced at Ford, who gave an almost imperceptible nod. "Well, they ain't much use to me."

Ford's contribution was quiet, almost thoughtful. "'Course, could be the sun really got in his eyes. Those dark glasses suggest sensitivity issues."

The observation was casual, but it felt like being ex-amined under a magnifying glass. Ford had noticed details I hadn't realized were visible.

"You're right," I said, affecting a casual indifference I'd perfected over years of undercover work. "Won't hap-pen again."

Hutch studied me for a long moment. "I hope not. Because when we hit that Wells Fargo stage, there won't be room for mistakes. That shotgun rider goes down, clean and quick, or the whole operation falls apart."

Ford added quietly, "Be a shame to lose such a famous man over something preventable."

Plain as day he suspected something. Every casual glance, every seemingly innocent comment now took on new meaning. The man missed nothing, and what he saw, he remembered.

As we rode back toward the bunkhouse, my mind churned with the implications. Hutch was clearly in charge, making decisions and giving the orders. But Ford's quiet observations carried a weight that Hutch respected. The dynamic was subtle but clear—Hutch led, but Ford influenced. Just how far did that influence go? And could it get me a bullet in my head?

I thought about Hayley, probably back at the bunkhouse fixing dinner, unaware that our carefully constructed covers were unraveling. She was smart, capable, and trained for this kind of work. But if Ford had doubts about me, how long before those doubts extended to her?

The weight of Auggie's gold button seemed heavier in my pocket, a reminder of what happened when I failed to protect someone I cared about. The metal felt warm against my chest, worn smooth by years of worry and regret.

I couldn't let that happen again. Not to Hayley.

By the time we reached the bunkhouse, I'd made my decision. Whatever Hutch was planning, whatever test Ford had in mind for the Wells Fargo job, I'd have to be ready. The stakes were higher now than just completing my mission.

Even if it meant crossing lines I'd never imagined crossing. Even if it meant becoming a man I'd spent my life hunting.

Because losing Hayley wasn't an option. And failure,

as Auggie's death had taught me, carried a price too high to pay.

25 – Auggie's Ghost

—————

J.J.

THE SATCHEL WAS empty.

I upended it again, shaking out every corner, my hands trembling as I pawed through the leather interior that had held my most precious possession for years.

Gone.

Auggie's button. Papa's button. Was gone.

My breath came in short, sharp gasps as I tore through my belongings a third time. Bedroll. Bible. Extra ammunition. Everything else was there, exactly where it should be. Everything except the one thing that mattered.

"No, no, no..." The words escaped as a whisper, then louder. "No!"

I dropped to my knees beside my bunk, running my hands along the floor, under the bed frame, searching every crack in the rough wooden planks. Maybe it had fallen. Maybe it had just rolled away.

It had to be here.

The gold was warm in my memory. The way it caught the light, the worn edges smooth from Papa's fingers, then Auggie's, then mine. The raised eagle was still visible despite years of being worried between nervous thumbs.

"This here's so you remember your papa, little man."

Papa's voice echoed in my mind, rough with emotion as he kneeled before six-year-old Auggie, pressing the button into those small, eager hands. *"I cut it right off my uniform. Keep it close, and you keep me close too."*

The headache that had been building all day exploded behind my eyes like a gunshot. I squeezed them shut, but that only made the memory sharper, clearer, more devastating.

Auggie clutching that button like a lifeline during the long months after Papa never came home. Sleeping with it under his pillow. Pulling it out whenever he missed Papa too much, which was every day.

And I—jealous, selfish, fourteen-year-old fool that I was—I took it.

"Just let me see it for a minute, Auggie. I promise I'll give it back."

But I hadn't given it back. I'd stuffed it in my pocket, told him I'd lost it, watched his face crumble like his world had ended. Which it had.

Twenty minutes later, Auggie slipped trying to cross that swollen river. Twenty minutes of him being so heartbroken over losing Papa's button that he wasn't paying attention to where he stepped.

And now I'd lost it too.

I was on my feet, frantic, tearing through my saddlebags, throwing clothes and gear across the empty bunkhouse. With my vision blurred from the pain in my head or the tears threatening, I couldn't tell.

"Where is it? Where is it?" I snarled at the empty air.

"J.J.?"

I spun around, and there was Hayley in the doorway, her gold eyes wide with concern. She stepped inside, closing the door softly behind her.

"What's wrong? I could hear you from—"

"Nothing." I turned away, wiping my face with my sleeve. "Just looking for something."

"J.J." Her voice was gentle but firm. "What are you looking for?"

I couldn't meet her eyes. Couldn't let her see me like this. Broken, desperate, falling apart over a piece of metal smaller than a silver dollar.

"Wagner," I corrected automatically. "We can't—"

"There's no one here but us." She moved closer, her boots soft on the wooden floor. "And right now, you don't look like Jay Wagner. You look like a man who's lost something that matters more than his own life."

The truth of it hit me like a physical blow. I sagged against the wall, all the fight draining out of me.

"A button," I whispered. "A gold button from a Union uniform."

Hayley waited patiently, giving me space to find the words.

"It was Papa's. From the 1st Texas Cavalry." My voice cracked. "When he went off to war, he cut it from his uniform and gave it to Auggie. Said it was so my little brother would remember him."

I slid down the wall until I was sitting on the floor, my head in my hands. "Papa never came home. Died at Antietam, they said. And that button... it was all Auggie had left of him. The only thing."

"J.J.—"

"I stole it." The words came out raw, torn from some deep place I'd kept locked for years. "I was fourteen, and I was jealous. Jealous that Papa gave it to Auggie instead of me. Jealous that he loved Auggie more. So I took it."

Hayley kneeled beside me, close enough that I could smell apple blossoms in her hair.

"I told him I'd just borrowed it, that I'd give it back. But I didn't. I kept it, and I let him think it was lost. You should have seen his face, Hayley. Like I'd killed Papa all over again."

My hands were shaking now, and I couldn't make them stop. "We were crossing this river a few hours later.

Shallow thing, barely knee-deep most times. But the spring rains had it running fast and high. Auggie was so heartbroken about the button, he wasn't watching where he stepped. His foot slipped on a wet rock, and the current..."

I couldn't finish. Couldn't say the words that had haunted me every day since.

"He was only twelve. A little boy who needed that connection to Papa more than anything, and I was selfish enough to steal it from him. And now..." I looked up at Hayley, and the tears I'd been fighting finally spilled over. "Now I've lost it too. The last piece of both of them, and I've lost it."

Hayley's hand found mine, her fingers warm and steady. "We'll find it," she whispered. "We'll tear this place apart if we have to."

I shook my head. "You don't understand. It's not just the button. It's..." I struggled for words that could capture years of guilt. "Heaven help me, Hayley, but sometimes I think Papa loved Auggie more because he saw what kind of man I'd become. Saw that I'd be the type to steal from my own brother. The type to get people killed."

"That's not—"

"It is." I pulled my hand away, unable to bear her kindness when I didn't deserve it. "I've spent years hunting outlaws, bringing in rustlers, telling myself I was doing God's work. But the truth is, I'm no better than the men I chase. Worse, maybe, because I hurt the people who trusted me most."

The silence stretched between us, heavy with the weight of confession.

"You want to know why I can't settle down? Why I can't let myself want things like a home, a family?" I laughed, but there was no humor in it. "Because men like me don't get those things. Men who steal from children and get their brothers killed don't get to be happy."

"J.J." Hayley's voice was soft, but strong. "Look at me."

Reluctantly, I met her eyes.

"You were fourteen. Fourteen and grieving and scared and probably angry at the whole world for taking your father away. What you did was wrong, yes. But it doesn't make you evil. It makes you human."

"Auggie's still dead."

"Yes. And that's a terrible tragedy. But torturing yourself for the rest of your life won't bring him back. It won't honor his memory. And it won't honor your father's."

She reached into her pocket and pulled out something small and golden.

Auggie's button.

I stared at it, unable to breathe, unable to move.

"I found it by the washstand," she breathed. "It must have fallen when you were getting ready this morning."

With trembling fingers, I took the button from her palm. It was warm from her touch, and the familiar weight of it settled into my hand like coming home.

"You know what I think?" Hayley continued. "I think your father loved both his sons equally. And I think Auggie would want you to forgive yourself. More than that. I think he'd want you to live. Really live, not just survive."

I closed my eyes, clutching the button tight. For the first time in years, I let myself remember Auggie's laugh instead of his drowning. His excitement when he showed me bugs he'd caught instead of the look on his face when I told him the button was lost.

"I don't know how," I whispered.

"Start with believing you're worth saving," Hayley said. "Because you are, J.J. You're worth saving, and you're worth loving, and you're worth more than this guilt you've been carrying."

When I opened my eyes, she was still there, still watching me with those gold nugget eyes full of compassion I didn't deserve but desperately needed.

"Thank you," I managed.

She smiled. Soft, real, beautiful. "Thank you for trusting me with the truth."

I slipped the button back into my vest pocket, over my heart where it belonged. Gray's words echoed in my memory. *Son, forgiveness isn't just about being forgiven. It's about accepting that grace and walking in it.*

The button was precious, yes. But it wasn't what made Auggie matter. It wasn't what would bring him back or honor his life. Living in guilt wasn't honoring him either.

Maybe Hayley was right. Maybe Auggie really would want me to forgive myself. Maybe holding onto this guilt wasn't honoring his memory. Maybe it was dishonoring it.

Maybe I was worth saving. Maybe I was worth forgiving.

But first, I had to make sure she was safe. Because losing her would destroy me in ways that losing Auggie's button never could.

26 - Brothers in Arms

J.J.

I COULDN'T SLEEP. Too much weighing on my mind, too much at stake come morning. The weight of Auggie's button against my chest felt different now, less like a burden and more like a reminder of what I had to protect. I slipped outside, careful not to wake the other men, and headed toward the barn to check on Magnus.

The night air carried the scent of sage and distant rain, crisp enough to clear my head but not quite cold enough to bite. Stars stretched overhead like scattered diamonds, and somewhere in the distance, a coyote called to its pack. The barn loomed ahead, solid and familiar, offering refuge I'd come to associate with honest work and decent horses.

The mustang nickered softly when I approached his stall, and I ran my hand along his neck, finding comfort in his steady presence. Magnus had carried me through more dangerous situations than I cared to count, never once failing me when I needed him most. His coat was warm beneath my palm. Muscles relaxed but ready, the way a good horse should be.

"Easy, boy," I murmured, checking his water and running my fingers through his mane. "Big day tomorrow."

"Figured you'd be out here."

I turned to find Shane emerging from the shadows near the back of the barn, Flynn and Grady behind him. Their faces were serious in the moonlight, etched with tension that came before dangerous work. Shane moved with that characteristic quiet confidence, Flynn's restless energy barely contained even in the dim light, while Grady carried himself with steady competence. A man who'd seen his share of trouble—and forgiven more than most. Grady had married into the Harper family despite their outlaw father ordering the execution of his parents. Had to respect a man like that.

"Couldn't sleep either?" I asked.

Shane shook his head, flicking his toothpick to the corner of his mouth. "Too much to think about. Mind if we talk?"

Flynn lit a small lantern and kept the flame low as we gathered near Magnus's stall. The light threw dancing shadows across the barn walls, illuminating stacks of hay, leather tack hanging from pegs, and the patient eyes of horses watching our midnight conference.

"This operation tomorrow," Shane began, working the toothpick between his teeth with deliberate precision. "It's bigger than just catching rustlers."

Flynn nodded, his wild blue eyes reflecting the lamplight. "Hutch's got connections we haven't mapped yet. Political ones, maybe territorial officials. If this goes sideways and he escapes, he could disappear into a network we can't touch."

"Or worse," Grady added, settling against a hay bale with careful movement. A man nursing old injuries. "He could come after all of us. Our families. My wife and children. Lilian and Deacon."

The implications hit me like a physical blow. Tomorrow had seemed simple in my mind. Bring in the outlaws and make sure Hayley stayed safe. These men were thinking about protecting everyone they loved from a network of corruption that stretched further than any of us fully understood.

"It won't come to that," I said, though even as the words left my mouth, I wondered if I was being naïve.

"You sound mighty sure of that," Grady observed, his tone careful but probing.

Shane studied me with that measuring look of his, weighing a man's worth in a heartbeat. "Flynn told us about Hayley being the bait. About you being positioned to protect her when Hutch makes his move."

"That's the plan."

"Plans have a way of falling apart when bullets start flying," Flynn said, his voice tight with barely controlled emotion. "What happens if you can't get a clear shot? What happens if Hutch's smarter than we think and sees through the whole setup?"

The questions hung heavy in the barn, mixing with the scent of hay and leather and the quiet sounds of horses shifting in their stalls. These men had fought together, bled together, trusted each other with their lives. Now they were asking if they could trust me with something infinitely more precious.

Flynn stepped closer, the lantern light casting harsh shadows across his angular features. "She's not just my sister, Westin. She's the heart of this family. When our father abandoned us, when our mother died, Hayley was the one who kept us believing we could be something better than what we came from."

"Flynn's right," Shane said quietly, his voice carrying the weight of years and responsibility. "Hayley's got more courage than sense sometimes, and more determination than the rest of us combined. But she's also..." He paused, searching for words. "She's what we fight for. What we protect. The reason we became lawmen instead of following our father's path."

Grady nodded, understanding crossing his serious face. "When Justine and I first met, Hayley was the one who convinced her to give me a chance. Said any man who'd stand up to corrupt men for the sake of justice was worth knowing." He smiled slightly. "'Course, she also said if I broke her sister's heart, she'd track me down and make me regret it."

"She would too," Flynn said, and for the first time that night, there was warmth in his voice instead of worry.

I felt the weight of their trust settling on my shoulders like a heavy coat. These weren't just lawmen asking me to do my job. These were brothers asking me to protect the most important person in their world.

"I know what she means to you," I said finally. "What she means to all of you. And I know you have every reason to doubt whether I can keep her safe."

"It's not about doubting your skill," Shane said, working the toothpick to the other side of his mouth. "We've all heard the stories about J.J. Westin. Forty-one successful apprehensions. Never lost a man you were protecting."

"Then what is it about?"

Flynn's jaw tightened, and I could see him wrestling with something. "It's about what happens when your heart gets involved. When it's not just another job, but the woman you love standing in danger."

The words hit home because they were true. This wasn't just another assignment. Hayley had become something precious to me, something worth more than my reputation or my life.

"You're right," I admitted. "My heart is involved. That could make me reckless, could make me take chances I shouldn't take." I paused, meeting each of their gazes in turn. "Or it could make me more careful than I've ever been in my life. Because losing her isn't an option I can live with."

Shane studied me for a long moment, then nodded slowly. "That's what I was hoping you'd say."

"This isn't just about tomorrow," Grady said, leaning forward in the lamplight. "If we all make it through this, if we bring down Hutch's network and keep our families safe, what then? What are your intentions toward Hayley?"

The question was blunt, without pretense. The question family asked when they needed to know where they stood.

"I intend to marry her," I said without hesitation. "If she'll have me. I want to build a life with her, something real and lasting. The Westin Detective Agency. Husband and wife, solving cases together."

Flynn's eyebrows rose. "You've given this some thought."

"Every day since I met her," I admitted. "She's got sand enough to stare down Hutch's entire crew and make them respect her. That's a woman worth changing your life for."

The silence that followed was comfortable, filled with understanding and acceptance. Finally, Flynn stepped forward, his expression serious but no longer hostile.

"Tomorrow, when the shooting starts, you remember that she's not just the woman you love. She's our sister. She's family." He paused, then extended his hand toward me. "And after tomorrow, if we all make it through this alive, so are you."

I gripped his hand firmly, feeling the calluses from years of hard work and harder choices. "For Hayley."

"For family," Shane corrected, and somehow that meant even more.

Grady stood, brushing hay from his vest. "We should get some rest. Morning's going to come whether we're ready."

As they prepared to leave, Flynn turned back to me. "One more thing, Westin. That light sensitivity of yours, the headaches. How bad are they really?"

I'd been wondering if anyone had noticed. "Bad enough. Bright sunlight can throw off my aim if I'm not careful."

"Then we'll make sure you're positioned with the sun at your back," Shane said matter-of-factly. "Every advantage we can give you, we will."

After they left, I remained in the barn with Magnus, listening to the quiet sounds of horses breathing and hay settling. The weight of their trust was heavier than any respect I'd ever earned, more precious than any reputation I'd built.

Tomorrow, Hutch would make his move, and I'd have to be ready. Not just as J.J. Westin, the famous rustler hunter, but as the man who loved Hayley Harper and had been accepted into the family that would die to protect her.

I thought about Auggie's button, warm against my chest, and for the first time in years, it didn't feel like a burden. It felt like a blessing. A reminder that love was worth fighting for, worth protecting, worth every risk I'd have to take come morning.

Magnus nuzzled my shoulder, and I scratched behind his ears. "What do you think, boy? Ready to bring our girl home safe?"

My mustang snorted softly, as if to say he'd been ready all along. All we had to do now was prove worthy of the trust that had been placed in us.

27 - The Wells Fargo Setup

Hayley

THE MORNING SUN cast long shadows across the canyon as I adjusted the ivory combs in my carefully arranged hair. The pale blue silk dress felt foreign after weeks in work clothes, with its pearl buttons and enough petticoats to make sitting properly a challenge. But appearances mattered in this business, and today I needed to look like a woman worth robbing.

"You sure about this getup?" Flynn asked, leaning against the boulder where I'd set up my impromptu dressing room. His wild blue eyes held a restless energy I knew meant trouble. "Seems like a lot of fuss just to get yourself shot at."

"It's called playing a part, little brother." I secured the final comb and turned to face him. "Rich ladies don't travel in work dresses."

Flynn snorted, but I caught the worry beneath his dismissive tone. Shane stood nearby, silent as always, but his dark eyes tracked every movement in the canyon below where Grady and Xavier Mack were positioning the Wells Fargo stage. My Pinkerton training automatically cataloged their positions—good sight lines, multiple escape routes, defensive cover if needed.

"How's baby Amy?" I asked Grady as he approached, hoping to ease some of the tension crackling between my brothers.

His face softened immediately. "Growing like a weed. Justine says she's got my stubborn streak already. Won't go to sleep unless someone's singing to her." He chuckled, then his expression grew more serious. "Justine made me promise to tell you to be careful. She's got a bad feeling about this whole thing."

"Smart woman," Shane whispered. It was the first thing he'd said all morning, which meant he was thinking hard. Shane went silent only when he was calculating risks—and finding too many variables he couldn't control.

"She is smart," Grady agreed. "Smart enough to know that what we're doing today could change everything for a lot of families. These rustlers have been bleeding ranchers dry for months."

I tucked my derringer into my reticule, making sure it was easily accessible but well-hidden. The Bowie knife went into a specially sewn sheath inside my skirt's waistband, hidden by the silk fabric but within easy reach. One shot and one blade. That's all I'd have if things went sideways, but my Pinkerton training had taught me to make every bullet count and every cut precise. The familiar weight of both weapons was reassuring, even if inadequate for a sustained firefight.

"The gold bars look authentic enough," I said, nodding toward the stage where Xavier was loading the painted lead weights into a strongbox. The bright red Wells Fargo coach gleamed in the morning sun, its yellow wheels dulled with trail dust that couldn't quite hide their cheerful color. It looked every inch of the valuable target we needed it to be.

"From a distance, no one will know the difference," Flynn said with a grin that didn't reach his eyes. "Until they try to lift them. Then they'll figure out real quick that lead weighs a lot less than gold."

Shane stepped closer, his voice low. "Positions are set. We've got men hidden along the ridge, and Grady's contacts are covering the back trail. Soon as Hutch makes his move, we'll have him boxed in."

I mentally reviewed the positioning, my training automatically identifying strengths and weaknesses in our setup. Good crossfire potential, adequate cover, but too many blind spots if they came from unexpected angles.

"What's our communication system?" I asked, my professional instincts taking over. "How do we coordinate if they split up or try to flank us?"

Shane pulled out a small mirror, angling it to catch the sunlight. "Light signals. One flash means they're coming. Two flashes mean abort. Three means we spring the trap."

"Range limitations on those signals?" I pressed. "What if dust or smoke interferes? Do we have backup communication?"

Grady nodded approvingly. "Hand signals for close range, whistle calls for long distance when it's quiet. Once the shooting starts, we're on our own until someone can move position."

"And if I'm in trouble inside the coach?"

"Drop your reticule out the window," Grady said. "J.J. will have eyes on the stage the whole time."

J.J. nodded from where he was checking his Winchester. "I'll be positioned with clear sight lines to both the ambush point and your escape routes. If things go sideways, there's a wash about fifty yards south of the road. Get there and stay low."

I studied the terrain with fresh eyes, plotting multiple escape routes from the coach to various defensive positions. The wash would provide good cover, but it also offered limited mobility. Better than being trapped in an overturned stage, though.

"What about prisoner handling?" I asked. This was

the part that separated professionals from amateurs. "We can't just leave wounded men scattered across the canyon."

"Xavier's got manacles in the stage boot," Grady replied. "Soon as the shooting stops, we secure whoever's left breathing."

Flynn checked his pocket watch. "Timing?"

"Stage hits the ambush point in exactly twenty-three minutes," Shane said with military precision. "J.J. takes his position in fifteen. Hayley enters the coach at eighteen. That gives us a five-minute window to make final adjustments."

The timeline felt tight but manageable. I'd worked with less preparation time on Pinkerton assignments, though usually with more backup and better equipment.

"Contingencies?" I pressed, pulling out my own notebook to jot down the key points. Allan Pinkerton had drilled into every agent the importance of detailed operational planning.

Shane's tactical mind was fully engaged now. "If they don't take the bait, we let the stage pass and regroup. If they outnumber us, we fall back to position two. That cluster of boulders near the canyon mouth." He gestured toward the natural fortification. "If they try to take hostages..."

"They won't get the chance," J.J. said quietly, but with absolute certainty.

Something warm unfurled in my chest at the steel in his voice. This was the legendary rustler hunter speaking, the man who'd made forty-one successful captures. But more than that, it was the man who'd held me close and promised to protect what mattered to him. The combination of professional competence and personal devotion sent a flutter through my stomach that had nothing to do with pre-mission nerves.

"I need to check my sight lines from the position," J.J. said, shouldering his Winchester. "Make sure there are no glare issues with the sun angle." He touched the brim of his hat toward me, then turned on his heel with that silent grace of his.

Grady turned to me, his expression serious. "Hayley, can we trust him not to actually shoot Xavier?"

The question hit closer to home than Grady knew. After yesterday's breakdown over Auggie's button, I'd seen J.J.'s soul laid bare. The man who'd cried in my arms over his brother's death, who'd shown such devastating vulnerability. Could I trust him to hold steady when the shooting started?

My eyes darted to where J.J. had disappeared among the rocks, remembering how he'd shattered at the memory of fifteen-year-old Auggie drowning. The guilt he carried was a wound that hadn't healed, might never heal. But beneath that pain, I'd also seen his fundamental decency, his desperate need to protect rather than destroy.

"He'll do what's right," I said, hoping my voice carried more confidence than I felt.

Flynn's eyes narrowed. "You sound mighty sure of that."

"I am."

"Hay," Shane's voice carried a warning. "Don't let your feelings cloud your judgment. Men have fooled you before."

Heat flashed through me at the reference to Stanton, but I kept my voice level. "This is different."

"Is it?" Flynn stepped closer, his protective instincts flaring. "Because from where I'm standing, it looks like you're sweet on a man who's been riding with rustlers and killers for weeks."

The accusation stung because it held a grain of truth. My feelings for J.J. had grown beyond professional respect, beyond the simple attraction I'd first felt. But my judgment wasn't clouded. It was informed by seeing him at his most vulnerable, most honest.

"Enough." I straightened to my full height, every inch

the Pinkerton agent I'd trained to be. "J.J. Westin has a reputation that speaks for itself. Forty-one successful apprehensions. He's not the problem here."

A movement in my peripheral vision made me pause. Something had shifted in the rocks above us—just a flash, like sunlight glinting off metal or glass. My trained eye caught details my brothers missed: the unnatural stillness after the movement, the way shadows seemed slightly off in one section of the ridge.

"Did you see that?" I asked, pointing toward the canyon rim.

Shane's hand moved to his gun. "See what?"

"There." I gestured again, but whatever I'd glimpsed was gone. "I could have sworn I saw movement. Deliberate movement, not natural."

Flynn was already scanning the ridge, his body coiled like a spring. "Someone watching?"

The feeling crept up my spine like icy fingers. A familiar Pinkerton instinct had kept me alive through two years of undercover work. The sensation of unseen eyes evaluating, cataloging, planning. We weren't alone, and whoever was up there knew exactly what we were doing.

"Grady," I called softly. "How many of your men are positioned on the north rim?"

"None. We kept everyone south to avoid being seen from the road."

Shane's jaw tightened. "Then we've got company."

Xavier looked up from the stage, his brow creased with concern. "You think they're onto us?"

Before anyone could answer, J.J. appeared from behind a cluster of boulders, moving with purpose. His dark glasses couldn't hide the tension in his posture or the way his hand rested near his sidearm.

"We're being watched," he said without preamble. "At least three men, maybe more. They've been there since before dawn."

My pulse quickened. Professional surveillance, then.

Not accidental discovery.

Flynn's hand went to his gun. "Hutch's people?"

"Has to be." J.J.'s voice was grim. "Question is, how much do they know?"

Shane stepped forward, his tactical mind already working through possibilities. "Could be routine scouting. Or..."

"Or Hutch has been playing us from the beginning," I finished, voicing what we were all thinking.

The silence that followed was heavy with implications. If Hutch suspected our true identities, if he knew about the trap we'd set, then everything we'd worked for was about to crumble. Worse, we'd be walking into an ambush of our own making.

"We abort," Flynn said immediately. "Get Hayley out of here and—"

"No." I cut him off, my mind racing through the tactical implications. "We've come too far to back down now."

"Hayley," Shane's voice carried a quiet authority that had kept our family together through the worst times. "If they know who you are..."

"Then they know who you are, too." I looked between my brothers, these men who'd spent their lives protecting me. "And they know about J.J. We're all in danger now, not just me."

The weight of command settled on my shoulders. Not as their sister, but as the Pinkerton agent with the most experience in situations like this. I'd been trained for hostile surveillance, for operations compromised by enemy intelligence.

J.J. nodded slowly. "She's right. Running now won't change what they might already know. But if we can spring the trap, take them by surprise..."

"It's risky," Grady said, wiping sweat from his forehead despite the morning chill.

"Everything we do is risky," I replied, falling back on

Pinkerton doctrine. "But this is our chance to end it. To stop them from hurting any more families."

I thought of Justine back home with baby Amy, of all the ranchers who'd lost cattle to the gang, of the mercantile owner who'd died in Canyon Diablo. This wasn't just about justice anymore. It was about protecting the people we loved from predators who saw them as nothing more than easy prey.

Flynn cursed under his breath, but I could see him wavering. Shane remained silent, which meant he was considering it, weighing risks against potential gains.

"If we do this," Shane said finally, "we do it smart. No unnecessary risks. First sign things are going completely south, we pull back."

"Agreed," I said quickly, before anyone could change their mind.

J.J. checked his rifle one last time, working the lever to ensure smooth action. "I'll be in position on the ridge. If they try anything, I'll have a clear shot."

"Just remember," Flynn said, his voice hard with warning, "some of us care more about Hayley coming home alive than we do about catching rustlers."

The look that passed between J.J. and Flynn was charged with an unspoken challenge. But J.J. just nodded, his expression serious. "So do I."

As the men moved to take their positions, I felt that prickle of unease again. Somewhere up in those canyon walls, hostile eyes were watching our every move. Hutch might know exactly what we were planning—might be planning something of his own.

But there was no turning back now. The die was cast, the trap was set, and in less than an hour we'd know whether we were hunters or prey.

I smoothed my silk skirts and walked toward the waiting stagecoach, every sense alert for signs of danger. The red paint gleamed like fresh blood in the morning light, and the leather seats creaked as Xavier made final adjustments to the harness.

The feeling of being watched followed me every step of the way, a constant reminder that this operation had already begun—and we might not be the ones controlling it.

28 – Crossfire

J.J.

THE WELLS FARGO stage rolled into view like a red and yellow beacon, dust billowing from its wheels as the six-horse team pulled it down the canyon road. My heart slammed against my ribs as I watched from my position on the ridge, rifle ready, sweat already beading under my dark glasses despite the morning chill.

My Winchester M94 lever-action repeating rifle felt solid in my hands. The familiar weight that had served me well through forty-one captures. The comforting bulk of my twin Remington six-shooters pressed against my hips, and I could feel my knife secured in my boot. An arsenal built for precision and reliability.

Sixty yards below, Hayley sat inside that bright red coach, looking every inch the wealthy passenger in her silk dress. One small woman with a derringer against whatever reckoning was about to break loose.

Keep her safe. Whatever happens, keep her safe.

The stage driver called out to his horses, leather traces creaking as the team slowed for the bend where Hutch waited with Derek and Mac. My finger found the trigger of my Winchester, the metal cold and familiar against my skin.

Hutch's voice drifted up from the rocks below. "Remember, Wagner. Clean shot. No hesitation."

I could smell the gun oil on my rifle, the dry sage crushing under my boots, and the metallic taste of fear coating my tongue. Somewhere to my left, Flynn was hidden among the boulders with his Colt Peacemaker, probably fighting every instinct to charge down and drag his sister to safety. Shane would be positioned south with Grady's men, his own Winchester ready, calculating angles and escape routes with that methodical mind of his.

Xavier sat tall on the driver's bench beside the stage driver, shotgun across his knees, playing his part perfectly. The man had nerves of steel. Had to, knowing I was supposed to put a bullet in him any second now.

The stage hit our predetermined ambush point.

"Now!" Hutch roared, spurring his horse into the road.

Everything exploded at once.

Derek and Mac flanked from both sides, guns drawn. Derek wielding a nickel-plated Smith & Wesson, Mac with an old cap-and-ball Navy Colt that looked like it had seen twenty years of hard use. Their shouts echoed off the canyon walls as the stage horses reared and snorted, eyes rolling white with terror.

Dust erupted in choking clouds as hooves pawed the air.

"Hands up! Nobody move!"

Xavier's hands tightened on his shotgun. A double-barreled twelve-gauge that could cut a man in half at close range. The signal we'd agreed on.

This was it. The moment they expected me to kill an innocent man.

I sighted down the barrel of my Winchester, centered the crosshairs on Xavier's chest. The rifle's balance was perfect, the action smooth as silk from years of careful maintenance. My heart hammered so hard I could hear it in my ears, drowning out everything else.

Lord, guide this shot.

I shifted my aim six inches to the right and squeezed the trigger.

The Winchester bucked against my shoulder, the thirty-thirty cartridge cracking through the canyon like thunder. The spent brass ejected cleanly as I worked the lever, already chambering the next round. Powder smoke stung my nostrils and burned my eyes.

Through the haze, I saw Xavier's shotgun spin from his hands. The walnut stock splintered where my bullet had struck instead of flesh.

"What the blazes?" Hutch's bellow cut through the chaos.

Xavier tumbled from the driver's bench, clutching his arm where splinters had cut him, playing wounded but very much alive. The stage driver hauled back on his reins, the horses dancing and snorting as leather traces snapped taut.

That's when the trap sprang.

Gunfire erupted from the southern ridge at Shane's position. Muzzle flashes sparked from the rocks as Grady's men opened up on the gang. A mix of Winchester repeaters and single-shot Springfields that had seen service in the Indian Wars.

The canyon filled with the sharp crack of rifles, the deeper boom of shotguns, ricochets whining off stone like angry hornets.

"It's a dadblasted trap!" Derek hollered, wheeling his horse as bullets chewed up the surrounding ground.

His Smith & Wesson barked repeatedly as he fired wildly.

Smoke billowed through the canyon, thick and choking. The acrid smell of gunpowder mixed with dust and horse sweat and the metallic scent of blood. My ears rang from the gunfire, making it hard to track who was shooting at what.

I worked the lever on my Winchester again, the action cycling smooth and fast. Brass cartridge cases glinted as they ejected onto the rocks beside me. The rifle held fifteen rounds, and I'd already burned two.

Had to make every shot count.

Movement to my right. Flynn broke cover, charging down the slope with his Colt Peacemaker blazing. The forty-five caliber rounds boomed like cannon shots in the confined space.

His wild blue eyes were fixed on the stage, on his sister, every protective instinct driving him toward the fight.

"Flynn, stay back!" I shouted, but my voice was lost in the maelstrom.

A bullet spanged off the rock beside my head, showering me with stone chips. I rolled left, bringing my rifle up, searching for the shooter.

There was Carter, crouched behind the overturned stage, firing wildly with what looked like an old Army Colt conversion. Cap-and-ball revolver modified to take cartridges. The modification made it unreliable, which explained his poor shooting.

I put a Winchester round through his shoulder. The thirty-thirty spun him around like a child's top. He went down screaming, his converted Colt clattering across the rocks.

But where was Ford?

Through the smoke and chaos, I caught glimpses of the gang scattering. Mac's horse went down, spilling him hard onto the rocky ground, his old Navy Colt flying from his hand. Derek had abandoned his mount and was scrambling up the canyon wall on foot, blood streaming from his arm, his fancy Smith & Wesson forgotten in the dirt.

And Hutch.

The big man was charging straight for the stage, a Remington in each hand. Same model as mine, but his were ivory-handled and engraved. Rage twisted his face as he realized this was a setup, and he planned to attack the nearest target.

Hayley.

"No!" The word tore from my throat as I swung my Winchester toward him.

A rifle cracked from somewhere to my right. The distinctive sharp report of a Sharps fifty caliber buffalo gun, not Shane's position. Through the smoke, I glimpsed a muzzle flash from the rocks where Ford had been positioned with the gang.

Hutch jerked like a puppet with cut strings, both ivory-handled Remingtons flying from his hands as the massive Sharps bullet took him center mass. The fifty-caliber round nearly cut him in half.

He stood there for a heartbeat, swaying, then toppled backward onto the blood-soaked ground.

Dead before he hit the rocks.

My blood chilled as the realization hit me. Ford had shot Hutch with a buffalo rifle. Not Shane. Not Grady's men.

Ford had killed his own leader with the precision that spoke of years behind a rifle scope.

But why would Ford kill Hutch? The quiet man had been more dangerous than any of us realized.

The gunfire began to slacken, individual shots instead of the continuous roar. Grady's voice echoed from somewhere below. "Throw down your weapons! You're surrounded!"

But something was wrong. My skin crawled with the certainty that this wasn't over, wasn't going according to plan. Ford shooting Hutch changed everything.

There was more to the quiet cowboy than any of us had suspected.

Behind me, Magnus snorted and stamped, sensing my tension. My mustang's ears were pinned back, nostrils flaring at the smell of gunpowder and blood. He knew danger when he felt it, and right now, every instinct was telling him to run.

Where was Ford?

I scanned the canyon frantically, Winchester ready, trying to spot the quiet man who'd been watching me too closely for weeks. The smoke began clearing, revealing bodies scattered across the rocks.

Mac lay motionless beside his dead horse. Carter was down, but breathing, clutching his wounded shoulder. Derek had vanished up the canyon wall, leaving a trail of blood on the rocks.

And Ford was nowhere to be seen. That Sharps rifle was still out there somewhere, waiting to cut down anyone foolish enough to try closing the distance.

That's when I heard Hayley scream.

The sound cut through the gunfire and chaos like a blade, freezing my blood. I spun toward the stage just in time to see a figure in black dragging her from the coach, one arm wrapped around her waist, a gun pressed to her temple.

Ford.

He must have circled around during the fight, using the smoke and confusion as cover. Now he had the one thing that would stop all of us cold.

"Well, well," Ford called out, his voice carrying easily in the sudden quiet. "Reckon we got ourselves a genuine Wells Fargo passenger, after all. Right pretty little thing, ain't she?"

Hayley's silk dress was torn, her carefully arranged hair falling loose around her shoulders. But her eyes, those gold nugget eyes, blazed with fury instead of fear.

Even with a gun to her head, she looked ready to fight.

I brought my Winchester up fast, trying to find a clean shot. Ford kept Hayley between us, but for just a moment, just a heartbeat, his head appeared over her left shoulder.

I had him.

The sun chose that instant to reflect off the canyon wall behind Ford, a brilliant flash of light that hit my eyes like a physical blow. Pain exploded behind my temples, and tears flooded my vision.

I squeezed the trigger anyway, trusting muscle memory and desperation.

The Winchester cracked, echoing off the stone walls.

But through my watering eyes, I saw Ford jerk Hayley to the side at the last second. My bullet sparked off the rock where his head had been a fraction of a moment before.

I'd missed.

"I wouldn't try that again, Westin," Ford said, calm as Sunday morning. "See, I know exactly who you are. J.J. Westin, the famous rustler hunter. Been huntin' men like you my whole life. Reckon I can smell a lawman at fifty paces."

The words hit like physical blows. He knew. Had known all along.

"Oh yes," Ford continued, backing toward a cluster of horses hidden in the rocks. "You think I'm some kind of greenhorn? Think I didn't recognize the Rustler Hunter when he showed up at my operation? Think I couldn't tell this here gal was law the minute she started askin' too many questions?"

Flynn appeared from behind the stage, his Colt Peacemaker trained on Ford, but he couldn't shoot any more than I could. Not with Hayley in the way.

"You see, boys." Ford's voice was easy, like he was discussing the weather. "Y'all been dancin' to my tune from the very start. Been plannin' this little shindig for weeks, soon as I cottoned on to what you really were. This whole Wells Fargo business? Shoot, I knew about it 'fore you did."

My blood turned to ice. If Ford had known from the beginning, if he'd been playing us all along...

"Now, here's how this is gonna play out," Ford said, still backing toward the horses. "I'm takin' this little lady as surety. And if any of you boys get notions about followin', well... reckon even the best lawman training don't stop a fifty-caliber bullet."

The canyon fell silent except for the sound of my heart hammering in my ears, the wheeze of wounded men trying to breathe, and the echo of my failure ringing off the stone walls.

I'd had one clear shot. One chance to save her.

And I'd missed.

Just like with Auggie, my weakness had cost someone I loved everything. The light sensitivity that made me wear those dark glasses, the headaches that came with bright sun, the tears that blurred my vision at the worst possible moment.

I was supposed to be the Rustler Hunter. The man who never missed.

But when it mattered most, when Hayley's life hung in the balance, I'd failed her completely.

Ford was backing away now, dragging Hayley toward the hidden horses, and there was nothing I could do. Nothing but watch the woman I loved disappear because I wasn't good enough, fast enough, steady enough when she needed me most.

I'd failed again. Just like with Auggie, I'd let someone I cared about walk into danger I should have seen coming.

But this time, I was going to get her back.

Even if it killed me.

29 - The Real Tall Hog

Hayley

FORD'S GRIP ON my arm was iron-strong as he dragged me up the rocky slope toward a cluster of weathered buildings tucked into the canyon wall. An old mining operation, by the look of it. The place where a man could disappear and never be found.

"Easy now, missy," Ford said, his voice carrying the same calm tone he'd used back at the bunkhouse. "No call to make this harder than it needs to be."

I kept my mouth shut and my eyes open, cataloging everything like Allan Pinkerton had trained me. Three buildings, including a main cabin with a stone foundation and thick timber walls, a smaller storage shed with a corrugated metal roof, and what looked like an old assay office with boarded windows. High canyon walls on three sides formed natural barriers, with only one narrow trail in or out unless you fancied scaling sixty feet of sheer sandstone.

Smart choice for a hideout. Defensible position, clear sight lines, multiple escape routes through the mine shafts if things went sideways.

Ford shoved me through the door of the main cabin and pushed me down into a wooden chair near a cold stone fireplace. The place reeked of stale tobacco, unwashed men, and something else. Gun oil. Lots of it. This wasn't just a hideout. It was an armory.

"Now then," Ford said, producing a coil of rope from a wooden crate. "Let's get you settled properly."

I studied the rope as he approached. Three-strand manila hemp, about half-inch in diameter. Strong enough to hold a struggling horse, but not impossible to cut if you had the right blade and enough time. Ford might be cautious, but he wasn't a sailor. His knots would have weak points.

He tied my wrists behind the chair back with what looked like a bowline variation, then bound my ankles to the chair legs with simple hitches. The rope was rough hemp, thick and strong, but not impossible to work with if I could get to my knife. The blade was still concealed at the small of my back, pressed flat against my spine beneath the torn silk dress. Ford hadn't thought to search a helpless woman too thoroughly.

Mistake number one.

"Comfortable?" Ford asked, stepping back to admire his handiwork.

I tested the bonds, letting him see me struggle just enough to satisfy his expectations. The wrist binding had maybe an inch of play if I compressed my hands just right. "Been better."

Ford chuckled and settled into a chair across from me, finally relaxing now that he had the upper hand. That's when I noticed something peculiar. The man was downright chatty suddenly.

In all the weeks I'd known him at the Diablo Bunkhouse, Ford had barely strung together more than a couple of sentences in my presence. Quiet, watchful, measuring every word like a man counting coins. But now? Now he seemed eager to talk. The careful mask he'd worn for months had finally slipped away, replaced by the arrogant satisfaction of a man who believed he'd already won.

No surprise there. Men like Ford wanted folks to know what they'd done. Like it was part of why they did such heinous things. Glory, ego, and evil were all wrapped up together.

"You know," Ford said, leaning back in his chair, "when you told Carter about being Galen Harper's daughter, it got me thinking. Galen and me, we rode together for near on three years."

He knew. Had known all along.

"Smart man, your daddy. Ruthless when he needed to be. Made quite a reputation for himself before the law finally caught up," Ford continued, clearly enjoying himself.

"I wouldn't know," I said carefully. "Wasn't much of a father."

"No, I don't reckon he was. But he was one masterful outlaw." Ford's eyes glittered with something like admiration. "Which makes you quite the disappointment, I'd imagine."

The words should have stung. Instead, I felt a warm glow of satisfaction deep in my chest. If Galen Harper would have been disappointed in me, then I must be doing something right.

"How so?" I asked genuinely curious.

"Working with lawmen. Playing house with some rustler hunter." Ford shook his head in mock sadness. "Galen always said the worst thing a Harper could do was go soft. Bet he's cursing your name from that Yuma cell if word's reached him."

I let a flicker of hurt cross my face, just enough to keep Ford talking. "You said you knew my father. What else did he tell you?"

"Oh, plenty. Had strong opinions about his young'uns, that man did." Ford leaned forward, warming to his subject. "Take that boy of his, Flynn, wasn't it? Galen always said that one was too soft, too eager to please.

Said Flynn would never make a real outlaw because he was always trying so hard to win his daddy's approval."

Heat flashed through me at the insult to Flynn, but I forced it down. Ford was fishing, trying to get a rise out of me. But he was also revealing useful information. *Keep him talking, Hayley. Let his pride hang him.*

"And you figured all this out because of my name?" I asked, letting a hint of anger creep into my voice. Just enough to seem believable.

"That, and that you ask too many questions for a simple cook and laundress. Plus, your boyfriend there has quite the reputation. J.J. Westin don't just show up at random bunkhouses." Ford's smile turned cold. "Took me about a week to put it all together. Galen Harper's daughter and the famous rustler hunter working together. Had to be law."

I bit back a dozen questions and focused on the most important one. "So you've been playing us from the beginning."

"Every step of the way, darlin'. See, when word came down Mossman was taking over the Aztec Land & Cattle Company, I knew things were about to get complicated. New manager meant new rules, new attention. Had to make some arrangements."

Ford stood and walked to the window, peering out at the canyon below through a gap in the wooden shutters. His movements were confident, relaxed. A man completely in control of his domain.

"Lucky for me, I had help on the inside."

"Inside what?"

"Mossman's operation." Ford turned back to me, that chilling smile widening. "You ever wonder how I knew about your little Wells Fargo trap before you did? How I stayed one step ahead of the famous rustler hunter and his Pinkerton friend?"

My heart started hammering, but I kept my voice level. "I wouldn't know anything about the Pinkertons."

"'Course you wouldn't." Ford chuckled. "Point is, I had me an advantage. A man on the inside feeding me information about every move Mossman made, every plan he hatched. Every meeting you attended, every strategy you discussed."

"That's impossible. Mossman's careful about who he trusts."

"Is he now?" Ford's eyes glittered with malicious amusement. "Tell me, darlin', you remember that scar-faced fellow who brought you and Westin to see Mossman a few weeks back? Big man, goes by Winston?"

The blood drained from my face. Winston. Mossman's right-hand man, the one who'd coordinated our entire operation. The man who knew everything.

"I can see you remember him," Ford said, clearly enjoying my reaction. "Well, old Winston and me, we got an understanding. See, back in January when word came that Mossman was headed to Arizona, I sent Derek to pay Winston's wife a little visit. Sweet woman lives in a nice little house in Prescott. Be a real shame if something happened to her."

The pieces clicked into place with sickening clarity. Every meeting with Mossman, every plan we'd made, every strategy we'd discussed. Winston had been there. Winston had known it all.

And Winston had told Ford everything.

"You're lying," I said, but even I could hear the uncertainty in my voice.

"Am I? How else you think I knew to have men watching your little setup this morning? How you think I knew exactly when and where to position myself for the best view of the whole show?" Ford returned to his chair, settling back with obvious satisfaction. "Winston's been real helpful. Told me all about your real identities, your mission, even that fancy trap you thought you were setting."

My mind raced, cataloging the implications. If Winston was feeding information to Ford, then J.J., Flynn, and Shane were in even more danger than we'd realized. Any rescue attempt, any plan they made, Ford would know about it before they did.

I had to get free. Had to warn them.

But I also needed to know more. How deep did Ford's network go? How many other operations were compromised? Information was a weapon, and right now, I needed every advantage I could get.

Slowly, carefully, I began working my right hand toward the knife at the small of my back. The rope around my wrists was tight, but I'd practiced escaping from bonds during my Pinkerton training. Compress the hand, work the thumb, find the weak point in the knots. The key was patience and steady pressure.

"So what's your game?" I asked, hoping to keep Ford talking. "You've got your inside man. You know who we are. Why not just kill us and be done with it?"

"Because, darlin', I got bigger plans than just killing a few lawmen." Ford's eyes took on that fanatic gleam I'd seen in too many criminals. "See, this here territory's about to become a state. When that happens, there's gonna be opportunities for them that's smart enough to position themselves right."

He stood and began pacing, hands clasped behind his back like a general surveying a battlefield. "I got operations running from here to New Mexico, darlin'. Rustling's just the start. I got men in half the territorial offices, judges in my pocket, railroad officials who look the other way when my trains roll through. And now, an inside man with the biggest cattle company in the Southwest."

Behind my back, my fingers found the handle of my knife. The leather grip was warm from being pressed against my skin, familiar as an old friend. Just a little more work on these ropes, and I could start cutting.

"You're talking about more than rustling," I said. "You're talking about taking over."

"Smart girl. Smarter than your daddy gave you credit for, I'd wager." Ford stopped pacing and fixed me with a cold stare. "When Arizona becomes a state, I intend to have a hand in who runs it. Governor, legislature, territorial judges. And that means clearing out troublesome lawmen like your boyfriend and those brothers of yours."

"You can't kill every lawman in the territory."

"Don't need to. Just need to kill the right ones. The ones that can't be bought or scared off." Ford's smile was purely predatory now. "Speaking of which, I expect Westin and your brothers will be along directly, trying to rescue you. Winston's probably telling them where to find us right about now."

My knife slipped free of its sheath, the blade flat against my palm. The steel was cold, sharp, perfectly balanced. I'd chosen this knife specifically for concealment and cutting power. Now came the tricky part—cutting the rope without Ford noticing.

"You're using me as bait."

"Smart and pretty. Galen would've been proud." Ford returned to his chair. "See, I could've killed you all during that little gunfight. But where's the fun in that? This way, I get to watch the great J.J. Westin walk into a trap with his eyes wide open. Get to see if he really is as good as his reputation."

I began working the knife against the rope, tiny sawing motions hidden by the chair back. The hemp was thick, maybe twenty individual strands twisted together, but my blade was sharp enough to shave with. Just had to be patient and work systematically through each fiber.

"And if he is as good as his reputation?"

"Then it'll be a fair fight. And may the best man win." Ford chuckled. "Either way, by sunset tonight, the rustler hunter problem gets solved permanent-like."

The rope around my right wrist gave slightly. Not enough to slip free, but enough to know I was making progress. Maybe ten more strands to cut through, then I could work on loosening the knots. A few more minutes and I'd have enough room to maneuver.

But did I have a few more minutes? And more importantly, if Winston was feeding information to Ford, was the rescue party walking into their own deaths?

The sound of hoofbeats echoed from the canyon below. Distant but getting closer.

Ford's head snapped toward the window. "Well, well. Right on schedule."

My pulse quickened. J.J. and my brothers were coming, riding straight into Ford's trap. I had to make a choice, and I had to make it now. Try to escape and warn them, or stay long enough to learn more about Ford's network and maybe expose Winston's betrayal.

It was the calculated risk I'd been trained for as a Pinkerton. The kind that could save lives or get me killed.

But as the hoofbeats grew louder, I realized something Ford hadn't counted on. He might know about J.J.'s reputation and my Pinkerton training, but he didn't know how resourceful I was.

Sometimes, the best way to win a fight was to change the rules entirely.

I kept working the knife, kept cutting, kept listening to Ford's boasts about his criminal empire. But now I had a plan. A harebrained idea that would have Flynn calling me seven kinds of fool and Shane working his toothpick faster with worry.

But it might just even the odds.

And if there was one thing Galen Harper's daughter had learned from her outlaw father, it was that sometimes you had to bet everything on a single, desperate play.

Ford was still talking, bragging about his network, his genius in staying ahead of the law. He had no idea that the helpless woman tied to his chair was about to turn his carefully planned ambush into the fight of his life.

Because if I was wrong, the people I cared about most in the world were about to die.

And I'd be joining them.

30 - Failed Legend

J.J.

I SAT ON a boulder with my head in my hands, the weight of my failure crushing down like a mountain of rock. The canyon had gone quiet except for the moans of wounded men and the creak of leather as Xavier secured the prisoners with practiced efficiency.

I ain't fit to shoot at when you want to unload and clean your gun.

The words rolled through my mind, bitter as wormwood. That's what I was now. Worthless. The famous Rustler Hunter who couldn't make the one shot that mattered. Eight years of building a reputation, forty-one successful captures, and it all crumbled because of a flash of sunlight and these cursed eyes that couldn't handle it.

"You had ONE shot!"

Flynn's voice exploded behind me, raw with fury. I didn't turn around. Didn't need to see those wild blue eyes blazing with the kind of rage that could tear a man apart.

"ONE chance to save my sister, and you missed!"

Heavy footsteps pounded toward me. I braced for the blow I deserved, but it never came. Instead, I heard

Shane's voice, low and controlled.

"Flynn. Back off."

"Back off?" Flynn's voice cracked like a whip. "He had Ford dead to rights! Clear shot at maybe sixty yards! Perfect position, no wind, target standing still for three full seconds! And his hands shook like some green kid with his first gun!"

Shane shifted the toothpick between his teeth, his dark eyes unreadable. "I said back off."

I finally looked up. Flynn stood ten feet away, fists clenched, body coiled like a spring ready to snap. With one hand on his brother's chest, holding him back, Shane still clamped the toothpick between his teeth. Grady stood nearby, his face grim but understanding.

The tactical part of my mind automatically cataloged the scene. Flynn's stance was aggressive, but not quite committed to violence. Shane's positioning was protective, ready to intervene if needed. Grady's hand rested near his sidearm, not threatening but prepared. Even in my failure, I couldn't stop thinking like the hunter I'd trained myself to be.

"Go ahead," I said, my voice hoarse. "Say what you're thinking. All of you."

Flynn snarled. "You ain't half the man your reputation claims! My sister's gonna die because the great Rustler Hunter can't handle a little sunlight!"

Each word hit like a physical blow, but I didn't flinch. Couldn't argue with the truth. False legend. That's what Flynn was saying without saying it. The great J.J. Westin, brought low by something as simple as reflected light hitting his eyes at the wrong moment.

"Flynn." Shane's warning carried steel, but his voice stayed level, controlled.

"No, Shane! Don't you dare defend him!" Flynn pointed a shaking finger at me. "Hayley defended him. Said he'd do the right thing. Said we could trust him. And now she's gone because he's too weak to make the shot when it counts!"

The words cut deeper than Flynn knew. Hayley had trusted me. Believed in me when I'd given her every reason not to. And I'd repaid that trust by failing her when she needed me most.

Grady stepped forward. "That's enough. We all saw what happened. The light hit at the wrong moment."

"Light?" Flynn laughed, but there was no humor in it. "What kind of gunfighter can't handle a little reflected sunlight? What good is he if he falls apart the moment things get bright?"

The question hung in the air like gun smoke. What good was I? I'd built my entire identity around being the man who never missed, who always brought in his target, who could be counted on when things got desperate. Now that identity lay shattered in the canyon dust, as broken as my confidence.

I stood slowly, every muscle tense with failure. My gun hand trembled slightly. Whether from adrenaline or from shame, I couldn't tell.

"You're right."

Flynn blinked, thrown off by my agreement.

"I failed her," I continued. "Just like I failed my brother years ago. Just like I'll probably fail everyone else who's fool enough to count on me." I met Flynn's blazing stare. "But I'm going after her. And this time, I won't miss."

"Like blazes you will." Flynn took a step forward. "You'll get her killed. Get us all killed."

"Boys!" Xavier's voice cut through our argument. The grizzled shotgun rider approached, wiping blood from his hands where he'd been tending the wounded. "Y'all can settle this family squabble later. Right now, we've got information."

Behind him, Glenn sat on the ground with his hands bound behind his back, looking ashamed but cooperative. Mac and Carter were secured nearby with rope and rawhide, though Carter's sullen glare suggested he'd put up quite a fight before Xavier got the drop on him.

"Glenn here's been mighty helpful," Xavier continued. "Seems he's grateful to Miss Hayley for patching him up after that bullet to the shoulder."

Glenn nodded eagerly. "She saved my life. Didn't have to, considering I was riding with outlaws. But she did it anyway. Used her own knife to cauterize the wound, risked her cover to keep me breathing."

"So you're talking," Shane said. It wasn't a question.

"Everything I know," Glenn confirmed. "Ford's got a hideout in an old mining operation about ten miles north of here. Place called Skull Canyon. He's been using it as a base for months. Three buildings set against the canyon wall, with mine shafts running back into the rock."

My mind immediately began working on the tactical problem. Mining operations meant multiple levels, potential escape routes through the tunnels, defensive positions among the equipment and structures. It would be like attacking a fortress.

"How many men?" Grady asked.

"Hard to say. Ford keeps his cards close. But I seen at least six others come and go from that place. Could be more holed up in the mine shafts. He's got rifles, shotguns, even some dynamite left over from the mining days."

Xavier spat into the dust. "Six against how many of us?"

"Four," Shane said, counting quickly. "Me, Flynn, J.J., and Grady."

"I can handle myself," I said, though the words sounded hollow even to me.

Flynn snorted. "Can you? Because the last time you tried, my sister ended up captured."

"That's enough," Shane said sharply. But then he fixed me with that measuring stare, working the toothpick to the corner of his mouth. "Flynn's got a point, though. You sure you can do what needs doing? Because if you freeze up again..."

"I won't." The words came out harder than I had intended. "I can't live with myself if I don't get her back."

But even as I said it, doubt gnawed at me like a hungry wolf. What if the light hit wrong again? What if my hands shook at the crucial moment? What if my cursed eyes failed me when Hayley's life hung in the balance?

Grady cleared his throat. "Glenn, what else can you tell us about this hideout?"

"Three buildings, like I said. Main cabin where Ford likes to conduct business. That's where he'll keep any prisoners. Storage shed full of mining equipment and supplies. Old assay office that's mostly collapsed. Canyon walls on three sides, only one trail in unless you can scale sixty feet of sheer rock."

"Defensible," Shane murmured, flicking his toothpick into the dust.

"Real defensible," Glenn agreed. "Ford chose it special. Natural chokepoint, clear fields of fire, multiple fallback positions. Man could hold off an army from up there if he had enough ammunition."

I closed my eyes, visualizing the terrain Glenn described. Three approaches: the main trail, scaling the canyon walls, or coming through the mine shafts if we could find another entrance. All of them dangerous, all of them playing to Ford's advantage.

Xavier checked his pocket watch, the brass case catching the late afternoon sun. "Sun's getting low. Y'all best get moving if you want to reach that canyon before full dark."

"What about Winston?" Grady asked. "He should coordinate with Mossman, let him know what happened here."

I watched as Shane and Flynn exchanged a look. Something passed between them, some silent communication I couldn't read. It reminded me of how Hayley and Flynn could speak without words, that bond forged by shared hardship and absolute trust.

"Winston can handle that," Shane said finally. "He'll know what to do."

Something about Shane's tone nagged at me, but I was too focused on the rescue to puzzle it out. Every minute we delayed was another minute Hayley remained in Ford's hands. Another minute for him to hurt her, interrogate her, or worse.

"We need to move," I said, standing and checking my weapons. Both Remingtons sat snug in their holsters, cylinders loaded with five rounds each. I had maybe thirty rounds of thirty-thirty ammunition for my Winchester, plus what was already chambered. Not enough for a prolonged fight, but it would have to do.

"Every second we waste gives Ford more time to hurt her."

Flynn's jaw tightened. "Or more time for him to kill her because you spooked him with that missed shot."

The words hit their mark, and I felt the familiar weight of Auggie's gold button in my vest pocket. Two lives hanging in the balance because of my failures. My brother, who'd drowned because I'd stolen his most precious possession. And now Hayley, captured because I couldn't make the shot when it mattered.

"That's why we're going to get her back," I said. "All of us. Together."

Shane nodded curtly. "Glenn, anything else we should know about Ford's operation?"

"He's smart. Careful. Don't underestimate him just because he's been playing the quiet cowboy for months." Glenn's face darkened. "And he's got a mean streak wide as the Rio Grande. I seen him gut-shoot a man just for talking back. If he thinks Miss Hayley knows too much..."

The unfinished threat hung in the air like smoke. I touched the button in my pocket again, feeling its worn edges. *Lord, don't let me fail her like I failed Auggie. Give me steady hands and clear eyes when the moment comes.*

Xavier stood, brushing dust from his chaps. "I'll get these three back to town, turn them over to the territorial marshal. Y'all bring that girl home safe."

As Xavier began organizing the prisoners, Grady pulled Shane aside. I caught fragments of their conversation about supplies, backup plans, contingencies. The kind of tactical discussion I should have been part of, but my mind kept circling back to that moment when the sun flared and my shot went wide.

One chance. One clear shot at Ford's head. Perfect position, steady rest, target in the open. Everything a marksman could ask for.

And I'd missed.

Flynn appeared beside me, his anger now tempered with something that might have been worry. "You really think you can do this?"

I met his eyes. "I have to. She's..."

"I know what she is to you." Flynn's voice was quieter now, but still edged with steel. "That's what worries me. Man makes mistakes when his heart's involved."

"Then why are you going?" I asked. "Your heart's involved too."

Flynn's smile was sharp as a blade. "Because she's my sister. And because if you fail her again, I'll put a bullet in you myself."

The threat should have angered me. Instead, it felt like a promise I could understand. Flynn would do whatever it took to protect Hayley, even if that meant putting down the man who'd failed her.

"Fair enough," I said.

Shane called out from where he was saddling his horse. "Time to ride. We burn daylight, we lose our advantage."

I swung up into Magnus's saddle, feeling the familiar creak of leather, the solid weight of my weapons. My Winchester rifle sat snug in its scabbard, with the shotgun secured on the other side. Both were clean, oiled, and ready.

The mustang sensed my tension, ears flicking back, muscles coiled beneath me like steel springs.

Around me, the others mounted up with the efficient movements of men who'd spent their lives in the saddle. Shane checked his rifle action one final time before sliding it home. Grady secured his rope and adjusted his saddlebags. Flynn's hands moved in a practiced sequence, checking revolver, rifle, spare ammunition, canteen. All present and accounted for.

We were as ready as we'd ever be.

As we rode out of the canyon, leaving Xavier with the prisoners and the wreckage of our failed trap, I touched the gold button in my pocket one more time. The metal was warm from my body heat, worn smooth by years of worry and guilt.

I won't fail you again, Hayley. Not like I failed Auggie. This time, I'll get it right.

Even if it kills me.

The sun was setting behind us, painting the sky blood red as we rode toward Skull Canyon and whatever trouble Ford had waiting. In the distance, I could see storm clouds gathering on the horizon. Rain would make tracking harder, but it would also mask our approach.

Maybe God was giving me one more chance to prove I was worthy of the name J.J. Westin.

Maybe this time, the legend wouldn't be false after all.

But as Magnus carried me toward what might be my final test, I couldn't shake the feeling that Ford was expecting us. That everything we'd done, every plan we'd made, had been anticipated.

And if that was true, we weren't riding to rescue Hayley.

We were riding into a trap that would claim all our lives.

31 - Captive Audience

Hayley

THE ROPE AROUND my right wrist was nearly cut through. I'd been working the blade in tiny, careful motions while Ford paced the cabin like a caged wolf, muttering about his plans and his network. The hemp fibers were stubborn, but my Bowie knife was sharp as a surgeon's scalpel, and patience was something Allan Pinkerton had drilled into every one of his agents.

Keep your wits. Stay calm. Gather intelligence.

The Pinkerton motto echoed in my mind as I worked. Each fiber that parted under my blade brought me closer to freedom. Twelve strands cut, maybe eight more to go. The key was steady pressure and controlled movement. Too fast, and Ford might notice. Too slow, and J.J. and my brothers would walk into his trap before I could act.

Ford had been talking for the better part of an hour, his earlier chattiness turning into full-blown bragging. Men like him couldn't help themselves once they got started. They needed someone to appreciate their cleverness, even if that someone was tied to a chair and planning their destruction.

"You see, darlin'," Ford said, stopping by the window to peer out at the canyon through a gap in the wooden shutters, "most folks think small. Steal a few head of cattle, rob a stage or two, maybe hold up a bank if they're feeling ambitious." He turned back to me with a cold smile. "But I think big."

I gritted my teeth at the word. Ford had no right to call me darlin'. Only J.J. could make that word sound like music instead of mockery. When J.J. said it, the word carried warmth, affection, promise. From Ford's lips, it was nothing but calculated manipulation.

"How big?" I asked, keeping my voice just curious enough to encourage him without seeming too eager.

"Big as statehood itself." Ford's eyes took on that fanatic gleam again. "Arizona's gonna be a state soon, and when it is, I aim to have my fingers in every pie that matters. Cattle, mining, transportation." He chuckled, a sound like gravel in a tin can. "Politics."

Behind my back, I felt another fiber give way. The rope was getting loose enough that I could feel circulation returning to my fingers. Almost there.

"Transportation?" I prompted, working another strand with the knife tip.

"Trains, darlin'. The Atlantic & Pacific's been running gold shipments through here regular as clockwork. Every second Tuesday of the month, like you could set your watch by it. Next week, there's a special transport coming through. Military payroll bound for Fort Whipple. Enough gold to fund my operations for the next five years."

I filed that information away carefully. A train robbery targeting military payroll. That was federal jurisdiction, which meant Flynn's people would want to know about it. The kind of crime that brought federal marshals and cavalry troops down on a man's head like the devil himself.

If any of us lived long enough to tell them.

The sound of hoofbeats outside made Ford's head

snap toward the window. I froze, praying he wouldn't notice the nearly severed rope or the way my right hand could almost slip free of its bonds.

"Well, well," Ford muttered, moving to the window and peering through the gap. "Looks like Derek made it back."

A few minutes later, Derek stumbled through the door, his left arm hanging uselessly at his side, blood staining his shirt from shoulder to elbow. His face was pale as bleached bone, but his eyes burned with anger and pain. Buckshot wounds, by the look of it. Someone had given him both barrels.

"They got 'em," Derek gasped, slumping against the doorframe like a man who'd ridden hard and fast. "Glenn, Mac, Carter. All of 'em."

Ford's expression darkened like storm clouds gathering. "Dead?"

"Captured. That shotgun rider, Xavier something. He was taking them back to town when I lit out." Derek's gaze found me, and his lip curled with contempt. "Guess your boyfriend really is who you claimed, missy. J.J. Westin himself. Saw him work the Winchester like it was part of his own body."

Ford nodded grimly. "I already figured that out. What else?"

Derek dragged himself to a chair, wincing as he sat down. Blood had soaked through the makeshift bandage on his arm, and his breathing was shallow. He needed a doctor, but Ford's expression suggested medical attention wasn't a priority.

"That brother of hers ain't just any cowboy, Ford. Heard that Xavier fellow call him Deputy U.S. Marshal Flynn Harper."

The words hit the cabin like a physical blow. Ford went completely still, his face turning pale beneath his weathered tan. For the first time since I'd known him, Ford Spencer looked genuinely shaken.

"Federal," he whispered.

"Gets worse," Derek continued, apparently unaware of the effect his words were having. "There're more lawmen than we thought. That Grady fellow who's been sniffing around? He's Livestock Commission. And I saw at least six other men with badges helping clean up the mess."

My heart sank even as a part of me felt fierce pride. Flynn had marshalled more help than I'd realized. But if Ford thought he was dealing with federal law enforcement, he'd become even more dangerous. Desperate men made deadly choices, and Ford had already proven he would kill to protect his operation.

Ford began pacing again, but now his movements were sharp, agitated. Like a man who could hear the gallows being built. "Federal marshals. Livestock Commission. This whole thing's been a setup from the beginning."

"What do we do?" Derek asked, trying to staunch the bleeding with his good hand.

"We finish it," Ford said flatly. "Kill them all. Every last one. Can't leave witnesses when you're dealing with federal law."

The cold certainty in Ford's voice chilled me to the bone. I'd heard that tone before, in my father's voice, when he talked about eliminating problems. No emotion, no hesitation, just the practical calculation of a man who viewed murder as a business expense.

Part of me wanted to see him get exactly what he deserved. A bullet, swift and final. Just like Daddy would have done. Eye for an eye, blood for blood. The Harper way.

But another part, the part that sounded like Lilian's gentle voice, whispered that maybe justice didn't always have to end in blood. Maybe some men could be redeemed.

Not Ford. He was too far gone, too deep in evil to find his way back. But others like Derek, who'd gotten swept up in something bigger than themselves, maybe they deserved a chance.

Behind my back, the last fiber of rope gave way. My right hand was free. Carefully, I began working on the knots around my left wrist, using the loosened rope to hide my movements. The blood flow returning to my fingers brought painful tingles, but also renewed strength.

"How many men we got?" Ford asked, checking his rifle action with practiced movements.

"Six here, counting us. Plus the three I sent to watch the canyon mouth." Derek shifted painfully in his chair, trying to find a position that didn't aggravate his wounded arm. "Should be enough to handle four lawmen, even if one of them is the famous Rustler Hunter."

Nine men total. J.J., Flynn, Shane, and Grady were riding into a trap with more than double their numbers. The odds were bad, but not impossible. I'd seen what J.J. could do with a rifle, and Flynn was faster with a revolver than anyone had a right to be. Shane was steady as granite, and Grady knew this country like the back of his hand.

But nine against four was still long odds, especially when the nine had defensive positions and time to prepare.

"What about the train job?" Derek asked.

"We'll handle that after we clean up this mess." Ford's smile held no humor, only menace. "Might even be easier with the local law dead. Less interference."

The rope around my left wrist came loose. Both hands were free now, though I kept them positioned as if still bound. The ropes around my ankles would be easier. Ford had tied them with simple hitches, more concerned with speed than security.

I began working on the ankle bonds, grateful that Ford was too focused on his planning to pay attention to me. My fingers were still stiff from restricted circulation, but I forced them to work, loosening knots with the patience of a woman who'd spent two years learning to pick locks and escape from every kind of restraint imaginable.

That's when I noticed the wooden crate in the corner of the cabin. Stenciled on the side in faded black letters: GIANT POWDER - DANGER.

Dynamite.

Of course. This had been a mining operation. They'd have used explosives to blast through rock, break up ore deposits, clear cave-ins. The crate looked old but intact, and dynamite didn't go bad easily. It just got more unstable with age, more likely to explode from shock or heat.

A crazy plan began forming in my mind. A plan that would make Flynn call me reckless, and Shane shake his head in disapproval. And Flynn calling anyone reckless was like a coyote calling a wolf too wild.

But it might just even the odds.

"You hear that?" Derek asked suddenly, his head tilting toward the window.

Ford held up a hand for silence. In the distance, very faint, came the sound of horses moving through the canyon. Iron shoes on stone, the creak of leather, the soft snorts of animals pushed hard.

"They're coming," Ford said with grim satisfaction. "Right on schedule."

He walked to the gun rack mounted on the wall and pulled down a Winchester rifle, checking the action with the smooth movements of a man who'd lived by his weapons for years. The lever worked smoothly, and I could see brass cartridges gleaming in the magazine.

"Derek, you stay here with the girl. Make sure she doesn't get any ideas. I'll position the boys."

Ford headed for the door, then paused with his hand on the latch. "And Derek? If this goes bad, you know what to do with her."

Derek's good hand moved to his gun, fingers curling around the grip. "I know."

The moment Ford stepped outside, I made my move. The rope around my ankles was looser than the ones on my wrists had been, and I had both hands free to work with. Within seconds, I was standing, blood rushing back into my legs with painful tingles that felt like a thousand needle pricks.

Derek started to rise from his chair, his good hand reaching for his weapon. Pain and blood loss had made him slow, but desperation could make even a wounded man dangerous.

I was faster.

My Bowie knife appeared in my hand like magic, the blade pressed against his throat before he could clear leather. The steel gleamed against his throat, sharp enough to part whiskers without pressure.

"Don't," I whispered.

Derek's eyes widened, but he slowly raised his hands. I could see the calculation in his gaze, weighing his chances. For about two seconds. Then his wounded arm swung up, trying to knock my knife aside while his good hand went for his gun.

I stepped back and brought the knife handle down hard on his wrist. Bone met wood with a sharp crack, and he yelped as his gun clattered to the floor. Before he could recover, I slammed my shoulder into his chest, sending him sprawling backward over his chair.

Derek hit the floor hard and didn't get up. Whether from blood loss, pain, or the knock to his head when he struck the cabin wall, he was out cold.

I looked down at Derek's pale face, blood still seeping from his wounded arm. He'd followed Ford's orders, yes, but I could see now what I'd missed before. He was young, maybe not much older than Flynn. Scared. In over his head.

There was a scared kid underneath the outlaw facade. Someone who'd made bad choices, but maybe wasn't evil to the core.

Daddy would have finished him off without a second thought. "Never leave an enemy breathing," he used to say. "Dead men tell no tales and shoot no guns."

But Lilian's voice echoed in my memory, gentle but firm. "Mercy isn't weakness, Hayley. Sometimes it's the strongest thing you can do."

I looked at Derek's unconscious form, then at the gun on the floor within easy reach. One quick motion, Ford would have one less man to call on. One less gun pointed at the people I loved.

My hand tightened on the knife handle.

Then I loosened my grip and stepped away.

I left Derek breathing.

That's when my attention returned to the wooden crate in the corner. GIANT POWDER - DANGER. The letters seemed to glow in the dim cabin light, promising destruction or salvation depending on how I used what was inside.

I pried open the wooden lid with my knife tip. Inside the crate, nestled in yellowed sawdust, were six sticks of dynamite and a coil of fuse. The explosives looked old but stable, wrapped in brown paper with red lettering. Each stick was maybe eight inches long and an inch thick. Enough to bring down a building or clear a mine shaft.

Or even the odds in a gunfight.

Perfect for what I had in mind.

Outside, I could hear Ford shouting orders, positioning his men for the ambush. The sound of approaching horses was getting closer, and I could make out individual voices now. J.J.'s calm baritone giving tactical instructions. Flynn's sharper tone asked about approach routes. Shane's quiet responses, steady as bedrock.

Lord, give me strength and steady hands. And please don't let me blow myself up before I can help J.J. and my family.

I grabbed two sticks of dynamite and a length of fuse, stuffing them carefully into my skirt pockets. The weight felt strange against my legs, but the fabric was thick enough to provide some protection. Then I picked up the whole crate, balancing it against my hip.

The sound of gunfire erupted outside, sharp cracks

echoing off the canyon walls like thunder. The rescue had begun.

And I was about to make it very interesting.

I kicked open the cabin door, the crate of dynamite balanced in my arms, and stepped out into the chaos of the gunfight. Smoke and dust filled the air, and muzzle flashes sparked from rocks and buildings like deadly fireflies.

My training had taught me to plan for every contingency, to rely on skill and preparation. But standing here with stolen explosives and gunfire all around, I knew that all the training in the world wouldn't be enough.

This was going to take a miracle.

And maybe, just maybe, a little of that Harper stubbornness that Daddy had passed down to all his children.

Time to show these outlaws what a Pinkerton agent with faith and grit could do.

32 - Crazy Calico

J.J.

THE CANYON ERUPTED in gunfire the moment we rounded the final bend. Muzzle flashes erupted from the rocks above like sparks from a forge, and bullets whined past my head close enough to part my hair. The sharp crack of Winchester rifles echoed off the stone walls, mixing with the deeper boom of shotguns and the rapid pop of revolvers.

"There!" Shane pointed toward the cluster of buildings tucked against the canyon wall. "Three buildings, just like Glenn said!"

I could see Ford's men spread out among the mine buildings, using the stone walls and old equipment for cover. They had the high ground, clear fields of fire, and twice our numbers. Everything Glenn had warned us about. Smoke was already beginning to fill the canyon as men fired from concealed positions.

"Split up!" Grady shouted over the gunfire. "Don't give them a concentrated target!"

Shane's voice cut through the chaos, calm and controlled. "Flynn, take the left flank. Suppress fire from that shed. Grady, center advance, draw their attention. I'll circle right and cut off their escape route up the canyon wall."

His commands were precise, tactical, the voice of a man who understood battlefield dynamics like reading a map. Shane had turned into the field commander none of us had expected, but all of us needed.

Grady nodded, understanding the plan immediately. Years with the Livestock Commission had taught him how to coordinate multi-agency operations, how to maintain communication during chaos. "I'll signal if we need the backup teams. Keep those escape routes covered."

Flynn peeled left, his revolver already blazing as he charged toward the storage shed. He moved from rock to rock, methodically and accurately picking off targets, using every piece of concealment available. Shane went right, his Winchester cracking steadily as he advanced on the assay office.

I caught glimpses of Shane through the smoke and dust. Not just fighting, but commanding. Hand signals to position Grady for better angles, tactical movements to cut off Ford's escape routes with the methodical precision of a seasoned field officer. This wasn't just a gunfight to him. It was a chess match, and he was thinking three moves ahead.

Grady took the center, drawing fire away from the main cabin, his shots exact and measured. He moved like a man who'd done this before, using the terrain to his advantage, making himself a target just long enough to pull attention from the rest of us.

And me? I spurred Magnus straight toward the heart of it all, my Winchester in one hand, reins in the other, every instinct screaming that Hayley was in that main cabin and I was running out of time.

A bullet *spanged* off a rock inches from Magnus's hooves, sending sparks and stone chips flying. My mustang didn't even flinch, just kept charging forward with that fearless heart that had carried me through years of hunting the worst men alive. His ears were pinned back against the gunfire, but his stride never faltered.

The air was thick with smoke and dust, making it hard to see over thirty yards in any direction. Bullets buzzed through the haze like angry hornets, and I could hear men shouting orders, cursing, calling for ammunition.

That's when I saw her.

The cabin door burst open, and Hayley stepped out carrying a wooden crate like it was a basket of laundry. Even from sixty yards away, through the smoke and chaos, I could read the faded letters stenciled on the side.

GIANT POWDER.

Dynamite.

My blood turned to ice water. "No, no, no..."

She was wilder than a mustang in a thunderstorm—and twice as dangerous. My heart hammered against my ribs as I watched her set the crate down behind a pile of rusted mining equipment. Ford's men were so focused on us charging up the canyon, they hadn't noticed the crazy woman preparing to blow them all to kingdom come.

I watched in horror as she pulled out what looked like a stick of dynamite with a length of fuse attached. The brown paper wrapping was unmistakable, and the red lettering caught the light. Old mining explosive, probably left over from when this place was a working operation.

Including herself in the blast radius.

"Hayley!" I yelled, but my voice was lost in the chaos of gunfire.

She struck a match.

Time slowed to a crawl as I watched that tiny flame touch the fuse. It caught with a hiss of sparks and smoke, and the fuse began burning toward the dynamite in her hand. Maybe ten seconds of fuse, enough time to throw it and take cover if she was smart.

But knowing Hayley, she'd probably stand there and make sure it hit its target.

She was going to throw it at Ford's positions. And if

she was standing that close when it went off, the concussion alone could kill her.

"Yaw!" I drove my spurs into Magnus's sides harder than I ever had before.

My mustang exploded forward as if he'd been shot from a cannon. I'd always known he was fast, but this was something beyond speed. This was a horse running for someone he'd learned to care about almost as much as I did. His hooves hammered against the rocky ground, eating up the distance in great, leaping strides.

The world blurred past us. Rocks, gunfire, shouting men. None of it mattered. There was only Hayley, a burning fuse throwing off sparks, and the shrinking distance between us.

I leaned far out of the saddle, my left leg hooked around the horn, my right arm reaching toward her as Magnus closed the gap with impossible speed. This was cavalry work, the kind of mounted maneuver that took years to master. But Magnus and I had been partners long enough that we moved like one creature.

Fifty yards. I could see the determination on her face, the way she held that stick of dynamite like it was salvation itself.

Forty yards. The fuse was burning steadily, sparks flying in a bright trail.

Thirty yards. She drew back her arm, preparing to throw.

Twenty yards. I could smell the gunpowder, the dust, and the sharp scent of a burning fuse.

The fuse was burning short, with maybe three seconds left.

Ten yards.

I could see her face clearly now, set in grim determination, ready to sacrifice herself to save the rest of us. Those gold nugget eyes were fierce with purpose, beautiful and terrible at the same time.

Not today, darlin'. Not on my watch.

"Hayley!"

She looked up just as Magnus thundered past. I swept her up in my right arm, lifting her clean off the ground, dynamite and all. The stick went flying from her hand as I pulled her against my chest, her body fitting against mine like she belonged there.

Magnus carried us both away from the mine buildings in a dead run, his hooves hammering against the rocky ground as we raced toward safety. I could feel Hayley's heart beating against my chest, fast and strong.

Behind us, the world exploded.

The dynamite Hayley had thrown detonated first, a sharp crack that sent rock and debris flying. I felt the heat wash over us, heard the whistle of flying stone. But that was nothing compared to what came next.

The blast set off the entire crate of giant powder.

The explosion was like the devil crawling up from the pit to reclaim his own. A wall of flame and thunder that shook the canyon walls and sent boulders the size of houses tumbling down from the rim. The concussion hit us like a giant's fist, and I felt Magnus stagger beneath the impact, his stride faltering for just a moment.

The sound was beyond hearing, beyond description. It was felt more than heard, a pressure wave that seemed to squeeze the life from my lungs and set my bones vibrating like tuning forks.

But my mustang kept running, carrying us both away from the destruction, his ears pinned back against the noise but his stride never faltering. Debris rained down around us, chunks of rock and twisted metal that could have killed us if they'd struck home.

When we finally pulled up behind a massive boulder, the canyon was still raining debris. Dust and smoke filled the air so thickly I could barely see my own hand. My ears were ringing like church bells, and every bone in my body ached from the concussion. The taste of dust and gunpowder filled my mouth.

But Hayley was alive. Safe in my arms, her heart beating against my chest, her golden hair tickling my chin. Dust streaked her face, and her dress was torn, but she was breathing. She was whole. She was mine.

"Are you insane?" I shouted, though I could barely hear my own voice through the ringing in my ears.

She looked up at me with those dusty gold nugget eyes, dirt streaking her face, her hair wild from the explosion. Pretty blue dress shredded at the hem. She was beautiful. Absolutely, completely, impossibly beautiful.

"Did it work?" she asked, having to raise her voice to be heard.

I looked back toward where Ford's positions had been. The storage shed was gone, just a pile of smoking rubble and twisted metal. The assay office had lost its roof and half its walls, the remaining structure looking like a broken tooth. The main cabin was still standing, but barely, its walls cracked and one corner completely blown away.

And Ford's men? The ones who weren't buried under rock were running for their lives, scrambling up the canyon walls like scared rabbits. Some were wounded, limping, or holding injured arms. Others had simply lost their nerve and were fleeing as fast as their legs could carry them.

"Yeah," I said, grinning despite everything. "It worked."

That's when she kissed me.

Not gentle, not soft, but fierce and desperate and full of relief that we were both still breathing. Her arms went around my neck, and I forgot about the ringing in my ears, forgot about the dust and smoke, forgot about everything except the woman in my arms who'd just blown up half a canyon to save my life.

Or hers. I still wasn't entirely sure which.

When we finally broke apart, both breathing hard, I kept my arms around her, unwilling to let go just yet. The world could wait. Ford could wait. Everything could wait except this moment.

"Don't ever scare me like that again," I whispered against her hair.

"What, you didn't like my plan?" she asked with that sassy smile that made my heart do funny things.

"Darlin', that wasn't a plan. That was crazier than popcorn on a hot stove."

"But effective."

I laughed, short and breathless. "Darlin', you are the most magnificent, terrifying, impossible woman I've ever met."

"I'll take that as a compliment."

A gunshot cracked through the settling dust, and we both spun toward the sound. Through the haze, I could see Ford emerging from the wreckage of his cabin, blood streaming down his face, his rifle raised and searching for targets.

He was looking for revenge. Looking to take someone down with him.

I slid Hayley down from Magnus's back, putting the boulder between her and Ford. "Stay here."

"J.J.—"

"Stay here," I repeated, checking my weapons. My Winchester was still in my hands, with five rounds left in the magazine. "This is my fight now."

I stepped out from behind the boulder, my rifle ready, and faced the man who'd caused us all so much trouble.

"Ford!" I called out.

He turned toward me, his face twisted with rage and pain. Blood from a head wound had painted half his face red, making him look like something out of a fevered dream. His rifle wavered slightly in his hands, but his eyes burned with hatred.

"J.J. Westin," he snarled. "The famous Rustler Hunter. Come to finish what you started?"

"Something like that."

We stood there in the settling dust and smoke, two men who'd been playing a deadly game for weeks. All the lies, all the deception, all the careful maneuvering had led to this moment. Just him and me and the truth between us.

Ford raised his rifle, trying to sight on me through the swirling dust.

I was faster.

My Winchester came up smooth and steady, muscle memory taking over. I'd practiced this shot a thousand times, could make it with my eyes closed. Center mass, steady breath, smooth trigger pull.

My rifle cracked once, sharp and final. The bullet took Ford in the shoulder, spinning him around and sending his rifle flying. He hit the ground hard, clutching his wounded arm, blood seeping between his fingers.

He was down, but alive. Beaten, but breathing.

That was good enough for me. I didn't have to be like the men I hunted. I could choose mercy over murder.

"J.J.!" Flynn's voice called out from across the canyon. "You got him?"

"Got him!" I called back, keeping my rifle trained on Ford as he writhed in the rubble.

Within minutes, Flynn appeared through the settling dust, his badge glinting on his vest, handcuffs ready. Shane and Grady followed close behind, herding the last of Ford's surviving men. Shane had already organized the aftermath. Wounded men secured, the escape routes blocked, evidence preserved. His quiet authority had turned chaos into order, transforming scattered lawmen into a coordinated force.

Grady was already thinking beyond the gunfight, his Livestock Commission training evident. "We need to secure the scene, document everything. This evidence will put away more than just Ford's gang."

"Ford Spencer," Flynn said, his voice carrying all the authority of federal law, "you're under arrest for cattle rustling, murder, and conspiracy against the United States government."

Ford glared up at him through the blood and pain. "You got nothing that'll stick, boy."

Flynn smiled, cold as winter wind. "We'll see about that."

For a moment, the canyon was silent except for the whisper of falling dust and the distant sound of Shane securing the other prisoners.

Then Hayley was beside me, her hand slipping into mine.

"Is it over?" she asked.

I looked around at the destruction, at Ford being hauled to his feet by Flynn, at the scattered remnants of the rustling operation that had terrorized ranchers for months. Smoke still rose from the ruins, and the acrid smell of explosives hung in the air.

"Yeah," I said. "It's over."

In the distance, I could hear Shane's quiet voice coordinating with Grady as they rounded up the last of the gang members. "Grady, get statements from the wounded. Flynn, secure Ford for transport. I'll coordinate with the territorial marshal's office."

Grady was already moving, his experience evident in how he handled the wounded prisoners. Professional, thorough, making sure their statements would hold up in court. "We'll need documentation on every head of stolen cattle, every illegal brand. This network's bigger than just Canyon Diablo."

But all of that felt far away. Right here, right now, there was just me and Hayley and Magnus, standing in the ruins of Ford's criminal empire.

I'd finally gotten it right. Finally made the shot that mattered. Finally, I proved to myself that I wasn't just a false legend built on other men's defeats.

The famous Rustler Hunter had lived up to his name when it counted most.

Hayley squeezed my hand, and I squeezed back.

Some legends, it turned out, were worth living up to after all.

And some women were worth becoming a legend for.

33 - Justice and Truth

Hayley

THE WAGON WHEELS creaked steadily as we rolled toward Holbrook, carrying our cargo of captured outlaws. Ford sat in the back, his wounded shoulder bound with strips torn from his own shirt, but his eyes still burned with the cold fury of a man who'd seen his empire crumble in a single afternoon. Derek slumped beside him, nursing the knot on his head where I'd knocked him cold with my knife handle. Mac and Carter completed our collection of defeated rustlers, both silent and sullen, their hands bound with rope and their weapons long since confiscated.

J.J. sat beside me on the driver's bench, with Magnus tied to the back of the wagon alongside the other horses. My silver mare Telli walked with her head high, as if she knew we'd won something important today. Shane and Flynn rode escort, one on each side, their rifles across their saddles and their eyes constantly scanning the horizon for trouble. Grady brought up the rear, already making notes in a leather-bound journal about evidence collected and statements needed.

The late afternoon sun painted the desert in shades of

gold and red, and for the first time in weeks, I felt like I could actually breathe. The weight that had been sitting on my chest since we'd first arrived at the Diablo Bunkhouse was finally lifting.

"So," J.J. said quietly, his voice just loud enough for me to hear over the wagon wheels and the soft thud of hoofbeats. "Reckon we ought to talk."

I glanced sideways at him. Dust and gunpowder still streaked his face. He removed his dark glasses, revealing the exhaustion around his eyes. But there was something else there, too. Something that looked like peace. Like a man who'd finally found what he'd been searching for without knowing he was looking.

"About what?" I asked, though I knew exactly what he meant.

"About us. About what comes next." He shifted the reins to one hand and looked at me directly. "No more pretending. No more cover stories. Just the truth."

My heart did that funny little skip it always did when he looked at me like that. Like I was the only woman in the world, like I was worth risking everything for. "All right. Truth it is."

"I love you, Hayley Harper."

The words hung in the desert air between us, simple and honest and more powerful than any explosion we'd set off in the canyon. They carried the weight of weeks of pretending, of stolen moments, of a connection that had grown stronger despite every attempt to keep it professional.

"I've loved you since the day you pulled a knife on Carter," he continued, his voice warm with the memory. "Maybe even before that. And I'm tired of pretending otherwise."

I felt tears prick at the corners of my eyes, but they were good tears. Happy tears. The kind that came when something broken finally healed.

"I love you too, J.J. Westin. Even when you were being a tight-lipped, mysterious cowboy who wouldn't tell me his real name."

He chuckled, a low, warm sound that made my stomach flutter. "Sorry about that. Occupational hazard."

"Speaking of occupations," I said, studying his profile as he guided the wagon around a rocky outcrop with practiced ease, "what happens now? You going back to hunting rustlers?"

J.J. was quiet for a long moment, his hands steady on the reins as he considered the question. The silence stretched, but it wasn't uncomfortable. It was the silence of a man thinking through something important, something that would change the course of his life.

"No," he said finally. "I'm done with that life. Done being alone, done drifting from one job to another, done pretending I don't want something more."

"What do you want?"

He turned to look at me again, and I could see the sincerity in his expression. The vulnerability of a man who'd spent years building walls finally letting someone see over them.

"I want a home. A real one. I want to wake up next to you every morning and go to sleep holding you every night. I want to build something that lasts."

My heart was doing more than skipping now. It was practically galloping. The picture he painted was everything I'd dreamed of but never dared hope for. A partnership built on love and respect, a future that stretched ahead of us like an open road.

"That sounds wonderful. But what would we do for work?"

"Been thinking about that." J.J.'s mouth curved into a slight smile. "What do you say to the Westin Detective Agency? Husband and wife team solving cases together. All the adventure, none of the loneliness."

The idea hit me like a bolt of lightning. Perfect. Absolutely perfect.

"You want to work with me?"

"Darlin', after watching you blow up half a canyon with stolen dynamite, I figure we make a pretty good team."

I laughed, feeling lighter than I had in years. "The Westin Detective Agency. I like the sound of that."

Behind us, Ford made a disgusted noise. "Bunch of sentimental fools," he muttered.

I glanced back at him. "Says the man who got out-maneuvered by a cook and a saddle tramp."

Ford's glare could have melted steel, but I just smiled sweetly at him before turning back to J.J.

"So that's a yes?" J.J. asked.

Instead of answering with words, I leaned in and kissed him, right there with the prisoners grumbling in the wagon behind us and my brothers riding escort. It was a promise, a commitment, a beginning. When our lips met, I felt the last piece of my heart click into place.

When we broke apart, J.J. was grinning like a man who'd just struck gold.

"I'll take that as a yes," he said.

The rest of the ride passed in comfortable conversation about our future, our plans, and our dreams. We talked about where to set up the agency. Phoenix felt right, the territorial capital buzzing with activity and opportunity, large enough for steady business but not so overwhelming that we'd disappear into the crowd. We discussed what kinds of cases we'd take, how we'd divide the work, and what it would mean to build something together.

By the time Holbrook came into view, we'd mapped out the next chapter of our lives together.

Mossman was waiting for us at his office, along with Pearce and several other men I didn't recognize. Federal marshals, by the look of their badges. My stomach tightened when I saw Winston's scarred face among the group, knowing what I now knew about his betrayal.

But first, we had to deal with the prisoners.

Flynn took charge of Ford, hauling him down from the wagon with less gentleness than strictly necessary. "Ford Spencer, you're going to answer for a lot of crimes," Flynn said, his deputy marshal's badge catching the late afternoon light.

The federal marshals moved efficiently, each taking custody of one of the captured outlaws. Mac and Carter went quietly, but Derek looked around with the desperate eyes of a man who'd just realized how much trouble he was in.

As Flynn prepared to march Ford toward the jail, I stepped forward.

"Just a minute," I said.

Ford looked at me with those cold eyes, his mouth twisting into something that might have been a smile. "Well, well. If it ain't the little darlin' who nearly blew us all to kingdom come."

That's when I hit him. A solid punch to the gut that doubled him over and left him gasping.

"Don't," I said pleasantly, "call me darlin'. That's reserved for J.J."

Ford wheezed, glaring at me with pure hatred. "You crazy witch."

"Crazy like a fox," I replied. "And smart enough to figure out that Winston here's been feeding you information from the beginning."

The words hit the group like a thunderbolt. Winston's face went white, and several hands moved toward guns. But the scarred man just stood there, his shoulders sagging with defeat.

"That's enough," Mossman said quietly. "Winston, you're under arrest."

The scarred man didn't deny it. Didn't try to run. He just stood there as Flynn stepped forward with handcuffs, his shoulders sagging with defeat.

Pearce stepped forward, his weathered face grim with disappointment and anger. "Winston, how long?"

"Since February," Winston whispered. "Ford's men showed me drawings of my house. Knew where Emma bought her groceries, what time she walked to church." His voice cracked. "I couldn't let them hurt her."

"We'll make sure she's safe," Mossman said firmly. "And we'll put in a word with the territorial judge about your cooperation. But, Winston, twenty years of good service doesn't erase this."

"They threatened my wife," Winston said, his voice barely above a whisper as Flynn secured the cuffs. "Said they'd kill her if I didn't cooperate."

"We know," Mossman replied, not unkindly. "And that'll be taken into consideration. But you still chose to betray your word."

As Winston was led away, I felt a pang of sympathy despite everything. Fear for a loved one could make any of us do things we never thought possible. But that didn't excuse the damage he'd caused, the lives he'd put at risk.

"There's more to discuss," Mossman said, turning to the rest of us. "Let's go inside."

The next hour was spent unraveling the full scope of Ford's operation. Maps were spread on Mossman's desk, showing the network of corrupt officials, stolen cattle routes, and planned crimes that stretched across three territories. Red pins marked known hideouts, blue ones indicated corrupt officials, and green ones showed confirmed crimes.

It was staggering. Ford's network reached from Colorado to California, with tentacles extending into territorial governments, railroad companies, and mining operations.

"This is bigger than we thought," one of the federal marshals said, studying the map. "We're looking at the largest criminal conspiracy in territorial history."

"The train robbery Ford mentioned," I said, remembering his bragging in the cabin. "When is that supposed to happen?"

"Next Tuesday," Mossman confirmed. "Thanks to

your intelligence, we've already wired the authorities. They'll be ready."

"The Atlantic & Pacific has positioned extra guards and changed the route," Pearce added. "Ford's partners won't know what hit them. Should dismantle most of his network, though we suspect there are other operations we haven't identified yet."

J.J. leaned back in his chair. "What about the bunk-house operations? You can't just shut down the whole Diablo section."

"We're not planning to," Mossman said. "Ian Kelly here has been working for us all along. He'll help transition operations to legitimate hands."

I blinked in surprise. Quiet, polite Ian Kelly was one of Mossman's men? That explained why he'd always been so respectful to me and Luciana. And why he'd never seemed quite as rough as the other cowboys.

"Howard Stiles will take over as foreman," Mossman continued. "He's clean, experienced, and the men respect him. Kurt Fleming will stay on as ramrod. Between the three of them, they should be able to get the Diablo operation back to legitimate cattle work within a month."

"What about Luciana?" I asked, thinking of the sweet Mexican woman who'd worked alongside me.

Ian Kelly spoke up with a slight smile. "She's staying on as cook. Howard specifically requested her. Said the men have suffered enough without having to go back to their own cooking."

"Poor souls," J.J. muttered. "They'll miss your grub something fierce."

"What about the Pinkerton investigation?" I asked.

"Officially closed with a commendation," Mossman said with a slight smile. "Allan Pinkerton himself wants to meet with you when you return to Chicago."

J.J. and I exchanged glances. "About that," I said. "I think my Pinkerton days might be coming to an end."

Mossman raised an eyebrow. "Oh?"

"The Westin Detective Agency," J.J. said, reaching over to take my hand. "We're going into business together."

"Married business partners," I added, feeling my cheeks warm.

Flynn snorted from where he was cleaning his weapons. "About time you two figured that out. Rest of us could see it from a mile away."

Shane nodded his quiet agreement, and even Grady was grinning.

"Well then," Mossman said, standing and extending his hand to J.J. "Congratulations to both of you. And if you ever need work, the Aztec Land & Cattle Company could use a good detective agency on retainer."

As we shook hands and made our final arrangements, I felt a deep sense of satisfaction settle over me. Justice had been served. We caught the criminals. We protected the innocent. Ford's network would be dismantled piece by piece, and the territory would be safer for it.

And I was going to marry the man I loved.

When we finally stepped out of Mossman's office into the cool evening air, J.J. slipped his arm around my waist.

"So, Mrs. Westin," he said with a grin. "Ready to start our new life?"

I leaned into his warmth, watching Flynn load Ford into a prison wagon for transport to federal court. In a few days, we'd head to Phoenix to set up our detective agency. In a few weeks, we'd be married in a small ceremony with my family in attendance.

The daughter of Galen Harper, outlaw and rustler, was going to marry the famous Rustler Hunter.

There was poetry in that, somehow. Justice in it. My father had spent his life on the wrong side of the law, hurting innocent people for his own gain. But his children had chosen a different path. Shane working livestock protection, Flynn as a federal marshal, and now me partnering with the man who'd spent his life bringing men like our father to justice.

We'd broken the cycle. Found our own way to honor the badge instead of running from it.

"Ready," I said, standing on my tiptoes to kiss him one more time. "Let's go build something that lasts."

As the prison wagon rolled away into the gathering dusk, carrying Ford toward whatever justice awaited him, I felt the last shadow of my father's legacy lift from my shoulders.

The Harper name would mean something different now.

Something better.

Something worth passing on to the next generation.

Epilogue - Westin Detective Agency

Phoenix, Arizona Territory
Eighteen Months Later

Hayley

THE BRASS NAMEPLATE on our office door gleamed in the morning sunlight: *Westin Detective Agency - J.J. and Hayley Westin, Proprietors*. I traced the letters with my finger, still marveling at how much my life had changed since that chilly January morning when we'd burned down the Harper ranch and sworn our oath to justice.

Mrs. Hayley Westin. Even after fifteen months of marriage, the name still made me smile.

"Admiring our handiwork again?" J.J. asked, appearing behind me with two cups of coffee. My husband looked more content than I'd ever seen him, the lines of worry and loneliness that had marked his face when we first met now replaced by laugh lines and the easy confidence of a man who'd found his place in the world.

"Just thinking about how far we've come," I said, accepting the coffee and standing on my tiptoes to kiss his freshly shaved cheek. He'd given up the mustache after our wedding, claiming it tickled me too much during our morning kisses.

Our detective agency occupied the entire second floor of a sturdy brick building on Washington Street, right in the heart of Phoenix's growing business district. Our four rooms comprised a waiting area for clients, J.J.'s office, my office, and a case research library that doubled as evidence storage. The walls were lined with filing cabinets containing our completed investigations, maps of the Arizona Territory marked with known criminal operations, and a growing collection of law enforcement contacts across the Southwest.

In eighteen months, we'd handled everything from missing persons to corporate fraud to the occasional cattle rustling case. Three insurance fraud investigations, five missing person cases, two embezzlement schemes, and one particularly memorable case involving stolen mining equipment that led us all the way to California. Word had spread quickly that the famous Rustler Hunter and his Pinkerton wife were available for hire, and we'd had more work than we could handle.

The territorial newspapers had taken to calling us "Arizona's Premier Detective Team," which never failed to make J.J. shake his head in embarrassment. But the reputation brought steady business and the respect of law enforcement agencies throughout the territory.

"Speaking of how far we've come," I said, settling into the chair behind my desk, "I have some news."

J.J. looked up from sorting through the morning mail, his gray eyes immediately alert. After more than a year of marriage, he could read my moods like a favorite book. The way I held my shoulders when I was excited, the particular tone in my voice when something important was brewing.

"Good news or concerning news?" he asked.

"Good news. Very good news." I took a deep breath,

savoring the moment. "We have a new member of our detective agency."

J.J. blinked, his coffee cup halfway to his lips. "We're hiring someone?"

I laughed, shaking my head. "Not hiring. Growing our family."

For a moment, my husband just stared at me. Then, understanding dawned across his features like sunrise over the desert, and the coffee cup clattered to his desk as he stood up so fast his chair rolled backward.

"Hayley? Are you saying...?"

"I'm saying you're going to be a father, J.J. Westin."

In two long strides, he was around the desk and lifting me into his arms, spinning me around the office while I laughed and held on tight. His joy was infectious, complete, the happiness that came from a man who'd never dared dream of having a family but was now being blessed with one.

"A baby," he whispered against my hair when he finally set me down. "We're having a baby."

"We are indeed." I cupped his face in my hands, marveling at the wonder and joy I saw there. "Are you happy?"

"Happy?" J.J. kissed me thoroughly, with a kiss that made my knees weak and my heart race. "Darlin', I'm over the moon."

The baby would grow up knowing both parents, knowing love, knowing safety. Everything J.J. and I had been denied in our own childhoods, we would give to our child. The Harper legacy of abandonment and cruelty would end with us.

We were still wrapped in each other's arms when a knock sounded at the office door.

"Mr. and Mrs. Westin?" a familiar voice called. "You decent in there?"

I groaned and stepped back from my husband. "That's Flynn."

"Your timing's always been terrible," J.J. called out, but he was grinning as he straightened his vest and opened the door.

Flynn stood in the hallway, his Deputy U.S. Marshal badge pinned to his chest, his hat in his hands. Behind him stood Shane, looking as quietly competent as ever, and to my surprise, Ike, our youngest brother.

"Well," I said, moving to hug each of them in turn. "What brings the Harper boys to Phoenix?"

Flynn looked older, more seasoned than when we'd first worked together at Canyon Diablo. The star on his chest carried real authority now, earned through successful captures and a reputation for fair dealing. Shane remained the steady anchor he'd always been, but there was less tension in his shoulders these days. Working with Grady had given him purpose beyond mere survival.

And Ike. My baby brother had grown into a man while I wasn't looking. His law degree had given him confidence, but I could still see the idealistic young man who believed justice could be served through courts and legislation rather than guns and dynamite.

"Business," Flynn said, but his wild blue eyes were sparkling with something that looked suspiciously like mischief. "And maybe a little pleasure."

"Coffee?" J.J. offered, already moving toward the pot we kept brewing for clients.

"Don't mind if I do," Shane said, settling into one of our client chairs.

Ike took the other chair, grinning at me with the same boyish enthusiasm he'd had at seventeen. Law school had filled out his frame and given him confidence, but he was still the baby brother I remembered.

"So," I said, settling back behind my desk while J.J. distributed coffee, "what kind of business brings you all the way to Phoenix?"

Flynn's expression grew serious. "Train robber. Fellow by the name of A.C. Beaumont. Been hitting Southern

Pacific trains from here to California. Word is he's headed for Holbrook."

I exchanged glances with J.J. Holbrook. Where this whole adventure had started, where we'd first met Mossman and begun the investigation that changed all our lives.

"Remember Ford's network?" Flynn continued, his voice dropping lower. "We think this A.C. Beaumont might be connected to the operations we didn't catch. Same methods, same territory, same railroad line. Could be Ford had more partners than we realized."

J.J. leaned forward, interested. "You think Ford's operation is still active?"

"Parts of it, maybe. Beaumont's hits are too well-coordinated, too precise. Someone's feeding him information about the trains, just like Winston fed Ford information about us."

Shane nodded grimly. "We've been tracking the connections for months. Bank records, telegraph intercepts, witness statements. There's a pattern, but it's subtle. Professional."

"What do you need from us?" J.J. asked.

"Information mostly. You two have made quite a reputation for yourselves. Figured you might have heard something useful."

We spent the next hour discussing what we knew about train robberies in the territory, possible hideouts around Holbrook, and the networks of informants we'd developed over the past year and a half. Our files contained detailed information about criminal operations throughout the Arizona Territory, cross-referenced with law enforcement contacts in California, New Mexico, and Colorado.

J.J. pulled out our territorial map, marked with red pins for known criminal hideouts, blue for corrupt officials we'd identified, and green for reliable law enforcement contacts. "Beaumont's smart if he's using Ford's old routes. These canyons provide perfect cover, and most of the local law doesn't know the territory well enough to track him."

"We've documented at least twelve different hideouts Ford's people used," I added, consulting our case files. "Some might still be active."

But eventually, the conversation turned to family.

"So," Shane said, his attention shifting between J.J. and me, "you two look... settled."

"We are," I said, unconsciously placing a hand on my still-flat stomach. "Very settled."

Ike leaned forward in his chair. "I finished law school last month. Took a job with the District Attorney here in Phoenix."

"That's wonderful!" I said. "You'll have to come for dinner soon. I want to hear all about it."

"They've got me working on territorial corruption cases," Shane continued, his eyes flickering with enthusiasm. "Trying to clean up some of the mess Ford's network left behind. Turns out his operation reached deeper into the territorial government than we realized."

"The cleanup's been massive," Ike continued, his eyes lighting up with the satisfaction of justice served. "Mossman had to let go more than fifty cowboys across all the bunkhouse operations. Some for direct involvement with Ford's gang, others for turning a blind eye to the rustling they should have reported."

"That's over half of his entire workforce," J.J. said, impressed despite himself.

"It was necessary," I replied, thinking of all the honest ranchers who'd lost cattle while corrupt cowboys looked the other way. "Better to rebuild with honest men than keep bad ones who'd compromise everything Mossman's trying to accomplish."

Shane nodded approvingly. "The Livestock Commission's been working with him to recruit reliable hands. Between Howard Stiles, Ian Kelly, and Kurt Fleming running clean operations, they've had the Diablo section back to legitimate work for a while now."

Ike nodded approvingly. "Good work. Long overdue."

"Speaking of dinner," Flynn said, "we're all meeting at the hotel restaurant tonight. Shane's treat, since he's been bragging about how well the Livestock Commission pays."

Shane actually smiled at that, a rare occurrence. "Six o'clock?"

"We'll be there," J.J. said. "Wouldn't miss it."

After my brothers left to check into their hotel and conduct their official business, J.J. and I sat in comfortable silence, processing the visit and the news I'd shared.

"They're good men," J.J. said finally. "All of them. Galen Harper was a fool not to see what he had."

"His loss was our gain," I replied. "Look how we all turned out. Shane with his quiet strength, Flynn with his fierce loyalty, Ike with his brilliant mind. Even Lilian and Justine, built good lives with good men."

I thought about our family's transformation. Six children of a notorious outlaw, scattered by abandonment and abuse, are now united in service to justice. Lilian had found peace in marriage and motherhood. Justine had built a loving home with Grady. Shane had channeled his protective instincts into legitimate law enforcement. Flynn had turned his restless energy toward federal service. Ike was fighting corruption through the courts.

When justice is executed, it is a joy to the righteous but a terror to evildoers. The words of Proverbs that had bound us together that night we burned down the ranch echoed in my mind. We'd kept our oath. All of us. The Harper children had rejected their father's path in favor of justice, and we'd made that choice mean something.

And I had found my partner in every sense of the word.

"And you," J.J. said, reaching across to take my hand, "the strongest of them all. Beautiful, brave, impossible

Hayley Harper Westin."

"We did all right, didn't we?" I said, squeezing his fingers. "All of us."

"Better than alright." J.J. brought my hand to his lips, pressing a gentle kiss to my knuckles. "So, this baby of ours. Any preferences? Boy or girl?"

I pretended to consider seriously. "Well, if it's a girl, she's definitely staying home where it's safe."

J.J. snorted. "Like blazes she will. Any daughter of yours will probably be blowing things up by the time she's walking."

"And any son of yours will be tracking outlaws before he can read," I countered.

"Point taken." J.J. grinned. "What do you really think?"

"I think," I said, settling back in my chair and placing both hands on my stomach, "that our little one can be whatever they want to be. As long as they have your faith and my grit, they'll be just fine."

"Faith and grit," J.J. repeated thoughtfully. "I like that."

Outside our window, Phoenix buzzed with the activity of a growing city. Soon, Flynn would begin his pursuit of A.C. Beaumont, a chase that would probably take him back to Holbrook and the wild country where we'd first found each other.

But here, in our office, in our new life, there was peace. There was love. There was the promise of a future that stretched ahead of us like an open road.

I was Hayley Harper Westin, wife of the famous Rustler Hunter, former Pinkerton agent, current detective, and soon-to-be mother. The daughter of an outlaw who'd found her calling in justice, the sister of lawmen, the partner of a man who'd shown me that true strength wasn't just in fighting. It was in building something worth protecting.

J.J. reached across the desk and took my hand again,

his calloused fingers intertwining with mine.

"Ready for our next adventure, Mrs. Westin?"

I looked at my husband, thought about the baby growing inside me, remembered my brothers and their continued fight for justice, and smiled.

Outside, Phoenix stretched toward the horizon, a growing city full of opportunities and challenges. The Arizona Territory was changing, moving toward statehood, and we would be part of that change. Our detective agency would grow with the territory, helping to build the kind of place where justice prevailed and families could thrive.

The Harper name would mean something different now. Something better. Something worth passing on to the next generation.

"Always, Mr. Westin. Always."

Author's Note

THE ARIZONA TERRITORY of 1898 was a crossroads between lawlessness and civilization, where family legacy could either condemn you or define you. The Harper children's transformation from outlaw heritage to territorial lawmen reflects the biblical truth that guides their mission: "When justice is executed, it is a joy to the righteous but a terror to evildoers." (Proverbs 21:15)

The Rustler Hunter launches the Harper's Justice series, but each book stands alone while building the larger family saga. J.J. Westin represents the legendary private stock detectives whose reputations often exceeded their physical stature, while Hayley embodies the groundbreaking female Pinkerton operatives who used society's assumptions to their advantage.

The Aztec Land & Cattle Company's million-acre operation was real, as was the organized rustling that threatened the Southwest's economic foundation. Burt Mossman's innovative law enforcement methods helped transform the frontier from chaos to order—the same transformation the Harper family makes in their own lives.

The techniques, challenges, and moral dilemmas faced by J.J. and Hayley draw from extensive research into the real detectives, marshals, and rangers who helped tame the American frontier through courage, faith, and unwavering commitment to justice.

Want exclusive historical insights, character backstories, and updates on the Harper family saga? Visit **rjsloanewesterns.com** to sign up for my newsletter and discover the real history behind the series.

R.J. Sloane

About the Author

R.J. SLOANE CAPTURES the raw spirit of the American frontier in action-packed westerns that don't shy away from the harsh realities of territorial justice. Drawing inspiration from modern classics like *Longmire*, *Yellowstone*, and *Murdoch Mysteries*, R.J.'s stories blend historical authenticity with the timeless struggle between law and lawlessness.

A passionate student of Southwest history, R.J. spends countless hours researching the legendary lawmen of the region—from the Arizona Rangers to the territorial marshals who tamed pivotal frontier towns like Phoenix, Tombstone, Prescott, and beyond. Growing up watching John Wayne, James Garner, and Clint Eastwood westerns with dad on lazy Sunday afternoons instilled a deep appreciation for authentic frontier storytelling. This combination of classic western influence and dedicated historical research brings depth and authenticity to every story.

The Harper Justice series follows a family of territorial lawmen as they navigate the dangerous transition from frontier chaos to civilized order, where doing what's right often means defying what's legal.

Website: https://www.rjsloanewesterns.com
Facebook: rjsloane.westerns
X (twitter): @RJSloaneWest

Books by This Author

The Harper name once struck fear in honest folk across the Arizona Territory. Now it strikes terror in outlaws. The six children of notorious criminal Galen Harper have turned their family legacy inside out, becoming the very lawmen their father spent his life outrunning. As Pinkerton agents, federal marshals, and territorial rangers, they're hunting down men just like the one who raised them. In the untamed frontier of 1898–1904, justice has a new name: Harper.

Blood Justice (Prequel) – Grady Thatcher

The Rustler Hunter (Book 1) - Hayley Harper

The Maverick Marshal (Book 2) - Flynn Harper

The Traitor's Badge (Book 3) – Shane Harper

Desert Life Media

There Is Life in The Desert

Entertainment-first Christian fiction set in the Southwest, featuring redemption, family, and faith

Publishing clean, wholesome, and uplifting fiction since 2010

If you enjoyed R.J. Sloane's The Rustler Hunter, check out more Western Adventures on our website:

desertlifemedia.com

The Maverick Marshal

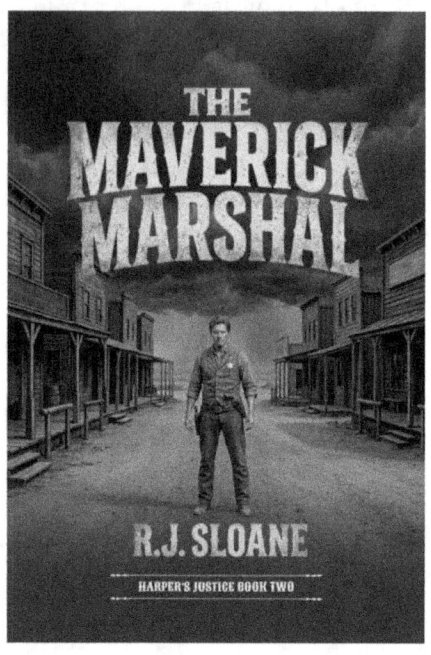

In a lawless land of guns and greed, one marshal won't back down.

Deputy U.S. Marshal Flynn Harper has built his reputation on one rule: bring them in dead or alive. When a federal warrant arrives for A.C. Beaumont, a master swindler bleeding the railroads dry, Flynn rides hard for Holbrook, expecting a routine arrest.

Instead, he finds a town tangled in lies. The evidence? Too perfect. The witnesses? Too rehearsed. And the terrified shopkeeper's daughter is desperate to protect a man she swears isn't a thief.

The deeper Flynn digs, the more tangled the trail becomes—until it leads to the last name he ever expected: his own.

Flynn's trusted his Colt .45 and unshakable instincts. But Holbrook isn't playing by the old rules, and neither is he. With corrupt officials, escaped convicts, and a criminal network closing in, this maverick marshal must decide if the badge on his chest still stands for justice or if it's just another brand of power.

Because in a land where justice hangs by a thread (and sometimes by a rope), Flynn Harper will learn the most dangerous enemy isn't the outlaw you're hunting. It's the system you're sworn to serve.

A gritty Western tale of betrayal, redemption, and moral courage, set against the raw beauty of the Arizona frontier in 1899.

Buy Now:
https://books.rjsloanewesterns.com/the-maverick-marshal